*Praise for the Novels of Marta Perry*

"What a joy it is to read Marta Perry's novels! . . . Everything a reader could want—strong, well-defined characters; beautiful, realistic settings; and a thought-provoking plot. Readers of Amish fiction will surely be waiting anxiously for her next book."
—Shelley Shepard Gray, *New York Times* bestselling author of the Sisters of the Heart series

"A born storyteller, Marta Perry skillfully weaves the past and present in a heart-stirring tale of love and forgiveness."
—Susan Meissner, bestselling author of *The Last Year of the War*

"Sure to appeal to fans of Beverly Lewis."
—*Library Journal*

"Perry carefully balances the traditional life of the Amish with the contemporary world in an accessible, intriguing fashion."
—*Publishers Weekly* (starred review)

"Perry crafts characters with compassion, yet with insecurities that make them relatable."
—RT Book Reviews

"[Perry] has once again captured my heart with the gentle wisdom and heartfelt faith of the Amish community."
—Fresh Fiction

# A
# CHRISTMAS
# HOME

# MARTA PERRY

JOVE
New York

A JOVE BOOK
Published by Berkley
An imprint of Penguin Random House LLC
1745 Broadway, New York, NY 10019

Copyright © 2019 by Martha Johnson
Excerpt from *Naomi's Christmas* by Marta Perry copyright © 2012
by Martha Johnson

A JOVE BOOK, BERKLEY, and the BERKLEY & B colophon
are registered trademarks of Penguin Random House LLC.

ISBN: 9781984803191

First Edition: October 2019

Printed in the United States of America
3   5   7   9   10   8   6   4

Cover images: Photo of woman © Claudio Marinesco;
Barn and house in winter by Conny Sjostrom;
Amish wagon cover logo by anton_novik / Shutterstock
Cover design by Sarah Oberrender
Book design by Alison Cnockaert

*This book is dedicated to the love of my life,
my husband, Brian.*

# CHAPTER ONE

The buggy drew to a stop near the farmhouse porch, and Sarah Yoder climbed down slowly, her eyes on the scene before her. Here it was—the fulfillment of the dream she'd had for the past ten years. Home.

Her cousin, Eli Miller, paused in lifting her cases down from the buggy. "Everything all right?"

"Fine." *Wonderful.*

Sarah sucked in a breath and felt the tension that had ridden her for weeks ease. It hadn't been easy to break away from the life her father had mapped out for her, but she'd done it. The old frame farmhouse spread itself in the spot where it had stood since the first Amish settlers came over the mountains from Lancaster County and saw the place they considered their promised land. Promise Glen, that was what folks called it, this green valley tucked between sheltering ridges in central Pennsylvania. And that's what she hoped it would be for her.

The porch door thudded, and Grossmammi rushed out. Her hair was a little whiter than the last time Sarah had seen her, but her blue eyes were still bright and her skin as soft as a girl's. For an instant the thought of her mother pierced Sarah's heart. Mammi had looked like her own mother. If she'd lived . . . but she'd been gone ten years now. Sarah had been just eighteen when she'd taken charge of the family.

Before she could lose herself in regret, Grossmammi had reached her, and her grandmother's strong arms encircled her. The warmth of her hug chased every other thought away, and Sarah clung to her the way she had as a child, when Grossmammi had represented everything that was firm and secure in her life.

Her grandmother drew back finally, her blue eyes bright with tears. She took refuge in scolding, as she did when emotions threatened to overcome her.

"Ach, we've been waiting and waiting. I told Eli he should leave earlier. Did he keep you waiting there at the bus stop?"

Eli grinned, winking at Sarah. "Ask Cousin Sarah. I was there when she stepped off the bus."

And she'd seen him pull up just in time, but she wouldn't give him away. "That's right. I was wonderful surprised to see my little cousin—he grew, ain't so?"

"Taller than you now, Sarah, though that's not saying much." He indicated her five feet and a bit with a line in the air, his expression as impudent as it had been when he was a child.

"And you've not changed much, except in inches," she retorted, long since used to holding her own with younger siblings and cousins. "Same freckles, same smile, same sassiness."

"Ach, help!" He threw up his hands as if to protect himself. "Here's my sweet Ruthie coming. She'll save me from my cousin."

Ruthie, his wife of three years, came heavily down the back porch stairs, looking younger than her twenty-three years. She looked from him to Sarah, as if to make sure

Sarah wasn't offended. "You are talking nonsense." She swatted at him playfully. "Komm, carry those things to the grossdaadi haus for Sarah. Supper is almost ready."

"Sarah, this is Ruthie, you'll have figured out," Grossmammi said. "And here is their little Mary." The child who slipped out onto the porch looked about two, with huge blue eyes and soft wispy brown hair that curled, unruly, around her face.

And Ruthie couldn't have more than a month to go before the arrival of the new baby, Sarah could see, assessing her with a shrewd eye. When even the shapeless Amish dress didn't conceal the bump, a woman knew it wasn't far off.

Eli loaded himself up with Sarah's boxes, obviously intent on getting everything in one trip. "Surrounded by women, that's what I am," he said cheerfully. "And now there's another one."

He stopped long enough to give Sarah a one-armed hug, poking her in the side with one of her boxes as he did. "We're wonderful glad you're here at last, Cousin Sarah."

Sarah blinked back an errant tear. Eli hadn't lost his tender heart, that was certain-sure. And Grossmammi looked as if she'd just been given the gift of a lifetime. As for Ruthie . . . well, she had a sense that Ruthie was withholding judgment for the moment. That was hardly surprising. She'd want to know what changes this strange cousin was going to make in their lives.

*As little as possible*, Sarah mentally assured her. All she wanted was a place to call home while she figured out what her new life was going to be.

Eli, finally laden with all her belongings, headed toward the grossdaadi haus, a wing built onto the main house and connected by a short hallway. Grossmammi had lived there since Grossdaadi's death, and when Sarah walked into the living room and saw the familiar rocking chairs and the framed family tree on the wall, she felt instantly at home.

"You're up here, Sarah." Eli bumped his way up the stairs until Sarah retrieved one of the boxes and carried it herself.

He flashed her that familiar grin. "What do you have in there? Rocks?"

"Books. I couldn't leave those behind. I just hope there's a bookcase I can use."

"If there isn't, we can pick one up at a sale. The auction house is still busy, even this late in the year. Almost December already."

"Grossdaadi used to say that any farmer worth the name had all his work done by the first of December."

"Ach, don't go comparing me to Grossdaadi," he said with mock fear. "Here we are. I hope you like it." He stacked everything at the foot of the old-fashioned sleigh bed. "Ruthie says supper is about ready, so komm eat. You can unpack later."

She'd rather have a few minutes to catch her breath and explore her new home, but Ruthie was her hostess. It wouldn't do to be late for their first supper together. With a pause in the hall bathroom to wash her hands, she hurried downstairs and joined Grossmammi to step the few feet across the hallway—the line that marked off their home from Eli and Ruthie's.

The hall led into the kitchen of the old farmhouse. Ruthie hurried them to their places at the table and began to dish up the food. Sarah glanced at her, opened her mouth to offer help, and caught Grossmammi's eye. Her grandmother shook her head, ever so slightly.

So something else lay behind the welcome she'd received. Best if she were quiet until she knew what it was.

This was a little disconcerting. She'd dreamed for so long of being here, but those dreams hadn't included the possibility that someone might not want her.

Nonsense. Ruthie seemed shy, and probably she was anxious about this first meal she'd cooked for Sarah. The best course for Sarah was to keep quiet and blend in.

But once the silent prayer was over and everyone had been served pot roast with all the trimmings, it wasn't so easy to stay silent, since Eli seemed determined to hear everything about everything.

"So what was it like out in Idaho? I didn't even know there were any Amish there." Eli helped himself to a mound of mashed potatoes.

"Not many," she admitted. "It was a new settlement." She didn't bother to add that anything new was appealing to Daad—either they understood her father already, or they didn't need to know. "Ruthie, this pot roast is delicious. Denke." The beef was melt-in-your-mouth tender, the gravy rich and brown.

Ruthie's face relaxed in a smile, and she nodded in acknowledgment of the praise. "And your brothers and sister?" she modestly moved on. "How are they?"

"All married and settled now." They'd wisely given up finding a home with Daad and created homes of their own. "Nancy's husband is a farrier in Indiana, and the two boys are farming—Thomas in Ohio and David in Iowa."

"Far apart," Grossmammi murmured, and Sarah wondered what she was thinking. To say it was unusual to have an Amish family so widespread was putting it mildly.

"They all invited me to come to them," she said quickly, lest anyone think that the siblings she had raised were not grateful. "But I thought it was best for me to make a life of my own. I'm going to get a job."

Eli dropped his fork in surprise. "A job? You don't want to be working for strangers."

She had to smile at his offended expression. "Yah, a job. Some work I can do in order to pay my own way."

That wasn't all of it, of course. Her desire went deeper than that. She'd spent the past ten years raising her brothers and sister, and it had been a labor of love. What would have happened to all of them after Mammi died if she hadn't?

But that time had convinced her of what she didn't want. She didn't want to become the old maid that most large families had—the unmarried sister who hadn't anything of her own and spent her life helping to raise other people's children, tending to the elderly, and doing any other tasks that came along. She wanted a life of her own. That wasn't selfish, was it?

Even as she thought it, Eli was arguing. "You're family. You'll do lots of things to pay your own way. You can help Ruthie with looking after the kinder, and there's the garden, and the canning . . ."

He went on talking, but Sarah had stopped listening, because she'd caught an apprehensive expression on Ruthie's face. This, then, was what Ruthie was afraid of. She feared Sarah had come to take over—to run her house, to raise her babies . . .

Ruthie actually did have cause to be concerned, she supposed. She'd been in complete charge of the home for the past ten years, through almost as many moves and fresh starts. It wouldn't be easy to keep herself from jumping in—with the best will in the world, she might not be able to restrain herself unless she had something else to occupy her.

"I'll be happy to help Ruthie anytime she wants me," she said, using the firm voice that always made her younger siblings take notice. "But I need something else to keep me busy."

"And I know what," Grossmammi said, in a tone that

suggested the discussion was over. "Noah Raber needs someone to keep the books and take care of the billing for his furniture business. I've already spoken to him about it." She turned to Sarah. "You can go over there tomorrow and set it up."

Sarah managed to keep her jaw from dropping, but barely. She'd intended to look for a job, but she hadn't expected to find herself being pushed into one as soon as she arrived.

"But . . . bookkeeping? I don't know if I can . . ."

"Nonsense," Grossmammi said briskly. "You took those bookkeeping classes a couple of years ago, didn't you?"

She nodded. She had done that, with the hope of finding something outside the home to do. But then Daad had gotten the idea of moving on again, and she had given it up. Did she really remember enough to take this on?

"Mostly Noah needs someone to handle the business side," Grossmammi went on. "The man loves to work with wood, but he has no idea how to send a bill. That's where you come in."

"But Noah Raber." Eli looked troubled. "Are you sure that's a gut idea? Noah's situation . . ."

"Noah's situation is that he needs to hire someone. Why shouldn't it be Sarah?" She got up quickly. "Now, I think we should do the supper cleanup so Sarah can go and unpack."

Grossmammi, as usual, had the last word. None of her children or grandchildren would dare to argue when she used that tone.

Carrying her dishes to the sink, Sarah tried to figure out how she felt about this turn of events. She certain-sure didn't want to continue being in a place where she was only valued because she could take care of children.

But this job . . . what if she tried it and failed? What if

she'd forgotten everything she'd once known? Noah Raber might feel she'd been foisted on him.

And what was it about his situation that so troubled Eli? She tried to remember Noah, but her school years memories had slipped away with all the changes in her life since then. He was a couple of years older than she was, and she had a vague picture of someone reserved, someone who had pursued his own interests instead of joining with the usual rumspringa foolishness. Was he interested in offering her the job, or had Grossmammi pushed him into it?

But she'd already made her decision in coming here—coming home. She shivered a little as a cold breeze snaked its way around the window over the sink and touched her face. There was no turning back now.

"WHY DIDN'T YOU put your shoes together under the bed like you're supposed to?" Noah Raber looked in exasperation at six-year-old Mark, dressed for school except for one important thing—his right shoe.

"I did, Daadi." Mark looked on the verge of tears, and Noah was instantly sorry for his sharp tone. Mark was the sensitive one of the twins, unlike Matthew. Scoldings rolled off Matty like water off a duck's back.

"It's all right." He brushed a hand lightly over his son's hair, pale as corn silk in the winter sunlight pouring in the window. "You look in the bathroom while I check in here."

There weren't that many places where a small shoe could hide, but the neighbor kids were already coming down the drive, ready to walk to school with the twins. With a quick gesture he pulled the chest of drawers away from the wall. One sock, but no shoes.

From the kitchen below he heard Matty's voice, probably commenting on the fact that the King children were coming. But a woman's voice, speaking in answer, startled him out of that assumption. Who . . . ? Well, he had to find the shoe before anything.

When his mother had been here, this early-morning time had run smoothly—he hadn't realized how smoothly until he'd had to do it himself. Still, it had been high time Mamm had had a break from looking after his twins, and her longing to visit his sister Anna and her new baby was obvious. Naturally he'd encouraged her to go, insisting he and the boys would get along fine. If he'd known then . . .

"I found it!" Mark came running in, waving the shoe. "It was in the hamper."

He started to ask how it had gotten there and decided he didn't really need to know. The important thing was to get them out the door.

"Let's get it on." He picked up his son and plopped him on the bed, shoving the shoe on his foot and fastening it with quick movements. "There. Now scoot."

Mark darted out the door and clattered down the stairs, running for the kitchen. Noah followed in time to see Mark come to an abrupt halt in the kitchen doorway. He stopped, too, at the sight of a strange woman in his kitchen.

"Who—" He didn't get the question out before Matty broke in.

"This is Sarah. She's come to work for you, Daadi."

The woman put a hand lightly on Matthew's shoulder. "Only if your daadi hires me." She smiled. "Matthew and I were getting acquainted. This must be Mark." Her eyes focused on Mark, hanging on to Noah's pant leg, but she didn't venture to approach him.

"I'm sorry. I don't . . ." His mind was empty of everything but the need to get the boys off to school. "Just a minute." He turned to his sons. "Coats on, right this minute. And hats and mittens. It's cold out. Hurry."

Apparently realizing this was not the time to delay,

they both scrambled into their outer garments, and he shooed them toward the small mudroom that led to the back door. "Out you go."

"I think—" the woman began, following him.

"Just wait," he snapped. Couldn't she see he was busy? "Have a gut day, you two. Mind you listen to Teacher Dorcas."

He opened the door, letting in a brisk wind. A hand appeared in front of him, holding two small lunch boxes. The woman was standing right behind him.

"Aren't these meant to go?"

Instantly he felt like a fool. Or at least an inept father, chasing his sons out without their lunches. He grabbed them, handing them off to the boys, and saw to his relief that, by running, they reached the lane to the schoolhouse at the same time as the other children.

He gave one last wave, and then it was time to turn and apologize for his rudeness. The turn brought him within inches of the woman.

"Sorry," he muttered. "You must be Sarah, Etta's granddaughter. I didn't expect you so soon."

"No, I apologize. I shouldn't have come so early. My grandmother assumed you started work at eight, and I didn't want to interrupt."

Looking at her, Noah realized she wasn't quite so strange after all. Etta Miller had talked about her granddaughter coming, of course. He had said that he didn't remember her, but now it was coming back to him.

"You were a couple of years behind me in school, weren't you?"

She nodded, face crinkling in a quick smile. "That's right. By the time I was big enough to be noticed, you'd left school and started your apprenticeship, I guess."

"Sarah Yoder," he said, the last name coming to him. Her mother had been Etta Miller's middle girl, her father a newcomer from down in Chester County. If he didn't remember anything else, he should have remembered hair the color of honey and eyes of a deep, clear green. She was short and slight, but something about the way she stood and the assurance when she spoke made her hard to overlook.

He realized he was staring and took an awkward step back. It seemed suddenly intimate to be standing here in the narrow mudroom with a woman he hardly knew.

"You're here about the job." He reached past her to grab his wool jacket from the hook. "Let's go to the shop and talk. No need to be hanging out in here."

She nodded, buttoning her black coat as she stepped outside, then waiting for him to lead the way to the shop.

"Didn't your great-onkel used to live here?" He heard her voice behind him as they crossed the yard through frost-whitened grass.

"Yah, that's so. We moved in about eight years ago." When he and Janie had married. When he'd still believed marriage meant forever. "My great-onkel used this building as a workshop, so I started my business here."

He found himself looking at the building he called the shop, seeing it through a stranger's eyes. It wouldn't look like much to her—hardly more than a shed with a small addition on one end.

But when he looked at it, he saw the future—the future that was left to him after what Janie had done. He saw a thriving furniture business where his handcrafted furniture was made and sold. He saw his sons growing, working alongside him in the business they'd build together.

"I understand from my grandmother that you need someone to handle the paperwork so you're free to spend your time on creating the furniture."

He nodded, liking the way she put that—*creating*. Each piece of furniture he made was his own creation, with his hard work and whatever gift he had pressed into the very grain of the wood.

"I'd best show you the paperwork, since that's what would concern you." *If I hire you,* he added mentally. But who was he kidding? He hadn't exactly been swamped with people longing to work for him, especially ones who knew anything at all about running a business.

He held the door open and ushered her into the shop, stopping to put up the shade on the window so that the winter sun poured in. Fortunately he'd started the stove earlier, so the shop was warming already, and the sunlight would help. He'd added windows all along one side of the shed, because he needed all the light he could get for working.

"Over here, in the far corner." He gestured toward the office area—a corner of the workroom with a desk, some shelves, and a chair. At the moment the desk was piled high with papers. "I haven't had time to get at it lately."

He wasn't sure why he was explaining to her. It was his business. But he guessed it was obvious he needed help. "You can take a look at it. See what you think."

Instead of commenting, Sarah walked, unhurried, to the desk. He followed her, not sure how to conduct this interview, if that's what it was. She began leafing through the papers, seeming to sort them as she went. After a moment she looked up.

"Where do you keep the receipted bills?"

"Um, there should be a box . . . yah, that. The shoebox."

Sarah looked at it, still not commenting. Her very silence began to make him nervous. "It's not always such a mess." Just most of the time. "My mother has been away on a trip for several weeks, so I've had the boys to manage as well as the business."

"I see. Sorry. That must be difficult. If you'd like me to

see what I can do with this . . ." She hesitated. "I take it your wife doesn't help with the business?"

He froze, his stomach clenching. Didn't she know? Didn't she realize that was the worst thing she could possibly say to him?

SHE'D SAID SOMETHING wrong—very wrong. Noah looked as if she had hit him with a hammer. His strong-boned face was rigid, the firm jaw like a rock. His dark blue eyes had turned to ice. Remorse flooded her. If the poor man had lost his wife, why hadn't Grossmammi thought to tell her?

Standing here silent wasn't helping matters any. "Noah, I'm so sorry. I didn't know. I'd never have said that if . . . I suppose the family thought I knew your wife had passed away—"

"No." The word was a harsh bark. He swallowed, the strong muscles in his neck moving visibly. "Janie didn't die. She left us a few months after the twins were born. We haven't heard from her from that day to this."

Sarah struggled for words. "I . . ."

"There's no need for expressions of sympathy." His mouth clamped shut like a trap.

Whatever she did, she mustn't show pity. It wasn't easy, but she schooled her face to calm. "You are the fortunate one, then."

Noah gave a short nod, as if he understood her instantly. "Yah. I have the boys. They are worth anything."

He spun, turning away from her, and looked yearningly at his workbench. Clearly he didn't want to talk anymore. Did that mean he didn't want her around at all?

"What do you think?" he said, not looking at her. He gestured toward the desk with the papers on it.

Sarah touched the stack of papers in front of her, mentally measuring it. If Noah wanted to carry on as if nothing had happened, surely she could manage to go along with him.

"It might be best if I look through these and sort them. Then we'll have a better idea of where we are. If that's all right with you." She trod as carefully as if she were walking barefoot on broken glass.

"Yah, gut. Denke." He still didn't look her way. They were both being cautious and polite, trying to pretend nothing had happened. "However long it takes. I'll pay for the time it takes to decide if you want to do this or not."

"You don't need to—"

"The laborer is worthy of his hire." He flashed a smile. It was a feeble effort, but it was the first she'd seen from him. "That's what my daad always says."

She nodded, sitting down at the desk while Noah moved quickly to his workbench. Her family might have been better off if Daad had adopted that saying. His, unfortunately, had been more in the nature of *The grass is always greener on the other side of the fence.*

Somehow, no matter how often he had been proved wrong, Daad had clung to that belief. Still did, she supposed. But at least she wasn't going with him now, the way she'd had to for the sake of her brothers and sister.

They worked without talking, and the workshop was silent except for the gentle swish of fine sandpaper against wood. Sarah glanced around the room. It was well designed, she supposed, with that row of windows bringing in a lot of light so Noah didn't have to depend on gas lighting.

But there wasn't much space. The small addition, which she'd assumed was a showroom for his finished pieces, was instead filled with all the equipment he didn't have room for in here. She began mentally rearranging it, putting her desk and chair in the addition with a few display pieces and moving all the work into the larger space. It would still be crowded, but it would be a better use of the space.

Noah glanced up and caught her looking at him. "Did you want to ask me something? You can interrupt, you know. Unless I've got my fingers near a saw blade."

The attempt at humor encouraged her. He wouldn't bother, she thought, unless he wanted to make this work.

"I haven't run across any tax papers." Sarah said the first thing that popped in her head. "I suppose you do keep tax records."

"If you can call it that." He rubbed the back of his hand across his forehead. "If you can figure out the taxes, you're better than I am. The file is in the house. I'll get it when we stop for lunch."

Sarah nodded, but before she could go back to sorting, he spoke.

"So what do you think? You've probably never met such a mess in any of your other jobs."

The expectation revealed in the comment startled her. Clearly he thought she'd been working as a bookkeeper. What exactly had Grossmammi told him?

"It . . . it's just what I would expect if you haven't had time to do anything with it in the past month or so."

Noah grimaced. "Make that three. Or four." He looked a little shamefaced. "Even when my mother was here, I didn't spend enough time on that side of the business."

She nodded, unsurprised. "So I see." She hesitated. "Just so we're clear—I don't know exactly what my grandmother told you, but I haven't actually had a job in bookkeeping." Before he could react, she hurried on. "I took all the classes, and I'd accepted a job, but then we moved before I could start work."

"You moved a lot, did you?" His voice had grown cool quite suddenly.

So it did make a difference to him. Disappointment swept over her. She could do this job, she thought, but not if he didn't give her a chance.

"I kept house for my daad and took care of my brothers and sister. When Daad decided to move on, we went with him."

It wasn't as if she'd had a choice. So she ought to be used to disappointment by this time.

But she wasn't giving up on getting this job before she'd shown what she could do, so she continued.

"It looks as if it will take a week or so of full-time work just to get everything organized. Once a system is set up, you may only need to spend a few hours a day on it."

Sarah waited, giving him the opportunity to say that in that case, he wouldn't need her. Or to agree that he'd hire her. But he didn't say anything. He just nodded and turned back to his own work.

Well, she'd have to take silence as his permission to go on with the sorting, at least. Perhaps he was thinking that would buy him time to see how well it worked out, having her here.

Did her presence upset his work? She studied him covertly over a stack of receipts. His eyebrows, thick and straight, were drawn down a bit as if he were frowning at the curve he was sanding . . . the arm of a delicately turned rocking chair. The curves of the legs and the back were what many Amish would consider fancy, but the whole piece was so appealing that it seemed to urge one to sit and rock for a bit.

Maybe he wasn't disappointed in the work—that look might be one of deep concentration. His strong features could easily look stern, she supposed, even if that wasn't his feeling. The twins hadn't inherited that rock-solid jaw, or at least, it didn't show yet. Their faces were round and dimpled.

Did they look like their mother? She didn't even know if the woman was someone local or not. Obviously, Grossmammi had some explaining to do.

Thinking of the twins caused a pang in the area of her heart. She shouldn't let herself start feeling anything for those two motherless boys. She knew herself too well—she'd fall into mothering them too easily, and that wouldn't do.

Presumably Noah's mother would take over again when she returned from her trip. Noah had been fortunate to have her available when his world had fallen apart.

Grossmammi had offered to take Sarah and her siblings when her mamm died, but Daadi hadn't wanted it. And Sarah, at eighteen, had been fully capable of looking after the younger ones—not only that, but she'd felt it her duty. She couldn't regret the years she'd spent raising them, but she didn't want to do it again, not unless it was with her own babies.

She stole another glance at Noah, his closed face giving nothing away, his dark brown hair curling rebelliously as he worked. He hadn't offered her the care of his children. He hadn't even offered her the bookkeeping job yet.

And if he did . . . well, given how difficult his situation was, she wasn't sure she should take it.

# CHAPTER TWO

Reaching home after a long day, Sarah was promising herself a serious talk with her grandmother. First of all, why had Grossmammi sent Sarah off without telling her of Noah's situation? Now that she had framed the question, she realized Eli had said something like that at supper, but Grossmammi had cut him off. Clearly she hadn't wanted Sarah to be forewarned.

Had she thought Sarah would back off if she knew?

And secondly . . . but she never had time to list her second point, since her cousin came rushing out the kitchen door of the farmhouse with the look of a man running away. He'd left the door ajar, and through it she could clearly hear the sound of Mary's wails, closely followed by the sound of breaking glass.

Without stopping to think, Sarah raced in, half-afraid of what she'd find. But Mary wasn't hurt—just standing in the middle of the kitchen rubbing her eyes and giving vent to the wail of an overtired child. Ruthie stood at the sink, staring down at the remnants of what looked like a plate.

First things first. She scooped Mary up in her arms, patting her. "Hush, now, sweet girl. You're all right."

Mary stopped in mid-cry, probably surprised, and leaned back in Sarah's arms to study her face. Apparently reassured by what she saw there, she snuggled against Sarah, eyes closing.

Ruthie turned, looking torn between anger and tears. "I don't need . . ."

"Yah, you don't need my help," Sarah said gently. "But maybe I need to help you. Won't you let me?"

Ruthie stared for an instant, and then the tears spilled over. She stammered out a confused complaint about hosting worship on Sunday, all the things she had to do, and how Eli didn't understand.

"He . . . he said that I shouldn't bother, because nobody would notice if I'd cleaned or not!"

That was clearly his greatest offense, and Sarah had to suppress a smile. Yah, that sounded like Eli, bursting out with the worst possible response when faced with a crying woman.

"I wonder what he'd do if we said that about his barn or his milking shed," she said, putting a tentative arm around Ruthie. "Can you imagine what he'd do if worship was being held in his barn?"

Ruthie managed a watery chuckle. "All I was doing was cleaning the dish cabinet, and he said I shouldn't be standing on that stool. And I told him . . ."

She threatened to spill over with tears again, and Sarah hastened to interrupt, wondering where Grossmammi was while all this had been going on. "Of course you want the cabinet to look nice, but why don't you sit down and rock Mary a bit? She's ready to fall asleep in your arms."

Ruthie let Sarah shepherd her to the rocker and settle her with Mary in her lap. "Just for a minute," she said, leaning back heavily.

"I'll pick up the glass in the meantime," Sarah said. "If that's all right with you?"

Ruthie nodded, looking almost as tired as Mary. For a few minutes silence ruled in the kitchen. Sarah cleaned up the fragments of the plate, glanced at Ruthie to see her eyes drifting shut, and went ahead to finish the cabinet.

The swing door to the hallway was pushed open a few inches. Grossmammi looked in, made sure all was peaceful, and slipped into the kitchen.

Ruthie blinked, her eyes opening. "Ach, I should . . ."

"You should go up and have a nice lie-down until supper," Grossmammi said. "You and Mary both. Sarah and I will take care of things."

"I don't think I . . ." But the tiredness was obviously overcoming her.

Sarah hurried to take Mary, and together with Grossmammi they managed to get both Ruthie and the toddler up the stairs and settled on the double bed. By the time Sarah drew the double wedding ring quilt over them, Mary was already asleep, and Ruthie close to it.

She and her grandmother slipped quietly down the stairs. When they reached the kitchen again, they exchanged glances. "I didn't hear all of that," Grossmammi said. "I'd guess Eli wasn't tactful."

Sarah chuckled. "Did you ever see Eli being tactful? He couldn't understand why Ruthie was fussed about hosting worship on Sunday."

"Ach, he should know better. But her sisters are coming to help clean on Saturday, and it wouldn't occur to him she'd want to do something first, before having her sisters looking in her cabinets. Ach, well, they'll come through worse than this in their marriage."

"I guess so." Sarah visualized Ruthie's tired face. "I wish she'd let me help her, but I understand. I'm still a stranger to her. And unfortunately, from her viewpoint, a stranger who's used to being in charge in the household. Naturally she's wary."

"And where would your brothers and sister be if you weren't someone who takes charge?" Grossmammi said. "It's not a bad trait, Sarah."

"Not necessarily." Sarah eyed her grandmother. "Is that why you didn't tell me about Noah and his wife before I went over there this morning? You thought I'd jump in and take charge?"

Grossmammi studied her, probably not sure how upset she was. "No, I didn't tell you because I was afraid you'd turn the job down without even trying if you knew Noah had two motherless kinder."

"Oh." That took her aback. Maybe she'd been a little too vehement in expressing her feelings about mothering other people's children when she'd written to Grossmammi. "I don't suppose I'd turn the bookkeeping job down, but he hasn't actually offered it yet."

"Why not?" Grossmammi's bristles went up at once. "How could he find someone more suitable than you?"

"I . . . I'm not sure. He gives me the impression that he'd rather not have a woman around at all. I guess I can understand that, after what happened with his wife."

"Yah, it was hard. And shocking when you first hear it. I guess after all these years, most folks have gotten used to it." Her grandmother pulled open the potato bin and gestured. "You start the potatoes while I get the chicken stewing."

Obediently she counted out enough potatoes for four adults and one small child, but she wasn't done with her questions. "Please, Grossmammi. Tell me about Noah's wife. I don't want to be a blabbermaul, but I stumbled into saying something that upset him once already, and I don't want to do it again."

"No, I guess you'd best know." Grossmammi rinsed the chicken pieces, waiting until she'd turned off the spigot to speak. "You remember Noah, don't you?"

"A little, I guess. I didn't know him well, for all we went to the same school."

"I'm not surprised. He was always the quiet one of the family. He just seemed to know what he wanted early on, heading straight into furniture making with his onkel."

Sarah nodded, remembering their neighbor. A bachelor, Noah's uncle had lived alone, seeming happy with his furniture shop.

"Noah had never fallen for a girl at all," Grossmammi said, "and then suddenly he was head over heels for Janie Burkhalter, and her barely eighteen and still enjoying her rumspringa. Too much, I'd have thought, to settle down, but . . ." She shrugged. "Who knows? She agreed to marry him, and it was all done in a rush because she wanted to be the first one married that fall."

Sarah thought she could see where this was heading. "So she was too young to be ready for marriage."

Grossmammi's forehead wrinkled. "Too young for motherhood, anyway. She seemed to enjoy their wedding visits, traveling around to stay with relatives and see different places. But naturally, when they came back Noah needed to get on with his work. He thought what everyone did, that she'd settle down when the baby came."

"Instead of one, it was two." Sarah could imagine the shock, going from being a carefree girl to having two babies so fast. "She didn't have much family, did she?" Sarah was starting to remember her, at least a little.

"Just her daad, Amos Burkhalter. It was all too much for her. Everyone tried to help, but Janie . . . she just kept talking about how she wanted to travel, to see places and meet people before she was too old. Noah promised her they'd travel after the kinder were grown, but one day she decided not to wait. She just left."

Sarah tried to absorb it, her heart hurting for all of

them. Janie must have been desperate to do such a thing, but—no, she couldn't understand a mother leaving her babies behind, no matter how desperate.

"I'm so sorry about Noah." She understood, now, his reaction when he realized how much she'd moved around. He'd thought she was like Janie, always looking for something new. He didn't realize that it had never been her choice.

"Yah, it's a sad thing. Noah is married to Janie, but she is out in the world somewhere." Grossmammi shook her head. "If she'd died young, that would be a great sorrow. But maybe this is worse—for him and those boys to live with thinking she didn't want them."

That was like a blow to the heart. No doubt Noah had tried to tell his sons something that would comfort them, but what would it be? There were no good explanations.

Her grandmother poked her. "Don't stand there dreaming. Get the potatoes on."

Sarah set the pot on the stove. "Not dreaming. More like a nightmare, ain't so?"

"Yah. But look at it this way. If you can help Noah get his business going forward, he won't have all that time alone to brood. You'll be gut for him."

Maybe, although Noah might not feel that way. And even if he did, she wasn't so sure that Noah and his sons would be good for her right now.

NOAH WAS ABLE to get the twins off to school the next morning without interruption. Waving good-bye, he yanked his jacket from the peg in the back entryway, closed the door, and started toward the workshop.

Colder this morning. He scanned the sky. They might get a flurry of snow before the day was over. That would excite the boys for sure.

So what did it mean that Sarah hadn't turned up yet? Had she decided one day was enough to waste trying to make order out of his chaos? Or maybe she'd been expecting a formal job agreement before she left. They hadn't really settled anything yesterday.

The truth was that he wasn't sure he liked the idea of having someone take over any aspect of his business—not if it meant having someone around all the time. Sarah hadn't been noisy, of course. She hadn't chattered—hadn't even spoken except when she'd needed to ask him something.

Still, her very presence was disruptive. He liked being alone when he was working—he always had. That was what troubled him, not Sarah as a person.

If she could take the work home to do—but that didn't make any sense, not at this stage. Sarah still needed to consult him on the scribbled notes and receipts. Maybe later. And maybe there'd be no need to think about it, if she didn't come back.

But when he went inside the workshop, Sarah was already at the desk, and heat flowed from the stove. A pot of what smelled like coffee sat atop it, staying warm.

She glanced up when he came in and seemed to catch his look at the stove. "I hope you don't mind. I thought you wouldn't have time for coffee when you were busy getting the twins off to school."

"No, that was a good thought." Already she'd made him feel like a stranger in his own workshop.

She had turned back to the shoebox of receipts she was sorting. Should he say something about the job? She didn't seem to expect it. Helping himself to a mug of coffee, he risked another covert glance.

Sarah wore green today—a deep, clear color that probably reflected the green of her eyes. She'd put on a black sweater in deference to the morning chill in the shop, and against it her hair, smoothed under her kapp, seemed brighter.

And he shouldn't be staring at her. He moved to the workbench, his back to her. Sarah would know about Janie by now. It would have been the first thing she asked when she got home yesterday, he supposed. She probably wondered what kind of man he was, that his wife had run away from him.

Well, she'd have sense enough not to bring up the subject, so he could be glad of that. Now he'd best get down to work and try to ignore her.

For the next few hours they worked in the same room, with only the occasional question and answer to break the silence. The rocking chair was finished, and he looked at it with satisfaction. That wasn't being prideful, was it? Rather, he felt pleased that the finished product matched the image that had been in his head when he'd started.

Would Sarah feel that when she'd finally dug her way to the bottom of the pile of papers on the desk? He glanced at her to find that she had made progress. At least, it looked like progress to him to have that haystack of paper reduced to neat piles.

"You're making progress."

She looked up at the sound of his voice, as if surprised that he'd broken the silence. "Some," she said. "Now that I have everything sorted, I can start bringing the ledger up to date."

With a sudden sense that he didn't want to relapse into silence between them, he said the last thing he'd intended. "Do you remember Janie? Janie Burkhalter?"

Sarah's eyes met his for an instant before flickering away. "Not really. She was a couple of years younger, I think. I . . . I am sorry about what happened."

"Yah." He shouldn't have brought it up. What could he expect her to say? Just the same as everyone else. *Sorry.*

"Noah . . ." She hesitated. "I am so sorry I spoke as I did yesterday. I hope you know I wouldn't have said anything like that if I'd known."

He nodded. He was sure of it—Sarah was obviously a kindhearted woman. She wouldn't willingly cause pain or embarrassment.

He turned back to considering what he'd work on next, feeling oddly relieved. Maybe it was just as well he'd spoken. It had cleared the air between them.

Maybe this would be a good time to discuss her job—

But the sound of a vehicle pulling up outside drove the thought away. It might be an Englisch customer. He moved toward the door, looking out to see if it was someone he knew.

The Englischer who slid out of the van looked slightly familiar, but he couldn't quite place him. Maybe someone who'd talked with him at the fall craft festival? There'd been plenty of people who'd wanted to talk about his work, and enough had ended up buying something to make the event worthwhile.

He opened the door as the newcomer came up the two steps.

"Good morning." The man had a quick smile at the sight of him. "Noah Raber?"

"Yah. Komm in." He stepped back, wishing he had mastered the skill of doing business with strangers.

"I'm Jeff Portman. Portman Furniture, out on the highway?" His tone made it a question, and while he talked his gaze darted around the workshop, seeming to take in every detail.

Noah nodded. He'd seen the huge store in passing, but never been inside. His mind jumped ahead hopefully. Was Portman interested in his furniture?

"What . . . what can I do for you? Is there something special you're interested in?"

Portman shrugged. "I've been hearing a lot about the work you do. Thought I'd like to see for myself. Mind if I just look around?"

"That's fine. There aren't a lot of finished pieces ready to show." He didn't like to admit it, but wasn't it better than having a roomful of things no one wanted to buy?

"Good, good. I don't want to disturb you and your . . . wife . . . is it?" He advanced on Sarah, hand outstretched.

"Bookkeeper," Noah corrected. "Miss Yoder is keeping the books for me."

Sarah seemed composed despite the man's attention. She responded politely and then turned back to her work with a decided air. He'd guess that, like a number of Amish women, Sarah didn't care for being forced into a handshake by a stranger.

"Most of the finished pieces are over here." He steered the man toward the few things he had ready—a dower chest, a nightstand, and the rocking chair he'd just finished.

Portman looked at each piece, nodding a little. Then he came back to the rocking chair, touching it so that it rocked smoothly back and forth, running his hand along the armrests.

"Nice," he said. "What are you asking for it?"

Noah did some rapid calculating in his head. "Let's say . . . a hundred and fifty?" He might get a bit more if he held it until the spring tourist season, but he could use the cash now.

Portman seemed to consider. "I'll tell you what," he said finally. "I could buy the rocker today for your price and sell it tomorrow for twice that, at least. But that's not my way. I like to build a relationship with a craftsman, so I can go to him often."

He wasn't sure what the man was driving at, but silence seemed the best response.

"So, anyway, how about if I take the rocker on consignment. That means . . ."

"Yah, I know." He'd finally caught up. "You want to display it in your store, and then if it sells, you keep a percentage of the price."

"That's it." Portman smiled again. Noah decided the smile must be part of his sales technique. "I always say you can't get the better of a Dutchman in a deal."

The possibility of consignment sales had occurred to him, but he'd never followed up on it. Now it seemed to have come to him. "What percentage were you thinking about?"

"Twenty-five percent." The number rolled off his tongue glibly.

For a moment Noah hesitated. Then he saw Sarah watching him. She shook her head.

"Twenty," he said promptly. "What price are you thinking of putting on it?"

Portman studied the rocker again, nodding slightly. "Okay, I think I can put four hundred fifty on it, at least. It's a nice piece, and it's unique, so far as I can tell. You aren't turning out chairs exactly like it every day, are you?"

He was probably joking, but to Noah the question was a serious one. "I would never create another piece exactly the same. Unless it was meant for a set."

"Sure, sure, I understand. A craftsman wants his work to be unique." Portman seemed concerned, as if he thought Noah might have been offended. He walked around the rocker again, looking at it. "Okay, it's a deal. So long as you understand that I might have to dicker on the price to make the sale."

Noah nodded. Everybody wanted to feel they'd gotten the best price. "All right. I agree." He managed to control his elation. Even with the commission, it was more than he'd make on his own.

If he could work up a regular business with the man,

he'd be able to give up the side jobs he took on and give all his time to furniture making. His dream of having a thriving business for his boys to take over could actually become a reality sooner than he'd thought.

"There's just one thing, though," Portman said.

Noah came back to Earth with a crash. There was a snag, then. "Yah?"

"If this goes as well as I think, I'm going to want more from you. I need to know you can produce new pieces regularly, and not put it on the back burner because you got busy with something else."

"This is my work," he said, trying not to think of all the small jobs he sometimes had to take on to make ends meet. "I won't be running off in some other direction." And that made it even more crucial that he have the help he needed, whether he liked it or not.

"Good, then we have a deal. We can load this in the van . . ."

He stopped when Sarah handed him a sheet of paper and a pen.

"The receipt," she said politely. "Mr. Raber needs a receipt showing your agreement, of course."

For a moment Noah was afraid the man would stalk off, but if that was anger Noah saw flash in his eyes, Portman quickly subdued it.

"Sure, of course." He took it, read it through, signed it, and handed it back to Noah. "Good thing you have Ms. Yoder to keep us both on track."

Noah wasn't sure the man meant that, but he seemed honest enough. He lifted the chair. Still holding the receipt, Noah hurried to open the door for him and then helped him load the rocker into the van.

Portman offered another handshake before climbing into his car. "I'll be looking forward to a long and profitable relationship. For both of us."

Noah nodded, trying to control his elation as he watched the vehicle drive off. He'd been so busy with the boys lately that he hadn't given much thought to the future of the business. It had been enough to keep his head above water.

Now . . . now a door had opened to a better future, and he was thankful. And thankful, too, he reminded himself, for Sarah's business sense. He glanced down at the receipt he still held. He'd have accepted a handshake deal, and that might have been a mistake. Not that he was suspicious of the man, but dealing with an Englischer with a big, prosperous business was a different story from agreeing to make a dower chest for a niece.

That being the case, he ought to firm up his agreement with Sarah. He knew perfectly well why he was hesitating, didn't he? If Sarah were a pleasant, grandmotherly married woman, he'd have settled it yesterday. She was pleasant, yes, but she was also an attractive single woman. And he was a married man without a wife, and with no hope of that situation ever changing.

That didn't seem to bother Sarah or her grandmother, but it bothered him, probably because he'd been far too aware of Sarah since the moment he set eyes on her.


IT WAS NEARLY time for Noah's boys to get home from school, and Sarah had made up her mind that she'd leave then for the day. She glanced at Noah. Was he really unaware that they hadn't settled anything about her job between them?

At first she'd been just as happy, since it gave her more time to decide if this was really what she wanted. But her doubts had begun to seem silly. Just because Noah had two motherless children, that didn't mean he'd expect her to mother them. She must be overly sensitive on that topic.

She could hardly accept the job until he asked her, now could she? Certainly at this moment he seemed to have forgotten she was even in the room. He was humming tunelessly under his breath as he worked, his face intent, his eyes focused on the wood under his hands.

Sarah shook her head slightly. She'd heard of losing oneself in work, but she'd never seen anyone who was quite as deaf to the outside world as Noah was. She amused herself with trying to think what it would take to distract him. A clap of thunder? She didn't think anything less would do.

Just then he glanced up and caught her watching him. Sarah felt a wave of heat reach her cheeks and hastily turned back to the paper in her hand, scanning it as if it were something crucial.

"Did you have a question, Sarah?" He straightened, stretching his back.

"No, I don't think so." She slapped the paper on its proper pile. "I have everything sorted, but I need a system for keeping bills and receipts and contracts stored. Some file folders would do. If you don't have any, I'll probably be in town sometime soon, so I could pick them up."

"Running errands in preparation for hosting worship?" he asked, seeming to indicate he was ready to take a break.

"Most likely. I'm looking forward to seeing folks at worship, but . . ."

"But this is pitchforking you right into it." He finished the thought for her. "I know what you mean. My sisters are convinced I'm incapable of hosting worship, so they descend on me the week before, cleaning everything that stands still."

Sarah smiled at the image. This was better. They were talking like friends, instead of like wary strangers. "I can imagine. Ruthie's sisters are coming tomorrow, so I foresee a busy day."

"I think there are some folders in the house . . ." He stopped at a clatter outside. From the sound of excited young voices, she'd say the twins were home.

"Daadi, Daadi!" The door burst open. "Is Sarah here?"

"Whoa, slow down." Noah caught hold of the nearest twin—Matthew, she thought. "Don't come in shouting."

"But it's Teacher Dorcas," Mark said. "She came home with us. She wants to see Sarah."

"Dorcas?" Her heart lifted at the sound of the name. Dorcas Beiler had been her closest friend since they were six-year-olds walking into school for the first time. And now Dorcas was the teacher at that same school. She couldn't get outside fast enough.

They met on the steps and nearly knocked each other over with the warmth of their hug. Dorcas let go, laughing. "Here, we'd best get off the steps. I have to preserve a little dignity. After all, I'm the teacher now."

"And that's impossible to believe, given how much of a schnickelfritz you used to be."

Happiness bubbling up in her, Sarah took stock of what the years had done to her friend. Dorcas was more mature, of course, but as pretty as ever with those flashing dark brown eyes and the smile that showed the dimples in her cheeks.

"Was Teacher Dorcas naughty?" That was Matthew, and he and his brother were watching the two of them wide-eyed.

"Matthew . . ." Noah began, sounding reproving.

"Not a bit of it," Dorcas said, laughing. "Sarah, if you tell any stories on me, you'll be sorry."

"I wouldn't dream of it," Sarah assured her. If anything were lacking to make her feel at home, it would be the friends of her childhood. "Ach, it's wonderful gut to see you. But did you come to talk to Noah?"

"No, I came to see you. The twins were full of the fact

that you're working for their daadi." Dorcas turned to Noah with the quick movement that was so characteristic of her. "Mind, now, you're not to keep Sarah working such long hours that she doesn't have time for her old friends."

There was an awkward little pause as Noah looked at her. It was logical enough for Dorcas to assume things were settled between them, but this was forcing the job subject with a vengeance. Sarah had intended to say something, but not this way.

Noah's eyes flickered as he focused on her intently, as if assessing her abilities. Or maybe whether he could stand having her around every day. But then he gave a small nod.

"Her hours are for Sarah to say. As much as it takes to do the job. If that's all right with you?"

For an instant she hesitated. Maybe he had been forced into it, but he could have made some excuse if he didn't want to hire her, couldn't he? He hadn't, so . . .

"Yah. That sounds fine," she said.

There. She had a job. One more step toward her future was accomplished.

# CHAPTER THREE

Matthew leaned against Sarah's skirt, and she put a hand on his shoulder without thinking. "Were you Teacher Dorcas's best friend? Like me and Mark?"

"You and Mark are twins, so I guess that's even better than best friends. But yah, Teacher Dorcas was almost like a sister to me when we were little."

"Not now?" he piped up.

Kinder did have a way of asking awkward questions. Before she could come up with an answer that took into account ten years apart, Dorcas took over.

"Now, too," she said firmly. "Now I'm going to walk home with my best friend. Don't you two forget to practice your spelling words. Tomorrow's Friday, remember?"

Matthew nodded, looking as if he'd rather not be reminded, but Mark tugged at him. "Let's go practice."

"That's right," Noah added, gathering the boys together and heading them toward the house. "Homework first, and then your chores." He glanced at Sarah. "I'll see you tomorrow, yah?"

She nodded. "Tomorrow."

But she wasn't thinking about work. She was thinking about what Dorcas had said. *Were* they still the best of friends after all this time? Once they'd told each other everything, shared every secret, but now . . . even the letters they'd exchanged might not have bridged the gap of the years.

Dorcas smiled, her dimples showing. "Ready to go? I promise not to take any shortcuts this time."

"Promise? No racing the bull to the fence?" Sarah reached inside to take her jacket from the hook near the door.

"I don't do things like that now." They fell into step on the lane that lead to the Miller farm. "I'm not eight any longer."

"Were we eight when that happened?" Sarah shook her head. "Old enough to know better, anyway. You should have heard the scolding I got."

"That's okay. I had one of my own, after your mother told my mother."

A little silence fell between them. Sarah wondered if Dorcas was looking back, as she was, and questioning where the time had gone.

"We were a little more sheltered than kinder are now, I think," Dorcas said, her usually smiling face looking grave. "Some of the things my scholars say startle me. They seem to know much more about the outside world than we did."

Sarah nodded, thinking about her own brothers and sister. Certainly they were more aware than she'd been in those days before Mammi's death had changed everything.

"How are Thomas and David? And little Nancy—it seems impossible that she can be old enough to be married."

"She was only nineteen." Sarah felt a familiar pang at the thought of saying good-bye to her baby sister. "I thought it was too young, but no one else did. And he's a gut man, with a fine job in his father's carriage business and a farrier on the side."

"But it was hard to part with her." Dorcas understood what she didn't say, just as she always had.

"She was the baby, after all—only nine when Mammi died, so I had to mother her more than I did the boys, in a way." Sarah shook her head, shaking off sad memories. "Enough about me. Tell me about you. How did you ever get to become a teacher?"

"After being such a wild teenager, you mean. Surprising, isn't it?" Dorcas's eyes regained their sparkle.

"Ach, you weren't that bad." But they both knew that Dorcas had gone very close to the line during their rumspringa.

"You don't believe that. If there was trouble around, I was sure to get into it. And if the school board members knew the half of it, they wouldn't want me near the school." Her voice went suddenly serious. "And I couldn't stand that. Funny that I never realized how much I'd like to teach until the opportunity fell into my lap. Now . . . it would be hard to give it up."

"I'm glad." She was. And maybe just a touch envious. Dorcas seemed to have no doubts at all about her path. "You're fortunate to have found something you love to do."

"I am. But what about you? Are you happy about this job you've taken on?"

The lane swung through a section of woods, shading them, and it was suddenly much colder. Sarah snugged her jacket around her more closely.

"I'm not sure *happy* is the word. I'm wonderful glad to have a job, though. My cousin Eli was all ready to sign me up to help his wife with the kinder and the house, whether she wanted me or not. I needed a job if I didn't want that to be my life."

Dorcas gave her a searching look. "Feeling regrets?"

"No, not regrets, exactly." She tried to find the words. "Sorrow, I suppose, that I missed the life I'd have had here. But I could never regret taking care of my siblings. Loving them, trying to make up for the loss of Mammi . . . that was the most important job in the world, it seemed to me."

"They couldn't have done without you, that's certain-sure." Dorcas hesitated for a moment. "What about your daad? What's he doing now?"

"He's off chasing a new life again, in Colorado this time. He urged me to go with him. I think he honestly didn't under-stand why I wanted to come home. It wondered me . . ."

She let that trail off, but she might have known Dorcas wouldn't be content with not knowing all of it. "What?"

"Was it my duty to go along and take care of him?" It was the first time she'd put the question into words. "I . . . I still keep second-guessing myself. He depended on me for so much, and I went off and left him on his own. If he gets into trouble . . ."

"That's nonsense." Dorcas was quick to respond. "What trouble could he get into? He's not a child. If he chose to go off someplace new, that's his business."

"I suppose." She wasn't convinced, but she saw no way of being sure she was right. "How did you get so much common sense? That was never your strong point."

Dorcas laughed. "It wasn't, was it? That I learned from sad experience." She sobered for a moment. "Anyway, you're here now and getting settled. If this job doesn't work out, at least it gives you time to look around for something else. Just promise me you won't go brooding about your daad. He can take care of himself."

"All right, I promise." And she'd try to keep that prom-ise. "You're right. I am getting settled, and I love living with Grossmammi."

"No problems with Ruthie, is there? She seems like a sweet girl."

"Yah, of course she is. But naturally, she wouldn't

want someone taking over her house and running it their way. No young wife would."

"And she thinks you couldn't help running things." Dorcas had a laugh in her voice. "We always knew Sarah was the one to take charge."

"As it turned out, that was just as well." Did she sound defensive? She didn't mean to.

"I know you did what you had to. It's just a shame—" She stopped, not finishing, but Sarah knew the rest of it.

"It's a shame we didn't stay here. But Daad was sure it was best to move. He wanted to get away from the memories, I think."

Dorcas looked at her skeptically. "Was it necessary to move all those times to get away?"

Anger flared for an instant, and then died like a spark sputtering out on stone. "You're right. I don't know why I'm still trying to defend him. He just likes to wander. When Mamm was alive, she could dissuade him." She made a face, trying to cover the sense of failure she carried. "I never could."

Dorcas reached out to clasp her hand for a moment in silent sympathy. "I'm just glad you're here to stay. I was afraid . . . well, afraid your daad would talk you out of it."

"He tried." She shrugged off the memory. "He just couldn't understand why I didn't want to take off to Colorado with him. But I was born without that wanderlust. All I ever wanted was a settled home."

"Now you have it. It's a shame poor Noah didn't marry someone like you. Janie . . . well, she was always thinking there was something she was missing in life."

"I just can't imagine any woman being willing to leave her babies behind like that. I could hardly believe it when he told me."

"He told you?" Dorcas blinked. "I've heard he never speaks about it to anyone."

"He didn't want to." She couldn't forget the pain and anger that had radiated from him. "I didn't know about it, and I blundered into saying something."

"How did he react?"

"About like you'd think. He was angry, but at least he understood that I hadn't known."

"It's a wonder he wanted to hire you, then."

Sarah had to smile. "You forced him into it with your teasing. What else could the man do?"

"We both blundered with Noah, I guess. But I'm glad it's working out, anyway." She put her arm around Sarah in a quick hug. "I'm wonderful glad to have you home."

"Not as glad as I am to be here." Her fears that they wouldn't be able to bridge the gap of the years had been foolish. Dorcas was still the same, and the gap she'd imagined had never been there at all.

They'd reached the path to the farmhouse. "Come in with me, why don't you? Grossmammi would love to see you, and I'd guess she has lemonade and cookies ready."

"I never could resist your grandmother's cookies."

Together they walked toward the house. Grossmammi evidently saw them coming, because she came out on the back porch, pulling a black shawl around her.

"Ach, Dorcas." Grossmammi swept her into a hug. "I wondered how long it would take you to come around after my snickerdoodle cookies."

"I think I must have smelled them all the way from the schoolhouse," Dorcas said, returning the hug. "Everyone thinks the kinder need a snack after school. The teacher needs it even more."

Grossmammi smiled in response, but Sarah detected something serious in the look her grandmother directed at her.

"What is it?" Her mind skittered from one thing to another.

"Nothing, nothing." Grossmammi patted her arm. "I was chust checking the answering machine in the phone shanty, that's all. There's a message from your daad."

Sarah stiffened. She'd thought Daad had finally realized she'd meant it about coming home. If he hadn't . . .

"Maybe he just called to see how you're getting settled," Dorcas suggested.

"Maybe." She tried to smile. "Forget it. We're ready for cookies now. I'll take care of calling back later."

But she couldn't so easily dismiss it from her thoughts. She'd have to call him back, and then what? Another fruitless argument? She'd always believed Daad wanted what he thought was best for his family. But she knew now that they'd never agree on what the best thing for her was.

ON FRIDAY MORNING Noah found himself unwillingly moving furniture. Sarah had decided that the workshop would function better if her work area and the finished pieces were in the addition, leaving the larger space for his works in progress.

Wasn't that just like a woman—coming into a man's workshop and rearranging it?

They each took an end of the desk. "Sure you can manage that? I could do this sometime when Daad is here." And maybe he could put it off indefinitely.

"I've got it," she declared. "Let's go."

Trying to control most of the weight with his hands, he backed toward the addition. The desk was a heavy oak piece that his grandfather had built years ago, and he wouldn't have thought of moving it if not for Sarah.

He could have said no, of course. But somehow he'd felt he owed Sarah something in exchange for embarrassing her yesterday. She had been embarrassed at having to admit that he hadn't actually hired her yet.

There hadn't been any good excuse for his hesitation, anyway. He needed help and she had the skills. The fact that he felt vaguely uneasy with her there wasn't a reason for denying her the job.

Teacher Dorcas had put an end to his waffling, that was for sure. With all of them looking at him, he'd had to firm up the job with Sarah.

That being the case, he ought to put a good face on this reorganization idea of hers. He lowered his end of the desk into place. "Here?"

She considered and then shook her head. "Just a little farther toward the back wall, I think."

"Right." He tried to sound cheerful about it as he hefted the heavy desk another foot or two. "This okay?"

"Fine." Sarah's eyes crinkled as she smiled. "Why do men hate to rearrange furniture?"

"Do we?"

"I think so. I always had to drive my brothers into getting the house in shape each time we moved. They'd just put everything down and leave it wherever it landed."

He couldn't help but stiffen at her reference to moving so often, but he tried not to let it influence him. Sarah couldn't know how he felt.

"Maybe if we understood the need for the rearranging, we wouldn't mind it so much," he suggested.

"Can't you see it?" Sarah stood behind the desk, looking around the small addition. They'd already moved her shelves and files, so he trusted they were nearly done. "When someone comes to buy, they'll come in here to see the finished pieces on display. And when they do buy, the records will be right here. No need to write receipts on a scrap of paper."

The last of his resistance disappeared in his amusement. "I take it you didn't think much of my record-keeping."

She smiled back, and there was another moment of what might be friendship between them. "I wouldn't say that. After all, you're my boss."

"Don't let that stop you. I'm used to criticism, with three older sisters."

Sarah shook her head, smiling. "I won't say a word, except denke for agreeing to move the furniture with me. I think this will work out better."

"Anything else you'd like me to do? Tear out a wall? Raise the roof?" He gestured toward the rafters, wanting to prolong her smile.

"No, I think this is enough for now." Laughter filled her eyes. "I'll just bring in the rest of the files, and you can get back to work."

It seemed like that was something he should be saying to her, but he let it slide. Sarah, like a lot of oldest sisters, had a way of taking charge. For the moment, he'd go along with it.

But by the time Sarah was happily settled organizing her files and he'd gotten back to work, he had to admit this was probably a better way of setting up the workshop. He had a sense of freedom now that he felt alone in the shop. Not that he was—Sarah was right around the corner. But still, it felt more normal to him, as if he had his work space to himself.

The telephone was the only thing he had yet to move. He'd have to pick up a longer cable to do that. But it rang so seldom that it was no hardship to stop work long enough to answer. Still, a business needed to have a phone, especially now that he hoped to be in contact with Mr. Portman about his furniture.

Thinking of furniture, it was time he got back to his business. He'd started work on a small table, and the piece of cherry he'd been saving would be perfect for the top.

He smoothed his hand over it, carefully considering the grain before he decided on any cutting.

Funny, really, that he found it easier to ignore Sarah just because she was out of his line of sight. He'd always thought he had better concentration than to let something like that distract him.

Had Sarah sensed his uneasiness in her presence? Maybe she'd come up with this arrangement to make him feel better. He didn't like thinking he was so transparent.

Or perhaps it was Sarah who felt ill at ease working alone with a married man. More to the point, a married man who lived apart from his wife.

Either way, this arrangement was probably the best way. Given how much he'd been grumbling since she'd suggested it, maybe he ought to tell her so. Turning from his work, he skirted the bench and went to the archway between the rooms.

Sarah was copying something into a ledger, but she looked up inquiringly at the sound of his footsteps. "Do you need something?"

"Just to tell you this was a gut idea, despite all the complaining I did about moving things."

Her lips curved. "Yah, I do seem to recall a few murmurs. But I'm wonderful glad you like it."

"When Mr. Portman comes back, I'll show him into the new display room." He nodded to the few finished pieces, noting that Sarah had grouped them in a way he wouldn't have thought of. Not that he thought most folks bought furniture because of the way it was displayed, but it did look nice.

"Have you heard anything more from him?"

He shook his head. "I wouldn't expect to this soon. Maybe next week he'll have some news."

Even as he said the words, the telephone rang, startling both of them. Sarah smiled. "Maybe he's calling."

But when he went back and picked up the phone, a strange male voice spoke in Pennsylvania Dutch, asking for Sarah. Startled, he put the phone down.

"Sarah? It's for you."

"For me?" He could hear the chair scrape the floor when she shoved it back and the quick, light sound of her footsteps.

The moment it took her to reach him was long enough to allow him to wonder who'd be calling her here. It certain-sure hadn't been anyone he knew. Maybe she'd left some man behind out west who was interested in her.

That wasn't his business, he lectured himself, handing the receiver to her.

He moved back to his workbench, trying not to listen, but he couldn't help noticing that she didn't seem very happy about the call.

"How did you get this number?" she asked.

The man had the sort of booming voice that seemed to use the phone as a loudspeaker. Loud enough, anyway, that Noah caught a reference to Sarah's grandmother. Whoever he was, Etta Miller had apparently thought it appropriate to have him call here. Nathan could hardly argue.

He turned back to the piece of cherry, but half his attention was still on Sarah. It sounded as if she were turning someone down. Saying no to him. Had she been courting before she moved back? Well, if she'd had any serious intentions, she wouldn't have returned, would she?

Come-calling friend or not, the man was persistent. He obviously didn't want to let Sarah go. And just as obviously, she was upset. He could hear the strain in her voice even when he couldn't make out the words.

"Daad, please don't." That came clearly enough that anyone would have heard it. Her father, then. And he was trying to persuade her to do something.

Nathan tried to think what, if anything, he remembered

about Jonas Yoder. It was little enough, since it wasn't as if he was the parent of any of Noah's close friends.

In the community, Jonas had had the reputation of being a good salesman, but not one who stuck to anything for long. Right now he was trying to sell Sarah on something, but she wasn't impressed, it seemed.

"I'm happy for you, Daad." He could hear the tremor in her voice that she was fighting to control. "But I won't change my mind."

There were a few more murmured exchanges, and Noah focused sternly on the workbench.

She hung up. He started to say something to her but he stopped at the sound of a muffled sob. Sarah stood with her back to him, her shoulders shaking.

Exasperation mingled with panic. Should he disappear outside and leave her in private? Or did this situation call for sympathetic words? He'd never been much use when a woman turned emotional.

Since he couldn't decide, he went over and poured a mug of coffee. "Here." He thrust it at her. "Maybe this will help."

"Denke." Her voice was hardly more than a whisper.

"You . . . you should take a break. Or go home if you want. You'll catch up with things later, when you feel better."

Shaking her head, Sarah wiped tears away with her fingers, like one of his sons when he'd been hurt. Noah's heart seemed to twist.

"No, I'm all right." Sarah straightened. "I'm so sorry. I don't mean to embarrass you." She stifled a sob, and he forgot his embarrassment in pity for her.

"I'm the one who's sorry. I should have left when I realized it was something private."

"Ach, why should you? This is your place of business." Sarah seemed to have herself under control now. "I guess you realized that was my daad."

He nodded. "I couldn't help hearing that much."

"He's in Colorado now." She stared down at the dark liquid in the mug. "He says it's beautiful there, and the Amish community is so friendly. It's the perfect place to settle."

"He wants you to come there, too." He was guessing, but he felt sure he was right.

"For sure." She rubbed her forehead tiredly with the back of her hand, like his mamm would do when she had flour on her fingers. *"It's wonderful, it's the perfect place . . . ,"* she mimicked. "I might believe that if it weren't that he said the very same thing about every other place he wanted us to move."

"He was the one who wanted to keep moving on. Not you." He'd jumped to conclusions, thinking she, like Janie, had been affected with wanderlust.

"Yah. The first time I thought . . . well, I felt it would be better for me and the kinder to stay here where we had family than to go off someplace else. But he insisted, and I couldn't let the young ones go off without me to take care of them."

"So you went along wherever he wanted to. If you'd tried to change his mind—"

"Don't you think I tried?" Her temper flared in an instant.

"I'm sorry. Yah, of course you did." He didn't like it when other people tried to tell him what he should have done about Janie, and now he was doing the same thing.

Her anger faded as quickly as it had come. "Mammi was the only one he ever listened to. I didn't realize it at the time, but I think he'd have moved on from here a dozen times if not for her. Once she was gone . . ."

Sorrow tinged her words, and he felt her pain almost as if it were his own.

He touched her arm lightly, wishing he knew something to say to comfort her. And wishing, too, that he'd left the workshop when he'd realized the call was for her. Cowardly, he supposed, but just listening to all of this seemed to cross the line between employer and employee.

"Sorry," she said again, attempting to smile. "I shouldn't be telling you all of this. Whatever happened, I'm sure Daad always wanted to do what was best for his family."

He had a few reservations about that. What she'd told him fit into an image he had formed of Jonas Yoder from rumors among the community . . . an image that Jonas was a man quick to hand off his responsibilities onto someone else.

"So you're sure now that you want to stay here?" For his own sake he needed to ask the question. He didn't want to rely on someone and then have her disappear.

"I'm not going to change my mind." Sarah spoke firmly, her gaze level and serious. "I'm back in Promise Glen to stay." Her smile flickered. "It really is my promised land."

# CHAPTER FOUR

Sarah woke later than she'd intended on Saturday morning and hurried through dressing, getting downstairs to find her grandmother already fussing over a tray of sandwiches.

"I know I slept in, but it's not lunchtime yet, is it?" She hugged her grandmother and headed for the coffeepot.

"Ruthie's sisters will be showing up any minute now, I'd guess. They'll all be primed to help get ready for worship tomorrow, so I thought I'd best have some sandwiches cut and ready for lunch later. They'll keep fine under a damp towel."

"What can I do?" She took a long swallow of coffee. She'd need it for the day ahead, she suspected. Hosting worship always led to an absolute frenzy of cleaning and preparation.

"Eat your breakfast," Grossmammi said, her face crinkling into a smile. "If I'd needed your help, I'd have called you. We'll go over in a bit and pitch in. Don't worry—there'll be plenty to do."

"I'm looking forward to it. Lately it seemed we weren't in one place long enough to host worship."

She'd said it lightly, but now she realized how true it

was. Hosting worship was a significant aspect of being part of the community. She had lost that for a time, and now she was set on enjoying it.

"It's gut to take your turn," Grossmammi said. She covered the sandwiches with a damp towel and poured herself a cup of coffee. "When I think of all the times we hosted worship in this house . . ." She fell silent, as if she were indeed thinking of all those occasions.

"You've lived here a long time," Sarah murmured, wondering how difficult it had been for her grandmother to give up her place in the farmhouse and move to the grossdaadi haus.

"When we were newlyweds and planning this house, your grandfather didn't want to have the front rooms built to open. He thought it would be easier to heat closed off." Her smile grew reminiscent. "He changed his mind when he realized how hard it would be to clean the barn enough to have worship there."

"You were right, like always."

"Ach, no, not always. Never think that. I made my share of mistakes, that's certain-sure. We all have to do that. How else would we learn?"

The sound of a buggy drew Grossmammi's gaze to the window. "It's Ruthie's sisters, Emma and Hallie. They must have gotten up with the cows. Finish up now, and we'll get started."

The moment they walked into the kitchen of the main house, they were enveloped in a babble of female voices. Amazing that three sisters could make that much noise. Sarah corrected herself—it was actually two sisters. Ruthie's sisters had apparently come in arguing about who was doing what—or maybe in what order they were doing it. Sarah couldn't be quite sure.

Silence fell long enough for Ruthie to introduce Sarah to her sisters. Emma was about her age and Hallie a little younger. Sarah remembered Emma from some teen sing-ings as a slip of a girl with the tiniest of waists. Five chil-dren later, she had spread out into a comfortably plump matron.

"It's been a long time," Emma said. "Wilkom. Ruthie will enjoy having another woman around to help her."

Sarah shot a glance at Ruthie, expecting a protest. Ruthie's eyes flashed, but she didn't speak.

"I'm wonderful happy to help Ruthie with anything she needs, but since I'm working all day—"

"Working already? I thought you just got here."

"The beginning of the week," Grossmammi said. "She has started to work doing bookkeeping for Noah Raber's furniture business."

"Noah Raber." Emma echoed the name, and she ex-changed glances with her sister. "I didn't know he wanted someone. I'm sure our cousin Elizabeth would have helped out if she'd known."

Since Sarah had no idea who Elizabeth was, she could hardly respond, but Grossmammi did it for her. "Yah, Elizabeth is always eager to help Noah, I'm sure. But she's not a trained bookkeeper, is she?"

"No." Emma looked as if it pained her to admit it, making Sarah all the more curious who this cousin of Emma's was. And had Grossmammi's words contained a barb? She'd have to corner Grossmammi and find out what was going on. Obviously there were perils to assum-ing nothing had changed in Promise Glen.

After considerable disagreement among the sisters, the jobs were finally assigned. Sarah found herself scrubbing the woodwork in the front rooms. Alone, she was happy to find. She could still hear the sisters in the kitchen, giv-ing advice to Ruthie as they cleaned her cabinets.

Grossmammi peeked in when she was about halfway

through the room. "I brought that other shoofly pie over and started coffee, whenever you need a break."

"That's okay. It's nice and peaceful in here." She lowered her voice to reach only her grandmother's ears. "I don't remember Emma being so bossy when she was younger."

Her grandmother shook her head. "She should have married someone who wouldn't let her get away with it."

Sarah hid a smile. Some might consider Grossmammi's ideas old-fashioned, but she wouldn't say so. "I'm sure she doesn't see it that way. But I think I understand why Ruthie is sensitive about anyone else taking over her house."

"Ach, it's no wonder. An oldest sister has to be careful about being managing."

That gave her pause. She was an oldest sister, and she'd been forced by circumstance into being a substitute mother as well. She hoped none of her siblings were thinking that about her.

Was she that kind of person? Her thoughts fled back to the disagreement about reorganizing the workshop. Noah had admitted in the end that it was a better arrangement. Still, maybe she could have found a more tactful way of going about it.

It seemed there were several places in her new life where she ought to tread lightly. She glanced at her grandmother. "Do you know who Elizabeth is, the one that Emma thought should have my job?"

"Elizabeth Schmidt." Grossmammi supplied the name. "She's a widow. No kinder. Her man was best friends with Noah when they were young."

Sarah raised an eyebrow. "Are you hinting that she has her eye on a new husband? But Noah isn't free. As far as anyone knows, the boys' mammi is still alive out in the world."

Grossmammi shrugged. "All I know is, she seems wonderful eager to see that Noah doesn't forget her."

It sounded like so much foolishness to her, but before she had a chance to say so, another woman bustled into the room. "Ach, here you are at last. Why haven't you been to see me yet, little Sarah?"

Only Aunt Anna would call her little when she was getting on toward thirty. Sarah rose to hug her mother's older sister. "How are you, Aunt Anna? I'm wonderful glad to see you."

It was fitting that Aunt Anna should show up just when they'd been talking about managing elder sisters. Aunt Anna had always had plenty to say about Sarah's mother's doings, including how she raised her young ones.

She'd been devoted to Sarah's mamm, Sarah reminded herself. And Mammi never seemed to mind Anna's advice. She'd just smiled, thanked her, and done it the way she'd intended. Remembering that, Sarah's hug was extra warm, and Aunt Anna looked gratified.

"There now. You're home where you belong at last. Just go on with what you were doing. We can talk and work at the same time." Anna seized a sponge from the bucket.

"I'm almost done," she protested, but her aunt kept right on scrubbing.

"So you'll be done twice as fast," she said. "Now tell me, what has been keeping you so busy that you haven't had time to visit your own aunt this week?"

"I just got here on Tuesday," Sarah said. "And I started my new job right away. Anyway, Grossmammi says we're coming to you for supper tomorrow evening, so I thought we'd catch up then."

Her aunt sat back on her heels for a moment, her broad face questioning. "Where did you find a job so soon?" She turned on her mother. "You didn't tell me about this."

"There wasn't any need for you to know sooner," Grossmammi said placidly. "Now you know."

"Not enough. Where are you working? Do you like it? Why did you want to get a job before you were even settled?"

"It didn't take any time to get settled," she said, answering the last question first. Aunt Anna always wanted to know all about everything. "And I like it fine. I'm doing the bookkeeping for Noah Raber and his furniture business."

She had become prepared for odd looks at this news, and Aunt Anna was no exception. She looked at Grossmammi first, as if asking if it were true, before shaking her head at Sarah.

"Ach, what was your grandmother thinking to let you take a job like that, a young single woman like you? You just tell him you can't continue, and we'll find a better job for you before you know it."

She reminded herself of her mother's tactics with Anna, but she knew she couldn't emulate her. Her temper was already rising, and it was all she could do to control it.

"Really, Aunt Anna—"

Before she could say something she'd regret, Grossmammi broke in. "I was thinking that here was a business that needed the skills Sarah has, and Sarah needing a job. That's all there is to it."

That had the benefit of distracting Aunt Anna's attention from Sarah, giving her a chance to cool off. She was further helped by Ruthie, who appeared in the doorway.

"Sarah, would you help me in the kitchen?"

Relieved, Sarah went to her quickly. "For sure." They headed for the other room. She didn't miss the fact that this was the first time Ruthie had wanted her help. Maybe this was a first step toward friendship. "What can I do?"

Ruthie smiled shyly, shaking her head. "I'm not really

that busy. But I couldn't help hearing—your aunt has a very carrying voice. I thought . . . well, maybe you'd like an excuse to step away for a bit."

She couldn't help but laugh. "You've got the right of it, Ruthie. Aunt Anna has a gut heart, but she surely likes to tell everyone what to do. Denke."

"It's all right." Ruthie hesitated for a moment, and then gave her a quick hug. "I know how it feels," she murmured, so softly Sarah could barely hear it.

Sarah's heart warmed. Maybe they could be friends after all.

NOAH TOOK ONE look at Matthew on Sunday morning and shook his head. "Not that shirt. Put on a clean one. It's Sunday."

Matthew grimaced, but turned to obey. Noah barely caught Mark's murmured, "Told you."

He hid a smile. Sometimes he thought it would be better if the little bit of naughtiness were distributed between the twins, but they were as God had made them, after all.

Matthew was back in a moment, making him think the shirt had been laid out and ready. Giving them no chance to dawdle, he hustled them out the door. Since worship was just down the road at Eli and Ruthie's place, they headed out on foot, the boys walking on either side of him. With their black jackets and black felt hats, they looked like solemn little versions of him.

Noah understood, too well, the reason for their delaying tactics on Sunday morning. Most young ones probably did so, not looking forward to three hours of sitting still on the backless wooden benches that would be set up in the front rooms of the farmhouse.

He had his own reasons for reluctance. It had been this way since Janie left, and he didn't see it getting any better.

He couldn't go to a gathering of the Leit without seeing himself as everyone else must—the odd man out, neither truly married nor single.

As they turned into the farm lane and approached the house, he managed to compose his face. At least no one should be able to tell by looking at him how he felt. A flake of snow touched his cheek, and another landed on Mark's hat. He glanced up at the leaden sky. Could be they were in for the first real snowfall of the winter. If so, it would be hard for the youngsters to contain their excitement.

Everyone was gathering outside the farmhouse in preparation for walking in to worship. That was the disadvantage at the Miller farm—with worship in the house, there was no convenient place to gather except outside on a cold morning. Still, it wouldn't be long.

It would be warmer for the service, so they'd be thankful for that comfort. It was better than sitting in the barn with the wind blowing through the cracks.

Matthew gave a little hop when he spotted his grandfather. "There's Aunt Susan and Onkel James and Grossdaadi. Can we run to say hello?"

Noah nodded, releasing their hands, and smiled as he watched them race to their grandfather. His sister Susan, who'd been looking after Grossdaadi while their mother was away, bent to whisper something to the boys. Her own kinder were in their teens by now, and she had a soft spot for the little ones.

He reached them in time to see her giving each of them a couple of wrapped candies. "Best save them until the middle of the service, when you'll start to get hungry."

"I'm hungry now," Matthew said, unwrapping one piece, while Mark carefully stowed his out of sight.

Noah exchanged smiling glances with his daad. They both knew what would happen. Matthew, unable to wait, would down both of his before worship even started. Then when Mark pulled his out halfway through the service, Matthew would manage to play on his brother's sympathy and get one of his.

He ought to stop that, he supposed. He'd told Mark he didn't have to share, but Mark didn't seem able to say no to his slightly older twin.

"I'd best get with the women," Susan said. "We're starting to line up." She paused to pat Noah on the cheek. "Don't forget you're coming to supper today."

"I won't." He couldn't, even if he wanted to. The pattern of Amish life went on quietly and securely, not changed by circumstances or personal feelings. He might not always appreciate it, but he wouldn't change it for anything else.

His gaze followed Susan to where the women were lining up for worship, oldest first, down through the young marrieds, the single, and finally the girls deemed old enough to sit with their peers instead of their mothers.

Without consciously looking for her, his gaze settled on Sarah. She was standing with the eldest of the unmarried women—her friend Dorcas and Dinah Hershberger, a childless widow who was about their age. Did they have his sense of not belonging? That might very well be. For a woman to be without a family in her late twenties was uncommon, though certainly not unique.

Sarah didn't seem to feel out of place. Her face was as calm as ever, and she smiled slightly as she listened to something Teacher Dorcas was saying.

Daad moved a tad closer to him, his sleeve brushing Noah's. "So you have hired Sarah Yoder to help you in the shop, your sister says."

He wasn't surprised—Susan always knew what was going on, sometimes almost before it happened.

"Yah. I was going to tell you when I saw you today.

Etta Miller asked if I'd consider it, since Sarah has training as a bookkeeper."

"Etta suggested it?" He sounded a little surprised.

"Why not?"

They'd started to move, and Daad shook his head slightly. "Are you sure it's wise? A single woman working alongside you?"

"Working, that's all. There's nothing else, so don't go thinking it."

Daad put his hand on Noah's shoulder for a moment. "I don't," he said, dropping his voice as they neared the porch steps. "I'm just concerned other folks might."

*People will talk*, in other words. He couldn't respond, because the line had begun to move. He could only grasp the twins' hands and follow his father into worship. But inside him the words were boiling—hardly a suitable feeling to carry into worship.

Hadn't people had enough of talking about him yet? He guessed not. A man living without his wife was bound to generate talk, no matter how carefully he lived.

Inside, the benches were set up in long rows, men on one side, women on the other. His position made it possible for him to watch as Sarah filed into place after Dorcas, followed by Dinah. They sat, taking a copy of the *Ausbund* from the bench.

Wherever she'd been going to worship in the past ten years, Sarah would have found the familiar hymnbook so that she could sing the familiar songs. Amish had been worshiping in houses and barns, singing from the *Ausbund*, for four hundred years, and they'd continue to do so. It was part of the continuity of Amish life.

Had Sarah found that a comfort throughout her frequent moves? He was just beginning to realize how difficult that life must have been.

Would Daad be reassured to know that Noah could

look at Sarah without a single touch of attraction? Even if he wanted to, which he didn't, he couldn't possibly feel anything other than friendship toward Sarah Yoder. Even friendship might be too much. He didn't have a place for a woman in his life, not any longer. Sarah seemed to understand that without being told.

Too bad if all the blabbermauls in Promise Glen weren't convinced.

As THE WORSHIP service drew to its end, Sarah had to blink away tears, hoping no one noticed. She was just so moved to be back here, worshiping God with those who had known her since she was born. No place had ever fit her like this place did.

Something touched her fingers, and she glanced toward Dinah Hershberger, sitting next to her. Dinah was looking straight ahead, but she slipped a handkerchief into Sarah's hand, next to her on the seat.

Dinah had noticed, obviously, and she was tactful enough not to draw attention to it. Blotting away the tears quickly, she stole another glance at Dinah. They had gone to school together, though Dinah was a year ahead of her. But while Dorcas's appearance hadn't changed in ten years, Dinah was a different woman. There was a new maturity in her face, and a gravity that surprised Sarah until she remembered that Dinah had recently lost her husband. That accounted, she supposed, for the wariness and sorrow in Dinah's eyes.

Life had dealt differently with the three of them, it seemed. Was it better to be married and widowed, or to have never experienced marriage at all? She didn't know.

The final words were spoken, and people stirred, standing to stretch, speaking to their neighbors. The men began making the adjustments that turned the benches

into tables for lunch. Given the December weather, everyone would eat inside, which would make it a bit of a crush.
Sarah wove her way through to the kitchen door. There'd
be plenty of work to be done feeding lunch to all these
people.

Somehow Grossmammi had made it to the kitchen before her. She was giving a final stir to the bowls of church
spread—the familiar mixture of peanut butter and marshmallow that was a staple of post-worship lunch. Sarah
joined Ruthie's sisters in getting out the bowls of jam, red
beets, and pickles that they'd prepared. She picked up one
of the platters of sliced cheese and checked to be sure the
bread was in place. They'd for sure be slicing more before
everyone was served, but they hadn't wanted to do it too
early. No one would want to serve stale food after church.
She suspected Ruthie's sisters would be more than upset
if such a thing should happen.

Eli slipped into the kitchen, going to put a protective
arm around his wife. "Sure you're not doing too much?"

"I'm fine." Her voice was edgy, and she flapped a dish
towel at him. "Just get out of the way."

For a moment Eli looked as if he'd argue, and Sarah
shook her head at him. The best thing he could do was
leave her alone, since she wouldn't relax until all was ready.

Eli obediently moved out of the way, looking back reluctantly at Ruthie. "Go on," Sarah murmured. "We'll see
she doesn't do too much."

It wasn't easy, but with an unspoken agreement, all of
them maneuvered the serving so that Ruthie did as little
as possible, and nothing at all that involved carrying anything.

When everyone had started eating, Sarah seized the
coffeepot Ruthie was reaching for. "Please let me. It will
give me a chance to greet the people I haven't seen yet."

Ruthie could hardly refuse, and by the time Sarah

reached the door, Grossmammi had persuaded Ruthie to sit down and sample the church spread. Sarah went out, smiling a little. How did people manage at times like this if they didn't have family to count on? Each of them might sometimes prefer to have less free advice, but she guessed it all balanced out in the end.

The sound of a hundred and some voices chattering while they ate eventually began to buzz in Sarah's head, and the house, which had been a little chilly when they'd begun, felt like the inside of an oven.

Sarah glanced longingly toward the side porch off the kitchen. No one would notice if she slipped out for a breath of air, would they? She spotted the snowflakes thickening, and that decided her. Grabbing someone's black shawl from the hook by the door, she stepped out onto the porch.

And was nearly knocked over by Noah's twins, erupting from the other house door. She caught hold of the first one—Matthew, of course.

"Here, slow down a bit. What's the rush?"

"It's snowing, Sarah! Don't you see? Mark whispered it was starting and he was right. It is."

"And it's the first snowfall of the season, ain't so? Well, I guess that's worth getting excited about. Just wait until you're off the porch to run."

"We will. Denke, Sarah." But despite his words, their pace went from a fast walk to a skip to a jump down the steps in a matter of seconds.

Sarah tried not to laugh. As she recalled, Noah had been a quiet boy, more given to thought than action. He'd have his hands full with these two.

The twins ran in circles, arms outspread, mouths open as they attempted to catch snowflakes on their tongues. Sarah resisted temptation for a moment. Then, taking a quick look around to be sure there was no one to see, she joined them.

"Look, Sarah, look. Do you think it will snow enough to get sleds out?" Matthew caught her hand.

Laughing, she swung him around. "I don't know. Maybe. But you'll have a whole winter to sled ride."

"The first snow is best," Mark said gravely.

It was, she realized, the first thing he'd volunteered to her, and she felt irrationally pleased. Maybe shy little Mark would like to be friends.

In a few more minutes she was swinging him around, turning her face up to feel the light kiss of snowflakes. The cloud-laden sky seemed close, blurring as she whirled. Dizzying, she slowed to a stop. She staggered a little, laughing at the sheer fun of it. Catching her breath, she said, "I think you're right, Mark."

"What is he right about?"

She spun around at the sound of Noah's voice, feeling her cheeks flush with embarrassment at being caught behaving like a child. Maybe he'd think it was the cold that brought the pink to her cheeks. She could hope, anyway.

"Mark thinks the first snowfall is the best. And I agree with him."

"I do, too." His face relaxed in one of his rare smiles. "But I don't usually make myself dizzy over it. I think you're just a child at heart, ain't so?"

"Better than being old at heart, don't you think?" For a moment they stood smiling at each other, in perfect accord.

Sarah had a sudden vision of Aunt Anna watching them. It was so clear she had to check the windows to be sure she wasn't there.

She wasn't, but it was a good reminder that anyone might see her and Noah together and get the wrong idea.

Noah seemed similarly affected. He was silent for a moment, and then he glanced at the boys. "I think I'd best get these two wild ones home."

Sarah nodded. "I'll see you tomorrow, then."

For some reason, those innocent words caused a change in Noah's expression. He looked for a moment as if he were thinking of something unpleasant.

"Sarah . . ." He stopped, glancing around as if he wanted to be sure he wasn't overheard. "I wasn't going to mention this, but maybe I should." His face tightened. "I've been told that people may talk about a single woman working with me. Because of my 'situation.'" His tone put annoyed quotes around the word. "It's ridiculous, but I thought . . . well, it should be up to you."

Sarah regained her emotional balance with an effort. "You haven't been talking to my Aunt Anna, have you?"

His jaw tightened. "So you've been hearing it, too. Maybe—"

"I heard, and my reaction was the same as yours. It's ridiculous. I don't intend to pay any attention, and I hope you won't, either."

He seemed to lose some of the tension. "Are you sure?"

"I'm sure. After all, we're the ones who'd know if it were a problem."

"Right." He seemed relieved. "Well, in that case, I'll see you tomorrow." He held out his hands to his sons.

Sarah stood on the steps for a moment, watching them walk down the lane. Then, reminding herself that she wasn't remotely interested in Noah, she went back inside.

# CHAPTER FIVE

Sarah returned to the kitchen and the cleanup job that awaited. It was a good thing each family only hosted worship once a year—she wouldn't want to be doing this again soon.

She reminded herself that it was an honor to host worship. Certainly Ruthie had been excited about it, but she'd been apprehensive as well. The timing could have worked out a little better, but when the calendar had been made up, there'd have been no thought of the impending birth.

Passing Hallie, the younger of Ruthie's two older sisters, who was laden with a tray of dishes, she stopped for a word. "Do you think we could convince Ruthie to get off her feet and rest for a bit?"

Hallie glanced at her little sister. "Gut idea, but she won't do it while so many folks are still here. I'll try it in a half hour or so." A smile flickered. "Or I'll get Emma to do it. It's harder to say no to her."

"Gut," she said, not specifying which part of Hallie's words she meant. So even Hallie, closer in age, found Emma's bossiness a bit much to bear.

Dorcas tossed a dish towel to Sarah. "Here. I'll wash, you dry."

"You don't have to help," she said, taking her place next to the draining rack. "With Ruthie's sisters and Grossmammi and me . . ."

"Another pair of hands is always wilkom, ain't so?" Dorcas plunged her hands into the hot, soapy water. "Besides, it gives us a chance to talk."

But by the time Sarah had the first platter in her hands, someone had stopped next to her. "You must be Sarah Yoder. We don't know each other—I'm Elizabeth Schmidt."

So this was the woman that Grossmammi had implied was interested in Noah. Looking at her, Sarah couldn't believe she was a woman to waste her time yearning over a man who wasn't free. Tall and confident, she had the determined look of a woman who was sure of her own place in the world.

"I'm glad to meet you, Elizabeth. You are Gus Schmidt's widow, ain't so? I'm sorry for your loss."

Elizabeth's face became grave. "Denke. It has been a lonely time since I lost him." She paused. "I don't know what I'd have done without Noah."

"I remember that he and Gus were always close friends." Naturally Noah would try to help his friend's widow. Surely Grossmammi was imagining things to think it was anything more.

"Poor Noah," she murmured. "And those poor little boys. I try to do what I can for them, too, naturally. We've always been so close."

She nodded. What was the woman driving at? There seemed to be some specific intent behind the words.

"I noticed you with the twins earlier." Elizabeth leaned in, lowering her voice as if this were just for Sarah's ears. "I just thought I'd give you a helpful hint, since you're working for Noah. He doesn't like anyone interfering with his boys. Very particular, he is."

So that's where this had been going. She was being

warned off. "I'm sure he takes advice from you, though, since you're such old friends."

"Yah, well, that's different." She shot Sarah a puzzled look, as if not sure how that was meant. "I just thought I'd let you know."

"Denke. That's kind of you." That wasn't what she thought, but she had to be pleasant. There was no point in making trouble.

Someone called to Elizabeth, and with a final smile, she moved off.

Sarah turned back to the dishes. Dorcas wasn't looking at her, but Sarah could see the amusement in her compressed smile.

"All right, go ahead and say it," she muttered.

"I wouldn't dare," Dorcas said, letting a giggle escape her. "That woman scares me. She obviously considers Noah her property."

"That's what Grossmammi thinks, too, but I don't see it. She must realize that Noah's not free."

"That's what I'd think, too, but she was warning you off, ain't so?" She darted a sudden glance at Sarah. "You're not getting interested in him, are you? If you want to marry . . ."

"I'm not interested in Noah in any way except that he's my employer," she said firmly. "As for marriage, why? Do you have some nice widower with a bunch of kinder who need a mother?"

"If I did, I might just snap him up for myself. On second thought, I probably wouldn't. I like my life too much the way it is. Although sometimes I think it's a shame there aren't any single men left our age."

"Well, then, maybe you ought to grab that nice widower you're imagining," she said lightly.

Dorcas shrugged. "I'll leave him for you. Wouldn't you be interested? Seriously?"

"I already spent ten years raising Mamm and Daad's kinder," she said. "I don't intend to marry unless I find someone who wants me for myself and not because he needs a mother for his children."

It was true, and a very good reason for not rushing into marriage. But even deeper was another concern. How would she know if she'd found a man she could trust? Daadi . . .

"I can see that," Dorcas said. "I guess I feel that way, too."

The noise in the house was dying down as more people took their leave. Dorcas seemed to become aware that what they said could be overheard.

"Ach, I'm nearly forgetting what I wanted to ask you. Would you be willing to help me plan the school Christmas program? I could use some new ideas."

Taken by surprise, Sarah turned it over in her mind. "Well, I guess I could. But won't the parents expect you to have them help you with it?"

"I'll let them help with the props once I know what I need." Dorcas sounded firm. "But if you'd ever tried to do it, you'd know why I don't want any mothers helping with the planning and directing."

Sarah had to laugh at the expression on Dorcas's face. "Surely it's not that bad."

"Foolish, very foolish," Dorcas said. "It certain-sure is that bad. Every mother is convinced that her child was born to take on the most important part. I've had the mother of a child who couldn't memorize a single line of poetry insist that he could learn three pages to recite." She shook her head. "The wishful thinking of mothers is beyond belief."

"I can see that," she said, mock seriously. "But won't they be angry with me for taking on the job?"

"You have to take some chances in life," Dorcas said. "After all, what are best friends for?"

She thought of all the times she'd tried to dissuade Dorcas from some action she'd thought dangerous, mostly failing. At least this project wasn't dangerous.

Besides, she'd been wanting to find a way of fitting in here. This might just be it.

"All right. I'll do it, as long as you promise to protect me from disgruntled mothers."

"I promise." Dorcas grinned, reaching out a wet, soapy hand to grasp Sarah's. "It'll be fun, working together again. Just like old times."


THE SNOW STILL lay on the ground by the afternoon on Monday—a good thing, as far as Noah was concerned. Even a scant two inches would make the boys happy when they got home from school. They hadn't had nearly enough of the snow yesterday.

Their snowman stood, half-finished, in the backyard. They'd left it with groans when he'd called them in to bed. Well, when they got home, the snowman could finally have his head.

He was focused on the curve of the cherry table when the telephone rang, and he stared at it, annoyed. Sarah hurried to answer it, and he heard the murmur of her voice as he returned his attention to the table, loving the grain of wood beneath his touch.

"Noah?"

He detached his attention again and looked at Sarah.

"I'm sorry to disturb you, but it's Mr. Portman."

Portman—had he already sold the chair? Brushing off his hands, Noah rounded the workbench and took the phone with a nod of thanks.

"Mr. Portman."

"Call me Jeff. I have some good news for you—I have a buyer who wants the chair. She's willing to pay top dollar for it, but . . ."

He paused, and Noah braced himself. What other option was there? She either wanted to buy it or she didn't.

"Yah?"

"The thing is, the buyer really wants a pair of chairs. So if you can do another one just like it, I can probably get at least seven fifty for the pair."

Seven hundred and fifty dollars. The figure danced in his head. He'd never gotten that much for his work before. But . . .

"We talked about this, remember? I want every piece I make to be unique. You said you understood."

"Well, yes, I do. But maybe you could think of this as a set. The two of them make a finished set. She's a good customer," he added. "If she likes your work, she's going to talk it up to her friends."

Something in him still held back. There was nothing wrong with someone wanting a pair of chairs, he supposed. He'd just never imagined he'd be copying himself.

Portman seemed content to wait for his answer. Maybe he knew what it was going to be. Noah had a family to support. He couldn't afford to pass up the opportunity.

"I'll have to put aside the piece I'm working on now, but . . . all right, I'll do it."

"Great. I'll stop by on Saturday. Have it ready then." Portman hung up before he could argue.

Noah frowned at the phone. What if he couldn't have it finished by then? He could, of course, but he didn't like being rushed, and the finish had to dry thoroughly.

Sarah took the receiver from his hand and hung it up. "Is something wrong?"

"Not exactly. I just . . . I don't like jumping around

from one thing to another on somebody's whim. But the customer wants two chairs, and I don't really have a choice if I'm not to lose the sale."

Sarah's head tilted slightly to the side as she considered it. "I guess that's the downside to working with a dealer. If you really want to be independent, you have to do the selling yourself."

"Yah, I know. And Portman can sell more and get higher prices than I've ever been able to." He shrugged. "Guess I'll get used to it."

She nodded, but she looked unconvinced. "You could probably sell more on your own if you advertised more. What advertising do you do now?"

Noah supposed he was looking blank, because that was how he was feeling. "None." Stupid that he had never given it much thought. His sales were generated by word of mouth.

"None?" She seemed to struggle with the concept. "But how will customers find you?"

"One person tells another. The way the Amish always sell and trade."

"The way the Amish used to sell and trade," she corrected. "Anyway, if you expect to sell to the Englisch, you have to let them know about your product."

When he didn't respond, she went on. "There's that little booklet the chamber of commerce puts out for tourists. You could have an ad in it. And you could put a sign out by the road, so people would know that you're here. And if you advertised on the Internet, you could reach a lot more people."

He was already shaking his head. "I wouldn't feel comfortable with all of that. I'm not sure the Leit would approve of advertising on the Internet."

"But plenty of Amish do advertise that way." Enthusiasm made Sarah's green eyes sparkle. "If you didn't want to do that, even just a colorful little brochure in the racks at restaurants and hotels would . . ."

"No." It came out more sharply than he had intended, but at least she stopped. "I'm not interested. Let's get back to work." He glanced at the clock.

Sarah pressed her lips together, her cheeks pink. She might not say anything, but her disapproval was plain. Well, she'd just have to get used to the fact that this was his business, not hers. He'd run it his way.

The sound of young voices put an end to the awkward moment.

"The boys are home. I'll have to go and see to them. You can leave now, if you want."

Sarah shook her head. "I'll finish what I was working on first." Her tone was cool.

Annoyed, he stamped out the door, grabbing his jacket as he went. The twins came running at the sight of him.

"Can we slide on snow saucers, Daadi? Please? We'll do our chores afterward, we promise." Matthew was in the lead, of course.

He had to smile at their enthusiasm, and his annoyance slipped away. "I guess you can do that first. I'll go in and fix your snack. Mind you come for it when I call you."

"We will," Matthew said, setting off toward the barn where the saucers were stored.

"Promise," Mark added before running after him.

Still smiling, Noah headed for the kitchen. He'd thought to make hot chocolate for them on this first snowy school day. That would warm them up after they'd come down the hill behind the barn a few times.

The boys had made him smile, but that didn't mean he'd forgotten his annoyance with Sarah. She was entirely too free with her opinions. This was his business, and how he ran it was up to him. She should keep her ideas to herself.

His conscience pinched him at that. After all, he was

the one who'd expressed his concerns over working with Portman. Maybe that had sounded as if he invited her response. But in any event—

A cry split the air, and the spoon he'd been stirring cocoa with landed on the floor. He was running toward the sound in an instant. Matthew—Mark—one of them was hurt—he should have stayed with them—why had he left them alone . . .

Sarah was ahead of him, running from the workshop toward the back of the barn, the shawl she'd wrapped around herself flying out in the wind. She'd get there first. If one of the boys was hurt . . .

He put on a burst of speed, his feet slipping in the snow. He rounded the corner of the barn. Sarah sat in the snow, her skirt pooling around her, cuddling one twin in her lap. Matthew, he saw in the next instant. Mark was wailing, too, standing over his brother, a red saucer dangling from his hand.

Noah slid to a stop and dropped on his knees. "How bad?" He choked out the words, his heart pounding.

"Not too bad." Sarah's voice was calm and soothing. She cradled Matty against her, gently trying to pry his hand away from his forehead. "Now let us look, there's a good boy."

"Don't touch," Matty wailed.

"I won't touch, just look," she said, and drew his hand away.

The lump that was coming up on his head was huge enough to make Noah's heart stutter. But Sarah never lost her calm.

"There now, that's not so bad. You've got a great big bump on your head. And you know what's going to happen?"

Matthew fingered the lump gingerly as he shook his head.

"You're going to have a black eye. Won't he, Daadi?" Sarah's frown ordered him to say something comforting.

"You certain-sure will," he managed. "Does it hurt anywhere else?"

Matthew shook his head again and then winced at the movement. "Just my head." He looked at his brother. "Hear that, Mark? I'm going to have a black eye."

He said it as if it were a badge of honor. Noah's fear faded and his lips twitched. He exchanged glances with Sarah, seeing that she had the same reaction.

"Now, let's get you inside and put something cold on your head. That'll make it feel better." She gestured to Noah, and he lifted Matty in his arms, a wave of thankfulness sweeping through him.

*Thank You, Lord.*

He strode toward the house, vaguely aware of Sarah saying something to Mark as they went.

Once they reached the kitchen, he set Matthew down on the table and glanced at Sarah. She was already getting out a dish towel.

She gestured to Mark. "Komm, Mark. You help me with this."

He was about to protest, wanting it done quickly, when he looked at Mark and saw what Sarah had obviously already noticed. Mark's face was dead white—his eyes wide and frightened.

Sarah repeated her request, and he blinked, losing that staring, terrified look. Together they made a pad with the dish towel, soaking it in cold water. He clung closely to Sarah as she put the pad gently into place.

Matty whimpered softly, but then relaxed when he realized it wasn't going to make his head worse. He leaned against Noah. Mark's face regained some of its color.

Noah tried to let go of his fear, but the size of the lump on Matty's head scared him. He caught Sarah's gaze.

"A doctor, do you think?" he asked softly.

"I don't think it's necessary." She smiled. "It looks worse than it is, maybe. His eyes are normal, and he didn't lose consciousness. But if you think it best . . ." She let that trail off, acknowledging that it was his decision.

"I guess we can wait a bit." He had to admit that if he had a lump like that on his own head, he wouldn't think a thing about it. But it was different with a child. He eyed Sarah. "How do you come to know so much about it?"

Her face eased into a smile. "You forget I raised two little brothers. I sometimes thought they were intent on destroying themselves. Or turning my hair gray."

"Did they get a bump on the head from saucer-riding?" Matty asked.

"Not from saucer-riding, but from plenty of other things. I remember one time when Thomas was chasing David through the house. I told him to stop, but he tried to argue and ran right into the wall. Not only did he get a big lump, like you, but he left a dent in the wall, and our daadi made him fix it."

Noah, watching them, realized that Sarah had known exactly how to handle the injury. Both boys became so engaged in the story that they peppered her with questions, forgetting what had happened to Matthew.

It occurred to him to wonder why she was working as a bookkeeper when she would clearly be wonderful gut at taking care of children. Sarah might be exasperating in some ways, but right now all he could feel was thankful that she was here.

"Denke," he murmured.

She glanced up and their gazes caught. For just a moment, it felt as if they were communicating without the need for words—as if she understood all that he didn't say. It was like standing in front of a roaring fire on a cold day.

Noah forced his gaze away, praying Sarah hadn't noticed. He wasn't free, and Sarah was a coworker, nothing more.

"HOW DO YOU decide what to do?" Sarah and Dorcas sat at the kitchen table at Dorcas's home, piles of booklets and papers spread out in front of them.

"You remember how it goes, don't you? We need a welcoming, a skit or poem for each of the grades, some songs, and a closing. That's all." Dorcas's eyes twinkled, as if she guessed how Sarah would respond.

"*All?* Sounds like a lot to me. I don't think we properly appreciated what our teacher did for us. So what are all these?" Sarah gestured at the papers covering the table.

"Past programs we've done or ones I've gotten from teachers at other Amish schools. When we had our area teachers' meeting before school started, we all shared materials and ideas. Believe me, it helps!"

"I can imagine. So what are you thinking about?"

"Suppose we sort things according to category— welcome, materials suitable for younger ones, middle grades, and oldest scholars, and then the closing. I'll let my scholars pick some favorite songs, I think."

Nodding, Sarah plunged into helping. She soon saw that most of the materials were marked for various ages.

It was a relief to have something to concentrate on other than her relationship with Noah. Those moments when she'd caught him watching her . . . that had shaken her. She'd been thinking of nothing more than helping the twins, and suddenly she and Noah were looking at each other as if . . . as if they shared something.

She'd like to be friends with Noah. It would make working together easier and more pleasant. But anything else was out of the question.

"How are things going with Noah and the boys?" Dorcas asked the question as if she knew what occupied Sarah's thoughts.

"Fine," she said quickly, and then realized that when Matty went to school with a black eye, Dorcas would wonder why she hadn't mentioned it.

"Well, actually, Matthew had an accident with his snow saucer after school. Got a nasty lump on his head."

Dorcas shook her head. "I should have known. A couple of kids usually manage to damage themselves in the first snow. You were there when it happened?"

"Yah, I was getting ready to leave. I heard him yell and ran out to help. Poor little guy—and Mark was as bad as if he'd been hurt, too."

"Those two are as close as any twins I've ever known. I wouldn't be surprised to know that it hurt Mark just as much." She hesitated. "Did Noah appreciate your help?"

Sarah couldn't help smiling a little. "Honestly, I thought he might bite my head off, but he seemed glad just to have someone there. He needed reassuring as much as the kinder did." She felt a wave of tenderness at the thought of his obvious fear for his child.

"So Elizabeth was wrong," Dorcas said.

"Elizabeth?" For a moment she couldn't think what Dorcas meant. Then she remembered the woman and her advice. "I guess she doesn't know him as well as she imagines."

She found she was picturing Noah's face, hearing his voice when he thanked her. She ought to put it out of her mind, she knew. But somehow she didn't think she would.

# CHAPTER SIX

Sarah glanced out the workshop window on Tuesday afternoon, wondering if there would be any snow left when the twins got home from school. They'd be disappointed if there wasn't, that was certain-sure.

Despite the fact that the sun had begun peeking through the layer of clouds, the ground was still covered with white in places where the sun didn't reach. The adults would probably be glad to see the last of it, but youngsters never wanted to let go of the first snow.

Noah was bent over the matching rocker, as he had been for most of the day, his forehead carved into a frown. Sarah couldn't tell whether his preoccupation was due to the necessity to repeat the same project or for some other reason. They'd moved a step toward friendship yesterday, but not far enough that she could understand his long silences.

She found herself thinking again about his difficult situation. There could be no divorce for Amish, of course, but she still found it strange that he'd never tried to find his errant wife. At least, Grossmammi said that was the case. Had he been so hurt by her running away that he couldn't bear to see her again? Or was it that the ending of his marriage seemed better than continuing to struggle? With no knowledge of Janie or the situation, she couldn't tell.

He looked up suddenly and caught her gaze, and the color rose in her cheeks. At least he couldn't know what she'd been thinking.

"You know what you said yesterday about advertising in that local tourist magazine?"

Startled, she nodded. "*Promise Glen Happenings*, it's called. They have it on racks at all the businesses in town, I noticed."

"You really think that might do some good for the business?"

He still sounded doubtful, but at least not annoyed, as he had yesterday.

"I haven't really looked into it, but I could." She didn't want to promise anything she couldn't deliver, but she couldn't help being enthusiastic. "Several Amish businesses advertise in it. It would be simple to talk to those people and find out. And I think a phone call would give us the information about how much it costs and when the next one comes out." She hesitated. "Would you like me to find out?"

Now it was Noah's turn to hesitate. Finally he nodded. "I guess it wouldn't hurt." He ran his hand absently along the curve of the chair back. "How do you know so much about this sort of thing?"

"I helped a friend with her business a while ago." She couldn't help a feeling of regret whenever she thought of Becky. "It was when we first went to Ohio. We had a neighbor a couple of years older than I was, and we got to be friends. Becky had a greenhouse where she grew plants for sale—mostly flowers." She smiled, remembering. "She got me interested, and I helped her a few hours a week."

"She did some of the things you were telling me about,

ain't so?" The frown had vanished from Noah's face, and his dark blue eyes studied her with what she thought was interest.

"Yah. I really enjoyed working with her, and she got me back into gardening. I hadn't done much after Mamm died." The memory of a sunny fall afternoon spent planting bulbs and talking made her smile. "I remember . . ." She let that trail off.

"What? Something else besides advertising?"

"Not exactly. We had made a lot of plans that fall for what we'd do in the spring—planting bulbs and starting some perennials. But then Daad said he'd heard about a wonderful gut opportunity in Indiana, so we were off again." She shrugged, trying to laugh it off. "Daad always thinks the grass is greener somewhere else."

Noah smiled, but she could read the sympathy in his eyes. "We used to have a buggy mare like that. Daad finally got tired of fixing the fences she broke and sold her."

Sarah nodded, but what he'd said made her think. She hadn't exactly done the same to Daad, of course, but she guessed letting him go on his latest adventure alone was the equivalent. She just hadn't been able to face starting over again one more time. She preferred her familiar pasture to anything else, regardless of how green it was.

Giving herself a mental shake, she came back to the present work. "I'd better make some notes about what I'm going to do before I forget." She raised her head, listening. "Sounds as if the boys are home. I hope Matthew's not planning on a saucer ride today."

"I'll try and get him started on something else." He was putting his tools in their proper places as he spoke. "Are you ready to leave?"

"In a few minutes. I'll get these notes down and tidy up first."

This was good, she thought, straightening her desk.

She and Noah were a little closer to being friends, and that would make working together more pleasant. It was too bad that had come at the cost of a black eye for Matthew.

However, she could hear Matthew's voice excitedly saying something to his father, so he must be feeling himself again. As for Mark . . . She frowned, considering. Certainly the twins' closeness was a fine thing, but she was a little worried about Mark. He seemed so content to be in Matthew's shadow. Wouldn't it be better for him to venture out on his own a bit? She'd have to see what Dorcas thought of it.

She had to laugh at herself. She'd been so determined to steer clear of involvement with Noah's children, but now that seemed a foolish plan. Apparently it wasn't in her nature to turn away from a child who might need something she could give. Taking an interest in them had nothing to do with her job or with their father.

WHEN HE GOT outside, Noah found that Matthew wasn't thinking of a saucer ride today. The twins came home from school excited about the snowman some of the older scholars had made during recess.

"We're going to finish our snowman, too," he insisted after they'd put their school bags inside. "Ain't so, Mark?"

Mark nodded. He seemed to be surveying the half-finished snowman critically. "Maybe we should start over and make it bigger."

"Yah, for sure. We can put it right here." Matty ran to the unbroken carpet of snow in front of the workshop, marked off only by two trails leading to the shop door—his and Sarah's. "You'll help us, won't you, Daadi?"

Noah pushed aside thoughts of getting supper started. The snow would soon be gone, but the boys would remember the first snowman they'd made this year.

The twins immediately started rolling a snowball to make the first part of their snowman. "Let's make it the biggest one ever," Matty said, making Noah smile.

That was Matthew, always wanting to do the biggest and the best. Mark was the more practical one. He was already pointing out to his brother that they shouldn't make the balls too big to lift.

Noah glanced toward the workshop. There was no sign of Sarah yet. He'd noticed that she always left things tidy at the end of the day, and he approved. A worker ought to put the tools of his trade back in their proper places.

He hoped he hadn't taken on too much in agreeing that she should look into the advertising idea. He hadn't really committed himself to following through, but he guessed Sarah could be really persistent once she got an idea in her head.

Sarah always seemed to be so cool and in control that he'd been a little surprised at the vulnerability she'd shown when she'd talked about that incident when she'd worked with her neighbor. Maybe she hadn't realized what she was giving away, but he'd seen the regret in her face when she'd talked about it. That disappointment seemed to have been more important to her than most folks would expect, and he couldn't help wondering what exactly it meant to her.

Maybe that was simply the moment at which she'd seen the life she was going to have with her father. When her mother died, she couldn't have done anything else but step in, but she might not have realized all that would mean. Life had a way of taking people by surprise. It certain-sure had with him.

The boys had nearly finished the first snowball, arguing a little over whether it was big enough. "We don't want him to have a big bottom and a skinny middle, do we?" Mark asked, and Matty reluctantly agreed.

They made the second ball with lots of chatter about how big it should be, and he helped them lift the snowman's middle on top of the base. They stood back to admire it for a moment.

Matty grew impatient first. "Hurry, let's make the head. Then we can decorate him."

He watched as they began rolling the third piece of the snowman. His mother would be home by Christmas, and he wasn't sure who'd be happier to see her—the boys or his daad. But one thing he'd already decided. He wasn't going to take advantage of Mamm when it came to the twins. She'd always be a big part of their lives, but now that they were in school, there was no need for her to be here all the time. He wasn't going to behave the way Sarah's father had.

They had just put the head on the snowman when Sarah came out of the shop. Matty rushed to her.

"Sarah, komm, see our snowman!" He tugged at her hand, practically dancing with impatience.

"Please, Sarah," Mark added.

"Let me see your forehead first." Sarah's smile blossomed as she tilted his face up. "Goodness, anyone can tell you apart today, can't they? That's quite a black eye."

"Teacher Dorcas says we all need lessons in how not to run into things," Mark said. "But we just have to watch out, ain't so?"

"That's right, but I'd guess the saucer didn't go the way Matthew wanted it to."

Noah noticed that she looked at each one of them when she spoke, her green eyes intent.

"It sure didn't." Matty sounded rueful. "I wanted to turn, but the saucer didn't."

Noah exchanged a laughing glance with Sarah. "I don't think the saucer has much to say. Komm, show Sarah the snowman and then let her go on home."

With the two boys pulling on her hands, Sarah advanced

on the snowman, admiring it. "What are you going to make its face with?"

"A carrot for the nose," Matty said. "Mark can get one from the bin in the barn."

Mark rushed off, never bothered by his brother giving him orders.

"How about some stones for his eyes," Sarah suggested. "He can wear my muffler if he wants to." She was taking it from around her neck as she spoke.

"Ach, don't bother." He put out a hand to stop her.

"No trouble." She handed the scarf to Matty. "I'm wonderful glad to have a part in Mr. Snowman."

Mark came rushing back then with a rather shriveled carrot, and Matty put the muffler on while they argued about just the right place for the nose.

"Mark went and got the carrot, so he gets to decide," Noah said, afraid they'd be standing there until the snowman melted if he didn't intervene. Sarah gave him an approving nod, pleasing him in a ridiculous way. Funny how nice it felt to share the twins' nonsense with someone else.

With stones for the eyes and the mouth, the snowman smiled at them. "One more thing," Noah said. "Run inside and get that black knit cap of mine."

They both rushed off, eager to be the one who got it first.

"What energy they have." Smiling, Sarah picked up a handful of snow and began molding it into a ball. "My brothers gave up snowmen for snowball battles very early, as I remember."

He eyed her warningly. "Don't you dare."

The boys came rushing back, quickly forgetting about the cap when they saw Sarah with the snowball. "Throw it, Sarah," Matty said, jumping up and down. "Throw it at Daadi."

Grabbing him, Noah pulled Matty in front of him. "If she does, she'll hit you."

"I'll do it." Mark sent a handful of snow toward him, but it disintegrated before it reached him.

"You have to pack it together, Mark." Sarah demonstrated, packing the snow in her hand. "You get it nice and firm, and then you throw it."

Before Noah could guess her intention, she threw the snowball right at him, catching him in the chest. The boys squealed with laughter and rushed to make snowballs of their own. In a moment the air was thick with flying snowballs.

Noah ducked one from Matty and then took one from Sarah right in the face. Brushing it off, sputtering, he grabbed a handful of snow. "I'll get you for that one."

Sarah ducked behind the snowman, dodging back and forth to evade him. The boys were helpless with laughter, and he wasn't much better by the time he finally connected with Sarah.

She brushed the snow into her hand and made an effort to toss it in his face. Suddenly they were very close. Her cheeks were rosy from the cold and the activity, and her green eyes sparkled with laughter. The moment froze, and then she ducked away, still laughing.

Sarah stopped abruptly, her laughter stifled. He followed the direction of her gaze and saw Elizabeth Schmidt coming toward them from the driveway.

"Well, this looks like fun on a winter day." She gestured with the basket she carried. "I brought peanut butter cookies for an after-school treat. And hot chocolate. Looks like you boys are ready to warm up."

"But we're playing," Matthew protested. "We don't have to go in already, do we?"

Noah managed to give him a reproving frown, although

he couldn't help but sympathize. No one ever wanted to stop doing something fun.

"It's wonderful kind of Elizabeth to bring you a treat," he pointed out.

"Yah, and I'd better be getting home." Sarah brushed off an accumulation of snow from her jacket. "I'll see you all tomorrow."

Elizabeth nodded good-bye to her and then turned toward the house. "Komm along. You can help me pour the hot chocolate and put out the cookies."

Noah's glare stifled any protest the boys might have made. He turned to Sarah, but she was already heading toward the lane. She turned and waved once, and then walked on.

Elizabeth was waiting for him, and he joined her quickly. He'd better try to make up for the boys' lack of enthusiasm.

"It's gut of you to think of us. The hot chocolate will be warming after being out in the snow."

"Not at all," she said, smiling. "You know I love doing things for the twins. They're such sweet boys."

She was being kind, he told himself. But . . .

"You could have asked Sarah to join us. She might have enjoyed a snack."

Elizabeth looked at him in surprise. "But she was obviously eager to leave." She shook her head. "You know, it probably would be better if you didn't let the twins impose on her."

He stiffened. "She doesn't seem to see them as an imposition."

"I'm sure you know best. But Sarah has told several people that she doesn't want to be involved with anyone else's kinder. Apparently she had enough of that raising her brothers and sister. I just thought it would be best to discourage them. Since she works for you, she can hardly say anything negative about your boys, can she?"

He didn't have an answer. He'd appreciated Sarah's response to Matty's saucer crash, and she'd seemed to enjoy those moments of playing in the snow.

Still, Elizabeth wouldn't be making that up. And given what he knew about Sarah's life after her mother died, it might well be true. He'd have to be more careful in the future when it came to Sarah. Theirs was a business arrangement, nothing else.

SARAH SET OFF for town the next morning in her grandmother's buggy, feeling as if she was playing hooky by taking the morning off. She hadn't realized how constricted her life had been since she'd been working all day every day.

Still, it was paying off. Organizing the business records had gone much faster than she'd anticipated, and she'd sent reminder bills to two people who hadn't yet paid for work completed.

Noah's reaction when she'd mentioned unpaid bills had made her shake her head. He'd actually seemed embarrassed at the idea of reminding people they owed him money. He really was much more a craftsman than a businessman. So that was her job, and she didn't mind it in the least. If she collected some of the money owed Noah, she'd feel as if she justified her salary. They hadn't actually talked about it, but she guessed he intended paying by the hour. At least, she hoped so. That would give her a bit more freedom once the books were organized.

The snow was melting off the fields along the road, with little left except in a few shady patches. The twins would be disappointed when their snowman started to vanish. She smiled, thinking of those few minutes playing in the snow with them the previous day.

And with Noah. That was the first time she'd seen him actually relax and enjoy himself. She hadn't realized how strained his usual expression was until she saw him laughing and playing with his boys. His love for them fairly shone in his face, and the years had slipped away, making him look like a boy again.

She'd decided to stop at Dinah Hershberger's bakeshop first to see what Dinah had to say about advertising. Since they'd talked at worship on Sunday, she'd been thinking about Dinah. It couldn't be easy for her to carry on with her business alone, but Dinah seemed to manage. She might have some suggestions about how to promote a business here in Promise Glen.

Just a week into working for Noah, and already she was acting as if she had a share in his business. Of course, if he didn't like the suggestions she came up with, that would be an end to it. She didn't doubt he was capable of rejecting anything he didn't want to do.

But she had come to see that some of the stress he carried related to making a success of his business. It was his path to taking care of his sons, and no doubt he felt the burden doubly because his wife had left.

Farms gave way to homes and then to businesses. Dinah's bakeshop was in one part of a frame building, sharing a storefront with Jacob Miller's harness shop. Jacob, yet another of her many Miller cousins, had been one of Noah's close friends when they were in school, as she remembered.

Sarah drew in to the hitching post along the side of the building, slid down, and patted the mare. "I won't be long."

The mare nuzzled her as if she understood. Dolly was getting up in years, but she covered the distance to town as easily as a two-year-old.

As she walked around to the front, Sarah tried to remember what had been in that part of the building. Jacob's father had had the harness shop before him, but the section Dinah was renting—odd that she didn't remember. She'd thought of this town so often in the years since they'd left.

A bell on the door jingled as she opened it, and she stepped into the aroma of baking bread and hot coffee. Dinah emerged from the kitchen at the sound, smiling at the sight of Sarah.

"Sarah, how nice. I thought you were working every day. Komm in."

In addition to the glass-fronted cabinets displaying baked goods, Dinah's shop had three small tables and chairs. Beyond them, a windowed door led into the harness shop in the other side of the building.

"I have the morning off to do some errands in town, and I wanted to see you. This is so nice. I didn't realize you were a coffee shop as well as a bakery."

Dinah was already pouring out a mug of coffee, looking as if Sarah's visit was the best part of her day so far. "I don't actually have that many people come in for coffee, but enough to make it worthwhile. Can you sit and chat for a bit, or are you in a rush?"

"I'd love to visit." That would make it easier to bring up the subject on her mind.

"Gut." Dinah's gentle, heart-shaped face brightened in a smile. "How about a cruller with your coffee?"

"Sounds great." She sat down, leaving the chair facing the door for Dinah, since she'd no doubt be keeping her eyes open for customers.

In a moment they were settled with coffee and crullers. Sarah took one crisp, delicious bite and smiled. "Wonderful. I'll have to take some home to my grandmother."

"How is she? Wonderful glad to have you home at last, ain't so?"

"She can't be any happier than I am." She sobered, putting her hand over Dinah's. "I'm so sorry about your husband. It must be hard."

Dinah nodded. "Denke. Yah, it is hard, but I'm thankful to have the shop to keep me busy. And you, I hear, are busy working in Noah Raber's business. Are you liking that?"

"Very much. Actually, that's one thing I wanted to talk with you about. Noah wants . . . well, actually, I suggested that he do some advertising for his business. A customer has to know he's there before they'll come out to find him. I thought you might have some ideas."

"I'm glad to help if I can. There's the *Happenings* magazine, of course, and sometimes they'll do an article about a business if you advertise with them. I'll tell you what— Jacob usually stops for coffee mid-morning, and he'd probably have more ideas. Let me ask him to join us."

She rose as she spoke and hurried to the door between the shops, disappearing into the harness shop. Dinah was probably wise—Noah's business had more in common with a harness shop than with a bakery.

Dinah reappeared at the door and Jacob followed her, shedding the heavy leather apron that protected his clothes.

"Cousin Sarah." He had a grin and a hug for her. "It's wonderful gut to have you back where you belong. Grossmammi has been like a dog with two tails about it."

"What an expression to use about your grandmother." She gave him a mock swat. "I see you haven't changed at all."

"I'm a bit bigger," he pointed out, looming over her for a moment before pulling out a chair and accepting the coffee Dinah handed him. "So Dinah says you've a mind to help Noah promote his business. That's our Sarah, organizing him already, and you've only been working there a week."

She couldn't help flushing slightly. "I just suggested trying to get a few more customers, that's all."

"You're exactly right," Jacob said, nodding. "Noah does fine work, but he needs to get involved in the business community, instead of holing up in his workshop all the time."

"Noah's not as outgoing as you are," Dinah pointed out. Obviously the two of them were friends as well as business neighbors. "He never has been."

"No, that's certain-sure. He was always the shy one of his family—more likely to be home working on a project than out getting into mischief like his brothers."

*Like Mark,* Sarah realized. That made sense. Noah had probably let his older brother take the lead, just as Mark did with Matthew.

Jacob leaned over, reaching out a long arm to the rack inside the door. "This is the place to start." He put a copy of *Happenings* on the table and opened it to the page with his ad. "He can put a box ad like this in for fifty dollars a month or in three issues for a hundred. That's what I do, but he might want to start with just one."

"Maybe so." Doubt assailed her. Would Noah feel he could afford to risk fifty dollars on an ad? "He hasn't really said for sure he's going to do it."

"It's not really that much." Jacob seemed to read her thoughts. Or maybe it was that he knew his friend well. "This little book is given out all over the county, not just here, so it's a lot of advertising for the money. If you stop over at the print shop, Len Reynolds will give you a sheet of information."

"I'll do that." She toyed with the idea of offering to pay for part of the ad herself. Trouble was that Noah's pride might be offended. Worse, he might consider her interfering.

"Tell you what," Jacob said. "Why don't I stop by and

see Noah sometime soon? The merchants in town are having an open house next week, where we'll all stay open late and there will be refreshments and door prizes in the different shops. Maybe Noah would display a few things in my shop. Kind of remind people he's there."

"That would be great. And it would come better from you than from me," she admitted with a smile.

"You've got a point, cousin. I'll do it." He shook his head, sobering a little. "The trouble is, Noah has retreated from the community ever since Janie left. I could understand at first—he had his hands full with the babies, and he was really cut up by it. But he needs to stop hiding."

Sarah looked at him with exasperation. "Honestly, Jacob. If you think that, why haven't you made a push to get him out of his shell before this? You were always one of his closest friends."

Jacob, predictably, looked uncomfortable. "I don't know. Guys don't like to interfere."

"Unlike me, you mean." She felt like giving him a swat for real. "Just be sure you see him soon and give him a little push. I'll take care of the rest."

Maybe she was a managing kind of woman. But maybe, in this case, that was just what Noah needed.

# CHAPTER SEVEN

Noah had a quiet morning in the shop since Sarah had taken the time off. She'd suggested that with the office work caught up, he might want her to work fewer hours, which seemed reasonable as long as she didn't mind. She'd probably be needed a bit more at the Miller place in the near future.

The second rocking chair of the pair was nearly finished, and he was looking forward to starting on something new. He had an idea for a desk and bookcase combination that he'd been playing around with. And there was the table he'd put aside.

He'd thought he'd enjoy having the place to himself, but instead he found he was glancing out the window for Sarah's familiar figure. Funny how quickly he'd gotten used to having her around. At least she wasn't a woman who had to be talking even when she had nothing to say.

Noah glanced out again, and this time he was rewarded by the sight of her slender figure crossing the yard toward him. Her cheeks were rosy with the cold and her step was light. All in all, she looked like someone happy with her life right now.

Sarah came in, smiling. "I hope I haven't been gone

too long." She slipped out of her wool jacket and hung it on the hook. Turning toward him, she held up several envelopes. "I was able to pick up quite a bit of information. Dinah Hershberger was helpful, and so was my cousin Jacob."

"Yah, Jacob's a gut businessman, just like his daad was. I'd forgotten he's your cousin. Lots of Millers in the valley, ain't so?"

"That's certain-sure." She came toward him and then hesitated, as if having second thoughts. "Whenever you'd like to look at it, just let me know."

He couldn't help smiling at the restraint in her voice. "What are you going to do with all that enthusiasm in the meantime?"

Sarah's eyes twinkled. "Ach, you're getting to know me too well. I do love getting started on a new project."

Maybe she felt the way he did when he worked on a new idea for a piece of furniture. He couldn't imagine it, but he was willing to admit it might be so. He gave the rocker another rub with a soft cloth and dropped it.

"Let's put those things out on your desk and you can tell me all about it." He'd have to be careful not to let her energy carry him away. He wasn't convinced about this whole idea of advertising. And after all, he'd already found a market for some of his work with Mr. Portman.

Sarah spread papers out and then picked one envelope up again and stuffed it in the desk drawer. "Oops. That's a letter from my sister. I picked it up from the mailbox on my way over."

"She's doing well out west, is she?" The sister was much younger, he knew, and he couldn't say he remembered her at all.

"Nancy's newly married. Once I saw her settled as well as the boys, I knew my work was done. Her husband's a farrier on the side and works with his father in a gut business, and they're living near his family in Indiana."

There was a trace of regret in her face as she said the last part of that. It would be hard, he guessed, to have her siblings settled far away. Far more usual to be like him, with all the members of his immediate family living within five miles of him except for one sister. Amish women tended to settle where their husband's work was, he supposed.

"Jacob and Dinah both advertise in *Happenings,* and Jacob explained how it worked and sent me over to the print shop to get the details. See, here it is." She put a sheet in front of him showing different sizes of ads along with a schedule of costs. He read through it, frowning.

"Kind of costly, isn't it? As I read this, the cheapest thing I could do would cost fifty dollars, with no guarantee I'd see anything back from it."

"That's true, but both Jacob and Dinah feel the ads bring in extra customers. After all, customers have to know you're there before they'll come into your shop."

"Most folks around here know where I am." Maybe he was being a bit stubborn about it, but he didn't have even fifty dollars to waste.

"Most of the Amish community, yah," she said promptly. "But what about the Englisch? And the tourists who come in the spring and summer?"

"Maybe." But to be honest, he hadn't even thought about who his customers were. How *would* people outside the Leit know about his business?

"Look at it this way." Sarah leaned toward him, her face intent. "How many new customers would it take for that fifty dollars to be worthwhile?"

Something else he hadn't thought about. "One, I suppose," he admitted. When she put it that way, it became a lot more reasonable. "Okay, we'll try it. Since you're so enthusiastic, I take it you know how to go about it."

Her smile lit up her face. "That's wonderful gut. I'll put it all together and show you. I can work on it this afternoon unless there's something else you want me to do."

"No, go ahead." He gave a wry smile. "I wish my sons had as much interest in the business as you do."

Sarah studied his face for a moment. "How did you become interested in furniture making? That isn't what your daad does."

"My Onkel James. He's the one who was into making things with wood. Not for sale, but just a hobby. He made things for presents mostly. He used to let me come into the workshop and help him with projects." He glanced around the familiar room where he'd first learned to work with wood. "That's how it started, and it wasn't long before I knew that was what I wanted to do."

Sarah's eyebrows lifted slightly. "I haven't seen you do that with Matthew and Mark."

She said it lightly, as if it meant nothing in particular, but it hit him like a bucket of cold water in his face. Sarah had it right. He didn't bring the boys into the workshop. At first he'd been afraid they'd hurt themselves, and it was too hard to keep an eye on both of them. Their grandmother usually kept them busy while he worked.

"You know, people might start thinking you have all the answers if you go around hitting the nail on the head like that all the time."

A pink flush showed in Sarah's cheeks. "If you're trying to tell me to mind my own business . . ."

"I'm trying to tell you that you're right about the boys. I can't believe I never saw that for myself." He shook his head at his own obtuseness. "With a gift like that, you ought to have a flock of kids of your own."

The instant the words were out of his mouth he wanted to take them back. If he'd hurt her feelings . . .

"I'm sorry. I should learn to keep my mouth shut if I'm going to say things like that."

There was the ghost of a smile on Sarah's face. "Don't worry about it. I'll take it as a compliment." She hesitated for a moment. "Can you guess how many offers of marriage I've had?"

Now it was his turn to blush, and he didn't suppose it was so becoming on him. "I don't know. A lot." He hoped that was the right answer.

She shook her head. "Three, actually. All three of them were widowers with families. One had eight kinder already, and he was quite open about it. He didn't know me himself, but he'd been assured I'd be a wonderful gut mother to them."

Her light tone eased the tension he'd felt. "It's too bad there aren't many single men your age in Promise Glen."

"According to Dorcas, there's only one, and he's my cousin." She was laughing as she said it, so he guessed she wasn't that troubled. "Don't get me wrong. I love young ones. But I think marriage needs more than that."

"Yah." The thought of his own marriage left a bitter taste in his mouth. "It does for sure."

It took another moment before he realized that they were talking like old friends. He'd never thought that could happen with a woman, not after Janie. But maybe he'd been wrong.


USING THE INFORMATION she'd brought back from the print shop, Sarah busied herself with planning possibilities for the ad. She could only hope she hadn't let her enthusiasm carry her away. Noah obviously had to watch

every penny. If he spent the money on her recommenda-
tion and then didn't see any results . . . well, that wasn't
something she wanted to imagine.

She'd brought back several issues of the local magazine, noting how Jacob changed his ad for different
months. It hadn't occurred to her to do that, but now that
she saw it, she could understand. Each one had the same
basic information about the shop, its location, and what it
offered, but each one showcased something different.

Gazing thoughtfully at the finished pieces she'd arranged in a display, she wondered which would work the
best to highlight. Maybe something that would make a
nice Christmas present, given the time of the year. The
small chest, for example. She could imagine a young man
giving it to his sweetheart.

By the time she'd completed several possibilities, she
heard the twins' voices outside, along with the low rumble of
Noah's answer. She hadn't even realized he'd gone outside.

Glancing at the clock, she began putting papers together. Obviously showing these to Noah would have to
wait until the next day. He'd be too busy with the boys,
and she had promised to meet Dorcas at the schoolhouse
to plan the setting and props for the Christmas program.

Slipping into her coat, Sarah snuggled a muffler around
her neck against the cold. Since she'd donated her other
one to the snowman, she supposed it would have to be
laundered before she could use it again. Smiling at the
memory, she stepped outside.

By the time Sarah reached the bottom step, both twins
were rushing to her. "Sarah, did you see our snowman?
He's melting away." It was Matthew who spoke, of course,
but Mark nodded vigorously.

"Yah, I see. He looks sad, doesn't he?" Indeed, the
snowman sagged as if depressed, and her muffler drooped,
dripping.

"Poor snowman," Matty said.

Mark nudged him. "Don't call him that."

The sudden objection was so unlike Mark that Sarah blinked. "Why do you say that, Mark?"

"I know." Matty wrinkled his nose. "It's because that's what *she* says about us."

Now she really was confused. "Who says what about you?"

"Elizabeth," Mark murmured, and then clamped his lips shut as if sorry he'd spoken.

"When she talks about us." Matthew finished his brother's thought. "Elizabeth calls us 'those poor boys.' We heard her."

"I see." This was a tough one. Caution told her not to meddle, but her instinct to help was stronger. After all, they'd said it to her. She hadn't brought it up. She brushed off the step and sat down, hoping it wasn't too wet. "Why do you suppose she said that?"

Inside, she was raging at Elizabeth. True, people might foolishly say "poor boys" about them because their mother had left, but it was inexcusable to let them hear it.

Mark stared at his toes, his face a mask of misery. Her heart hurting, she drew them toward her.

"'Cause we don't have a mammi," Matty said. "She went away and left us."

So they knew it. She'd wondered what they might have been told. "Well, I think they're foolish to say that," she declared. "Maybe your mammi isn't here, but you have a daadi who loves you more than anything in the whole world. I think that's enough for anybody. Don't you?"

The twins exchanged looks, brightening a little.

"I wouldn't say 'poor boys,'" she said. "I'd say 'smart boys' or 'lively boys' or sometimes 'silly boys.' Ain't so?"

Matty, the more volatile of the twins, grinned engagingly. "Silly," he said. "That's what we are."

She rubbed a gentle hand on Mark's shoulder. "What about you, Mark? Okay?"

As if in answer, he pressed a little closer against her before drawing back, nodding. Relieved, she saw that the shadow had left his eyes.

She smiled, thankful for the resilience of the young, but still seriously annoyed with Elizabeth. She ought—

Sarah lost the thought, realizing that Noah was standing a few feet away. How long had he been listening? And was she about to be told off for interfering with his children?

But he clapped the boys on their shoulders. "Your snack is ready, and I see Cousin Sally coming. You'd best say good-bye to Sarah and greet your cousin."

"Bye, Sarah," they chorused. Looking excited, they raced toward the driveway, where a teenage girl was climbing down from a buggy.

Sarah braced herself, but Noah's first words were mild enough. "I'm sorry if they delayed you. I told them not to bother you."

Standing, she brushed off the back of her skirt. "They weren't bothering me. We were talking."

"So I heard." His gaze met hers, and she thought she read pain there. "Denke, Sarah. You said exactly the right thing."

"I didn't bring it up," she said quickly. "But I felt I had to say something. Elizabeth . . ." She stopped, not wanting to voice her opinion.

"Elizabeth means well." He glanced away. "Anyway, I'll talk to them again about not bothering you."

"Please don't. I enjoy talking with them. Why would you think they bother me?"

"I . . ." He seemed at a loss for an answer. "Well, I'd heard you don't want to bring up someone else's kinder, not after raising your siblings. I mean, before we talked about it."

Somehow she thought she knew who had given Noah that bit of advice. What did Elizabeth hope to gain, anyway? If she was looking for another husband, she must realize that Noah wasn't free.

"I told you what I feel," she reminded him. "Just because I won't marry someone solely to mother his children, that doesn't mean I don't enjoy kinder. Especially the twins. They always make me smile."

"Well, gut. That settles it, then." He hesitated a moment and then said, "Weren't you going home?"

Without realizing it, she'd started walking toward the lane that led to the school. Laughing, she shook her head. "I guess that does look as if I don't know where I'm going. No, I have to stop by the school to help Dorcas decide some things about the Christmas program. She'll wonder what happened to me."

A smile chased across Noah's face. "She'll wonder it about me, too. She asked me to help build the props for the program. So if you'll wait a minute until I speak to my niece, I'll walk with you."

He hurried toward the house, not giving her time to respond. Maybe that was just as well, because what she was thinking was better not shared. What exactly was Dorcas up to? Just wait until she got her alone.

IT WASN'T FAR to walk to the school, and that was just as well, Sarah decided. The silence between them was a little awkward. Or was it just her, because she was afraid Dorcas had manipulated this?

Noah put out a hand to help her negotiate a slushy patch on the lane and then cleared his throat. "About Elizabeth—she means well. Her husband was one of my closest friends."

Sarah nodded, wondering just how much he'd heard of

that conversation with the boys. Did he realize how they felt about Elizabeth? "I'm sure she does . . . mean well, that is."

"She tries to be helpful, but she doesn't seem to know how to talk to the boys. Funny, because she's known them most of their lives."

So apparently he did realize how the boys felt. "It's hard to deal with something like that. You want your children to be polite, of course, but you can't make them like someone. Maybe it'll be better when they're older." She didn't really think so, but she could be letting her own reaction to Elizabeth affect her judgment.

He shrugged. "I hope." He glanced at her. "You seemed to know right away how to be friends with them. You must have a gift. I remember your mammi . . ."

Noah hesitated, as if wondering whether it was all right to talk about her.

"Yah, Mammi had that gift, that's certain-sure. She was always so interested in people. And it was real, not put on." She smiled, remembering.

"That was it. She always had a smile for each of the kinder when she saw us." He seemed to study her face. "You're like her, you know. In looks, but in manner, too."

"I couldn't ask anything better."

It was a nice moment. Maybe Noah realized how much she loved to talk about Mammi, or maybe it was chance, but either way, she appreciated it. Funny. She'd thought at first that he was so introverted he was difficult to talk to. It wasn't that, she realized. He only talked when he had something to say.

"Here we are." Noah opened the door for her and wiped his boots on the mat. "Teacher Dorcas will get after us if we make wet tracks in her schoolroom."

"That's right, I will." Dorcas was there to greet them. "So you walked over together—I thought you might."

"You didn't tell me Noah was going to be helping, too." She gave Dorcas a pointed look and got an expression of innocence in return.

"Didn't I? I guess I didn't have a chance. I thought Noah was the best person to tackle the carpentry that needs doing for the program." She waved them to the front of the room, where three chairs were arranged around her desk.

Hanging their jackets in the coatroom, they joined her. Sarah looked around the familiar room, so little changed since she'd been one of the scholars. Different posters, of course, but the arithmetic lesson on the chalkboard even looked like one she'd have struggled with.

"This is my first time working on the program since I was in it," Noah said. "You'll have to show me what you want done."

"No problem." Dorcas had an encouraging smile. It was the one she'd always used to lead other kids into trouble, as Sarah remembered. "Sarah and I planned what each group will do, and there are just a few props needed for them. The main thing today is to figure out how we can turn this area into a stage." She gestured toward the front of the room.

"It's hard to see how you can make it look like anything but a classroom," Sarah commented. "You can't get rid of the chalkboard or bulletin boards, although we could move your desk out of the way."

"Yah, for sure we'll do that. And I plan to have the scholars decorate the chalkboard and bulletin boards for the Christmas season. Maybe if we had a curtain, but I've done that before, and it's always a hassle to open and close."

"I'll say." Noah chuckled. "I remember one year when the whole curtain fell down on top of the teacher. We got her out from under it all right, but it knocked her kapp off and her hair came down."

"And you laughed, I'm sure," Dorcas said with mock severity. "The scholars always think it's hilarious when the teacher looks foolish."

"Guilty," he said, grinning. "So what else could we do?"

"What about a kind of archway?" Sarah stepped back, surveying the front area. "Some sort of frame that we could decorate with greens."

Dorcas was quick to nod, her eyes sparkling. "That could work. Then each class could step to the middle when it's their turn to speak."

Noah followed Sarah, his gaze seeming to measure the width of the room. "How big would it need to be? And how high? I'd have to be sure it was sturdy enough not to topple over, but I might be able to attach it to the side walls."

Looking toward the ceiling, Sarah visualized it. With a quick movement, she pulled a child's chair over near a table and climbed up. "About like this, do you think?" She held up her hand. "Or maybe a little higher?" Still gazing upward, she took the large step up to the table.

"Look out." Noah reached out to steady her, but before she could take his hand the chair wobbled, her weight shifted, and the chair slid out from under her.

She gasped, seeing the floor coming at her, reaching futilely for something to hang on to. But before she could hit, Noah grabbed her. His arms were steady around her, and she felt the strength of his muscles under her hands. Her breath caught, and she seemed to feel her heart pounding in her chest.

"Are you okay?" Noah clasped her arms. "Did your ankle twist?"

Sarah shook her head, unable to speak. That moment, when his arms closed around her, she'd had a surge of emotion that shocked her. Attraction—pure and simple, that lurch deep inside that made her long for his arms around her. She couldn't deny it. Her cheeks grew hot with embarrassment, and she couldn't meet his gaze, afraid of what he might see there.

She took a breath, steadying herself with a hand on the table. "I'm fine. Just clumsy, that's all."

Noah stepped back, looking relieved, and Dorcas gave her a quick hug.

"Enough excitement. I'll tell you what I tell my scholars. Chairs are for sitting, not climbing on."

"Do they obey?" Noah asked, maybe in an effort to ease Sarah's embarrassment.

"Always," Dorcas said, and then laughed. "Well, most of the time. Suppose you figure out whether we can build an archway. Sarah can sit down where it's safe and help me make a list of props."

Dorcas was amused, and she very obviously had noticed more than Noah had when it came to Sarah's reaction.

But how could she find it amusing? Attraction might be a natural enough thing, but Sarah had never felt anything so overwhelming in her life. And it was impossible. She couldn't feel that way. Noah wasn't free, and very likely he would never be.

# CHAPTER EIGHT

When they'd finished what they could do for the day, Dorcas insisted on driving both of them home, pointing out that it was on her way. Sarah would have gotten out of it if she could, but it was already dusk, and Dorcas wouldn't hear of it.

For that matter, Noah had been equally insistent, which further convinced her not only that he had felt nothing in those moments they'd been so close, but that he hadn't noticed her reaction. Relieved, she'd reluctantly agreed to a ride home.

They hadn't gotten out of the school lane before Sarah knew this was a mistake. Squeezed between Dorcas and Noah on a seat built for two people, she could feel Noah's every breath, it seemed. Even through the wool of her coat and Noah's heavy jacket, she was far too aware of the way her shoulder pressed against his arm and the slightest movement of his long leg.

"Sorry for the squeeze," Dorcas said cheerfully. "But it's not far to Noah's."

"Just drop me off at the end of the lane. That's plenty close enough."

That was exactly how she felt—the sooner the better.

And once she and Dorcas were alone, she was going to let her friend know exactly what she thought of her manipulation.

As Dorcas had said, it wasn't far to Noah's lane. When he finally jumped down she slid over on the seat, her tense muscles relaxing. Now maybe she could get her renegade emotions under control.

Dorcas shot her a sideways glance as she clucked to the horse. "Did you like my little surprise?"

"You did that on purpose. Dorcas, what is wrong with you? Don't you realize folks are ready enough to gossip whenever Noah looks at a woman?"

The teasing look Dorcas wore vanished abruptly. "I never thought of that, honestly, Sarah." To do her justice, at least she did sound sorry. "I just thought that since you're working for him, it might be easier if you and Noah got to know each other as friends."

Sarah didn't speak, because she was afraid that anything she said might give her away. Would this ride never end?

"You're not mad, are you? I didn't mean anything."

Sarah managed a wry smile. "Seems to me I remember you saying that in excuse just about every time one of your bright ideas got us into trouble."

"I know, I know. Sorry. I thought I'd gotten over being impulsive." She paused, but Sarah seemed to feel Dorcas studying her face. "It's something more than that, isn't it? Sarah, don't tell me you're falling for him."

"Of course not," she snapped. "*Falling for him.* Where do you get such sayings? You might try for a little dignity now that you're a teacher."

Dorcas chuckled. "I do. And usually I succeed. Seeing you again just takes me back to being a silly teenager at heart. But seriously, I'm sorry. I just didn't think about the fact that this might be a difficult situation for both of you."

"No harm done." She'd like to believe that. "You can drop me . . ." she began, but Dorcas was already turning into the lane.

"I'll at least deliver you to your door." She drew up to the back porch as she said the words. "There you are. Thanks, Sarah, for helping."

She nodded, sliding down quickly and skidding on a slushy patch. "Get off home now before it's completely dark. I'll see you soon."

Dorcas swung into turning with a final wave. Sarah hurried toward the door, relief sweeping over her. Now, if only she could dodge any lengthy conversations with her grandmother, maybe she could have the solitude she needed to forget having felt anything at all when Noah held her.

When she went into the kitchen, she found it empty. Where was Grossmammi? At this hour she'd normally have supper started. But she wasn't here, and in fact the whole grossdaadi haus felt empty. She walked into the living room, calling out, but there was no answer.

She wanted to be alone, but not like this. Hurrying now, she crossed over into the farmhouse. The instant she opened the door, she inhaled the aroma of chicken potpie. Her grandmother was at the stove and turned at the sound of the door.

"Grossmammi, what's happening? Where's Ruthie?" Little Mary, playing with her blocks in the corner, toddled over to her and tugged on her skirt. The expression on her grandmother's face set off her alarms. "What's wrong?"

"Nothing serious," Grossmammi said quickly, making an obvious effort not to look worried. "Ruthie had her check by the midwife this morning, and she decided Ruthie should see the doctor."

A chill clutched Sarah's heart. "Is it the baby?"

Mary chose that moment to hold her arms up, loudly voicing one of her few words. "Up!" she demanded.

Sarah picked up the toddler, patting her automatically. "Is it?" she repeated.

"The doctor was a little concerned that the boppli might come early. So she's ordered bed rest for Ruthie." Her voice trembled a little, and she shook her head impatiently. "I'm sure it will be all right. These things happen, and it's not that long until her due date."

Sarah nodded, but Grossmammi's apprehension was contagious. "We'll have to get organized to take care of things. I can take over supper if you have something else to do."

"Actually, Ruthie wanted to see you when you came in. Put Mary in the high chair first, and I'll give her a little snack. Then you'd best run upstairs."

"Right." She bounced Mary in her arms. "You'd like a snack, ain't so, Mary?"

Obviously understanding, Mary reached toward the high chair, and Sarah popped her in without any difficulty. Grossmammi produced a toddler cup and a graham cracker, giving them to Mary and crooning softly to her.

Taking advantage of the moment, Sarah hurried to the stairs. Her desire for solitude vanished in the midst of the family emergency, and in fact seemed foolish to her now. How self-centered she'd been—her feelings didn't count when something real and serious was happening.

Tapping lightly on the door, Sarah looked in. Eli sat next to the bed, holding Ruthie's hand and looking uncomfortable. He greeted her with a relief that was obvious.

"Here's Sarah now. You just tell her anything that needs to be done. She'll take care of it."

"That's right." She approached the bed, and Eli gave her his chair and retreated. "Grossmammi and I can handle everything. Not as well as you, that's certain-sure, but well enough to go on with."

Ruthie, propped up on pillows against the headboard,

grasped Sarah's hand. "Don't tell my sisters. Promise me. Don't let Eli tell them."

"Of course not, if that's what you want." She patted Ruthie's hand. "I'm sure Eli won't do anything you don't want him to do." She hesitated, but Ruthie had to know this. "I'm afraid they're bound to hear, though. You know how fast word spreads."

"I know. But not until tomorrow, at least. By then I'll feel able to cope with them." Tears glistened in her eyes. "You know how they are. I just want you and Grossmammi and Eli tonight."

"That's what you'll have, then," Sarah reassured her, suspecting that when Ruthie's sisters heard, they'd blame her and Grossmammi for not telling them. But Ruthie came first.

Ruthie sniffled a little. "That sounds thankless, I know. But you saw how they are. They'd rush to take over and not listen to a thing I said." A faint smile flickered. "I have to be a bit stronger to cope with them."

"I know. Big sisters can be a pain." She smiled, knowing Ruthie would appreciate the joke.

"I don't want Grossmammi to do too much." The worry came back into Ruthie's eyes. "She shouldn't be running up and down the stairs."

"I won't let her." She patted Ruthie's hand again.

"But your work . . ." Ruthie began.

"That's a fortunate thing. Noah and I decided that now that the office is organized, I won't be working full-time. So I can be here when you need me. God's timing is always right—that's what Grossmammi says."

"Yah." She settled back against the pillows. "Rest and don't worry, that's what the doctor said." Her round face crumpled suddenly. "Oh, Sarah, do you think my boppli will be all right?"

"I'm sure of it." She forced assurance into her voice.

"All you have to do is obey doctor's orders. Let your body take care of the rest, and the baby will be fine. I'm certain-sure."

Ruthie nodded, seeming to accept her words. "I'm glad you're here," she said, her voice soft. "At first, I didn't know how it would be, but now I do. It's a blessing."

Sarah found herself blinking back tears. She bent and kissed Ruthie's cheek. "Now you try to sleep a little. I'll be up in a little while with some delicious chicken potpie for you. Grossmammi's chicken potpie will heal anything."

A soft chuckle was her reward. She turned away, mentally listing all the things that must be done. If anything was good for taking your mind off yourself, it was someone else in trouble.

NOAH DISCOVERED THAT young Sally had left a pot of beef stew on the stove for their supper. Relieved, he dropped his harried search for something he could fix in a hurry. Somehow he'd never mastered the technique of putting a meal together quickly.

"Cousin Sally made that." Matty stood on tiptoe to watch his father stir the stew. "She said so. She made it this morning just for us."

"That was wonderful gut of her, ain't so?" He dished up some applesauce to go with it.

"She likes to play with us," Mark said. "She told us so."

"Maybe she could come again soon. She'd like that." Matthew scurried to his chair, apparently sure supper was about to appear.

"Maybe so." He shook his head at his son. "Wash up first. You know that."

Matty's grin showed his good-natured response to being caught. The two boys scrambled to the sink, jostling each other.

So Sally wanted to come more often. Or maybe that was wishful thinking on the twins' part. Either way, it made him think about how often he'd turned down opportunities to get together with family.

Was that as selfish as it suddenly seemed? He felt awkward in family gatherings—the only one without a spouse. That wasn't a good reason to deny the boys the fun of family times.

Maybe Mammi had been wiser than he knew to make her trip at this time. He'd begun seeing things in a new light since he'd been getting along without her help. His thoughts flashed to Sarah and what he'd learned about her father. That had shown him, clearly, the type of man he didn't want to be—a man who thought only of his own feelings.

Once they'd cleaned up from supper, Noah realized that he hadn't finished his work before he'd hurried off to the school. He opened his mouth to tell the boys he had to go back to the shop when he remembered what he'd told Sarah about his uncle.

"There's a little more work to do in the shop. Suppose you boys come and help me?"

Their faces, so alike, were easy to read—first surprise, and then sheer pleasure. "For real?" Matthew spoke, as usual, for both of them.

"For real. Run and get your jackets on. It's cold outside."

By the time he'd shrugged into his own coat and taken the flashlight from the hook by the door, the boys were waiting on the porch. "Come on, then." Shining the beam on the porch steps, he led the way.

"It's really dark." Mark's voice wavered a bit.

"Yah, it is. But look up at the sky."

The clouds had cleared away, and it was one of those crystal clear winter nights when the stars were so bright it almost seemed he could reach up and touch them.

"Wow." Mark breathed the word.

"There's the Big Dipper," Matty said, pointing. "See it, Mark?"

"Right you are. Can you find the Little Dipper? Remember how Grossdaadi taught you to find it?"

"Make a line through two of the stars in the Big Dipper." Matty began well enough, but then he faltered. "Which two was it?"

Noah squatted between them. "Look at the two stars that make the outside of the Big Dipper's bowl." He pointed. "See? Now draw a line between them and keep going until you come to a very bright star."

"There!" Mark bounced against him. "There it is."

"It's at the end of the Little Dipper's handle." Noah traced the shape, remembering when Daad had knelt between him and his brother to show them. Daad had been good at taking time to help them appreciate God's world. He needed to do the same.

"It has a long handle," Mark observed. His upturned face was rapt, and he looked as if he could stand there all night.

Matty was not so patient. "Komm on. Let's go to the workshop."

Running in and out of the flashlight's beam, the twins scurried across the yard. Once they were inside, he let Matty hold the flashlight for him while he pumped up and lit the gas lamp. When it was hung from the ceiling hook, it provided plenty of light for the few small things he needed to do.

Noah led them to the rocking chair, still on the workbench. "This just needs a last going-over with the cloth." He handed each of them a soft fabric square. "You two can do that while I clean up."

"Did it get dusty?" Mark asked as he drew his cloth carefully down the arm of the chair.

"You could say that. I go over it with very fine sand-paper, and that leaves some dust on it. So it needs to be wiped down."

"We'll do a gut job." Matty nearly climbed on the workbench in his eagerness. "You can count on us."

Amused at their enthusiasm, Noah left them to it while he put away the tools he'd had out. Normally he did that last thing before leaving the shop, but he'd been distracted this afternoon. His uncle had never let him leave the shop until everything was back in its proper place.

He was interrupted by a clatter as something hit the floor. He spun around to find Mark staring at the screwdriver on the floor. Mark looked up at his daad, his face white, eyes wide with dismay, and Noah's heart winced. His little boy shouldn't look that upset over a simple accident.

"Ach, I forgot to put that screwdriver away. Bring it over here, Mark, and I'll show you where it goes."

Mark bent to grab it, and when he came hurrying with it, his cheeks were rosy again. But all the while he was showing Mark how the tools were arranged and letting him put the screwdriver in place, Noah struggled.

Why was Mark so lacking in self-confidence? Was it something he'd done or something he hadn't done? Either way, he had to find a way to help him.

As they closed up the workshop and walked back to the house in the glow of the flashlight, Noah worried at it. If Janie had stayed, would she have known how to handle Mark's shyness? What kind of mother would she have been, if she'd stayed long enough to find out?

Inside, as he hung up his jacket, he noticed the list he'd left lying on the counter—the list of props for the program that Sarah had written out for him. He looked at it for a moment and then turned to the boys.

"I'm going to be making some things Teacher Dorcas

needs for the Christmas program. Would you two like to help with those?"

They didn't need to say anything. The pleased excitement on their faces was enough for him.


SARAH COULD HARDLY believe it was the end of the week already. In one way it seemed that the time flew by, yet in another she felt she'd been back in Promise Glen forever.

Leaving the lane, she crossed the yard to the workshop. She'd have to speak with Noah about her schedule for this week. Grossmammi insisted she could handle everything at home, but she'd wear herself out trying to take care of a toddler and Ruthie. Eli would help, of course, but he had his own work to do. She'd told them she'd be home early this afternoon, when she'd try to persuade Grossmammi to have a rest while she took over.

Noah hadn't arrived yet when she went in, so she stoked the stove and started making coffee. Still wearing her coat, she went to her desk. The crucial thing today was to get a decision from Noah on the advertisement. If they didn't send it in soon, it would be too late for the Christmas issue.

Organizing the folder of papers, she pulled open the drawer of the desk. There, on top of the ledger, lay the letter she'd received from Nancy yesterday. How could she have forgotten getting a letter from her only sister? Slitting it open with a paper knife, she spread it out eagerly.

Nancy's letter was like Nancy herself—cheerful and bubbling with enthusiasm. So far she liked everything about married life, it seemed, and she'd been assimilated into her husband's family without a hitch. She'd joined a quilting frolic with her sisters-in-law, and Daniel's mother had given her the recipe for that steak and onion casserole he liked so much. It was like having Nancy sitting across from her, chatting without a break as she always did.

*I was glad to hear you got the job you wanted right away. But I was wondering—is Noah Raber's wife the Janie Burkhalter who ran away from him and her babies to turn Englisch? Because there's a Burkhalter family in the church here in Indiana, and there's been some talk of an Englisch relative in the area. So I wondered if it's the same family.*

Sarah's breath seemed to stop with the shock. She read the paragraph again, but there was no mistaking what it said.

Could it really be Noah's Janie, surfacing in such an unexpected way? It seemed too ridiculously like a coincidence, but it was true that the Amish world was a small one. Just about every family in Pennsylvania had a relative or two in a settlement in Ohio or Indiana, if not farther out west. It wasn't really strange to think that Janie might choose to stay in an area where she already had people.

But would they welcome her? They'd have to know that she'd run away from her husband and left the Amish.

No, it was impossible. Nancy had to be wrong. She was building too much on the fact that her community had such a family. Nancy always had jumped to conclusions. When she'd received Sarah's letter about her new job, she'd taken off from there and imagined a connection.

That had to be it. Putting the letter down, she headed for the coffee, thinking she needed to clear her thoughts with a hot cup. Noah came in the door, wiping his boots on the rug she'd added in front of the door.

"Is that coffee I smell? Wonderful gut."

Smiling, she poured a mug and took it to him. "All

ready. I decided I needed it to get myself moving this morning."

"Did you have a bad night?" He took the coffee, his fingers brushing hers as he did so.

"Not exactly." Here was the opportunity she needed to settle her work schedule. "But Ruthie has been ordered bed rest by her doctor. It looks as if she'll need help for the next couple of weeks, at least."

"Ach, that's hard, that is. Does the doctor think . . ." He hesitated, and she knew he was trying to find out about the baby without mentioning Ruthie's pregnancy in mixed company.

"The doctor and midwife seem sure everything will be all right if she just takes it easy. I'll need to be helping, so I thought we could talk about my schedule."

"You must take whatever time you need," he said quickly. "Family comes first. If you want to leave now, just go ahead. I'll manage."

"No, not now. I'll take off early this afternoon, if that's all right. Grossmammi is taking care of Ruthie this morning, and I'm sure her sisters will turn up soon." She smiled, remembering Ruthie's comments. "I'll get the advertisement ideas for you."

She hadn't meant that as an invitation, but he followed her to her desk. She opened the folder with her ideas, covering the letter. "Here are some possibilities. If you want to do an ad, that is." *Don't push*, she told herself.

But he didn't seem to take it that way, bending over the desk to gaze intently at the papers.

"I used the ads that Jacob had for the harness shop as a kind of model for what you could do."

"I see that. I looked over the magazine again last night." He paused, studying them for another moment. "That one," he said, planting his finger on the one she'd thought was her best effort. "We'll use that."

"Does that mean you want to go ahead with it?" She held her breath, waiting.

"Who am I to argue with the wisdom of Jacob and you?" His eyes crinkled. "Yah, go ahead and send it in."

"I'll do it right away." In her excitement, she snatched up the folder, revealing the letter from Nancy. She started to put it down again, but he was too quick for her.

"That's the letter from your sister in Indiana, ain't so? Are you just now reading it?"

"I left in such a hurry yesterday that I didn't take it." Once again her cheeks felt warm at the thought of what had happened at the school. She stuck the letter back in the envelope and put it in the drawer, wishing she could forget its contents as easily.

Noah was frowning slightly. "Whereabouts in Indiana is she?"

"It's a nice rural area where there's a big Amish population. The nearest town is Standish. That's where we were living when Nancy met her husband." She hesitated, wondering how much she could ask without making him suspicious. "Do you know Indiana at all?"

"Not much." His face seemed to close. "Janie. My wife—she had relatives there. They came for our wedding. Her daad moved out there after . . . after Janie left."

Sarah's throat seemed to close so that the words came out with difficulty. "You've never heard anything about where she might be?"

Noah frowned, his eyes seeming to darken. "No." His tone was curt. He must think her a gossip, probing like that.

"I'm sorry. I shouldn't have asked." But if Janie's father was there, was it possible that Janie was as well?

Noah didn't respond. He stood still, frowning into a past only he could see. Finally he turned away. "I'd best get to work. You'll take care of the ad, yah?"

"I'll do it right away." She sank into her chair, her muscles weak with relief at ending this difficult conversation. But even as he moved away, her thoughts returned to what she'd learned.

Janie's relatives were indeed in the same community as her sister. That certainly increased the chances that Nancy's speculations could be right. Still, they might have any number of relatives who had gone Englisch.

She could ignore the whole thing, but was that the right thing to do? If she were sure that Janie was actually there, should she tell Noah? Would he even want to know?

The questions were unanswerable, at least without more information. So that's what she had to have. Her fingers tightened on the handle of the desk drawer. She'd write to Nancy again tonight. She'd try to find out if her sister really had any basis for her idea. And then . . . then she'd decide what, if anything, to tell Noah.

# CHAPTER NINE

Noah watched as Mr. Portland's van drove off down the lane, the second rocking chair secure in the back. It was a satisfying feeling to have a wad of money in his hand, with the promise of the other half of the payment within the week, once Portland had been paid.

Timely, that's what it was. With Christmas coming up, some extra cash was welcome. He still hadn't decided what to give the twins for Christmas. He could ask them outright, but then they'd know, and he'd like to surprise them. Maybe his niece would have some ideas after having spent time with them.

And thinking of Christmas reminded him that he hadn't done anything else to prepare for the holiday, either. Mamm usually did that—cutting greens to put around the house, setting up the crèche, making Christmas cards with the boys, to say nothing of all the baking she normally did.

Well, Mamm wouldn't be back until so close to Christmas that he'd have to take on some of those chores himself. Except for the baking. He drew the line there.

Noah turned toward the house, his usual Saturday

cleanup chores on his mind. No doubt he'd be calling the twins back from the barn to finish cleaning their bedroom—they always missed something.

A buggy turned into the lane just as he started up the porch steps. He turned, going to greet the visitor, and smiled in surprise to see that it was Jacob Miller.

"Jacob. What brings you out this way on a Saturday morning? Not enough business to keep you in the shop?" He took a lead line and attached the buggy horse to the hitching rail.

Jacob jumped down, grinning. "I'm giving my nephew a chance to run the shop this morning. Millie's boy, that is. He wants to come in with me as an apprentice, so I thought I'd give him a taste of it."

"I didn't realize Millie's son was that old." Time had certainly gotten away from him. He supposed he'd seen the boy at worship, but his age hadn't registered.

"Yah, he's in his last year with Teacher Dorcas. I may let him start next summer. In the meantime, he can try on the role and I can come visiting on a Saturday morning. Give us a chance to talk."

Surprise colored his thoughts as he nodded. When had Jacob ever stopped by just to visit?

"Come on in. The coffee's still hot."

"Sounds good. Where are those boys of yours?"

"There." He nodded toward the two small figures running from the barn. "Coming to see who's here. They've been in the barn the last hour. The barn cat finally brought her kittens out for them to see."

"Kittens at this time of year?"

"Yah. Christmas kittens, Matty calls them." He led the way into the kitchen and gestured toward a chair, heading for the coffeepot.

The twins burst through the door at that moment. They

skidded to a stop in front of Jacob, grinning. Each time they saw Jacob, he pretended not to know which was which, and for some reason that never grew less funny to them.

Jacob waited, studying them solemnly. Finally Matty couldn't stand it any longer.

"Guess which is which!"

"Ach, this time I know," Jacob said. "You're Matthew."

Matty's face fell. "How did you know?"

Jacob chuckled. "Because you're the impatient one. You couldn't wait for an answer."

Everyone grinned at that, including Matthew. Noah set two mugs of coffee on the table. "Okay, now you know, so run along and do your chores while we talk."

"But, Daadi . . ." Mark tugged on his arm. "Listen."

"Yah, listen." Matthew took up the plea. "It's going to be cold tonight. How will the kittens stay warm? We have to do something."

"Cats know how to keep their babies warm. You don't have to worry about them."

"But, Daadi," Mark said again, leaning against his knee. "They'll be cold. What if she can't keep them warm enough? They might freeze." His blue eyes were bright with tears, touching Noah's heart. Mark had such a tender spot for any creature's suffering.

He put his arm around his son. "Tell you what. Just in case, why don't you and Matty open another bale of straw and make a little nest for them. Straw is a good insulation—that means it will keep out the cold."

"You're sure?" His face was anxious.

"I'm sure." Noah patted his cheek. "Go on now."

Reassured, the two of them ran back out again, racing each other to the barn.

Jacob took a gulp of coffee and then smiled. "Those two. Do they run everywhere they go?"

"Just about. Didn't we, when we were that age?"

"Ach, I can't believe we ever were that age." Jacob shook his head.

Noah studied his face. Still rosy cheeked and clean-shaven since he wasn't married, Jacob didn't really look much older than when they'd left school.

"Sorry I don't have anything to go with the coffee," he said, conscious of his lack as a host.

"This is fine." Jacob gestured with his coffee mug. "I came to talk, not to eat, anyway."

"Talk about what?" He'd been sure Jacob wouldn't drive out here on a Saturday morning unless there was something on his mind.

"Well, it's this way. The town merchants are having an open house next week. Everybody stays open in the evening, and some of the shops serve food even. It's kind of a welcome to the Christmas season. And a chance to make some sales, that's for sure. The Englisch are great for buying presents at Christmas. The idea is to get folks to buy from us instead of going off to some shopping mall."

Noah nodded his understanding. It wasn't the Amish way of observing Christmas, but no Pennsylvania Dutchman would miss the chance to make a sale. Unless it was on the Sabbath, of course.

"So I thought maybe you'd be willing to display a few of your things for sale in the front of my shop." Jacob seemed to rush the words out. "Not many folks are buying harnesses or even saddles and bridles for Christmas presents, so I need something else to get shoppers into my store."

"You think my furniture would bring people in?" Jacob had made it sound as if Noah would be doing him a favor, but Noah wasn't so sure. "Did Sarah put you up to this?"

Jacob's cheeks grew redder. "Not exactly. I thought of it when I was telling her about advertising. It could be gut for both of us, ain't so? So what does it matter how I got the idea?"

He shrugged. There was a lot in what Jacob said, but even so . . .

"Yah, okay. I guess you're right. Denke, Jacob." He shook his head, smiling a little. "I don't remember Sarah being such a manager when we were young."

Jacob chuckled. "Me, neither. But we've all grown up."

"Can't have been easy for her, taking over when her mamm died and raising those kids. I guess she had to be the boss, from what I remember of her daad."

He might wish that Sarah's father hadn't taken his family to the very same place where Janie's kinfolk lived. Still, most Amish were connected in one way or another. Coincidences like that were normal enough not to be surprising.

"If you have time, you can help me pick out something to display." He stood. "I'd think something not too big, ain't so?"

"Yah, maybe so." Jacob looked relieved that his goal had been accomplished so easily. He probably didn't want to face Sarah if he didn't succeed.

Sarah could try to manage all she wanted, he decided, leading the way to the workshop. But not even Sarah would get him to do something he didn't want to do.


IT WAS MONDAY morning, and Sarah wasn't rushing off to work first thing. Thanks to Noah's cooperation, she'd go in after lunch today, and then she could go on to the school for rehearsal.

She and Grossmammi had fallen into a routine for

taking care of Ruthie and little Mary with help from Ruthie's sisters and various other relatives who'd rallied with offers of assistance as soon as word had gotten round. Grossmammi would take care of things this afternoon, and one of Ruthie's sisters was bringing supper.

Finishing the breakfast dishes, she looked over the kitchen. Needless to say, she wanted it to be neat and clean so that Grossmammi wouldn't think she had to do something to it. The way she'd planned it, keeping Ruthie company and putting Mary down for her nap would be the extent of Grossmammi's activities today, but it was always hard to predict what she might take it into her mind to do.

Collecting her workbag, Sarah headed upstairs for Ruthie's room. Yesterday had been a quiet Sabbath, since it was the off Sunday when there were no worship services. Grossmammi and Eli had taken Mary and gone to his brother's for a meal, bringing back supper for her and Ruthie. There'd be other times for her to see her cousins.

When she slipped into the room, she found Mary curled up against Ruthie, turning the pages of a storybook.

"It's nice and quiet in here," she said, drawing a rocking chair close to the bed.

"Mary's being such a good girl." Ruthie gave her daughter a hug. "I think she understands Mammi needs to stay in bed."

Sarah nodded noncommittally, unsure that at nineteen months Mary had figured that out, but she was a quiet child by nature, always willing to occupy herself with a book or a toy.

"Is there anything I can bring you? Some juice, or a cup of tea?"

Ruthie shook her head. "Not now. Did you bring your crocheting up with you?"

"That I did. I haven't had it out since I've been here, but when we started talking about handwork yesterday, it reminded me." She drew out a crochet hook and a ball of the softest white yarn, getting easily back into the circular pattern she'd started.

Mary leaned over for a closer look. "What is it going to be?"

"It's just a tiny circle so far." Sarah held it up. "But soon it will be a cap. Guess who for?"

Ruthie flushed with pleasure. "Ach, Sarah, how sweet. Denke."

"I'm enjoying it. I haven't had a chance to do something so small in a long time. I thought I'd do several, since you'll want one every day in this cold weather. Maybe a pale green and a pale yellow? Or maybe a pink and blue striped one. That way you're prepared for any eventuality."

Ruthie stroked Mary's head. "A boy for Eli would be nice. But I do like little girls. So long as it's healthy."

Sarah sent up a silent prayer. Their family had more cause to think of that than many, with the prevalence of some kinds of birth defects among the Amish. All they could do was pray and be happy with what the Lord sent.

Her circle began to curve into a cup shape, and she measured it against her hand. Newborn hats were so tiny, just the size of a grapefruit, she thought. Maybe a pair of matching booties would be good.

Ruthie looked at the hat shape as she held it up. "That goes fast, doesn't it? Maybe you should make a pair of them for the twins for Christmas."

The idea of giving something to the twins caught Sarah by surprise. She certain-sure couldn't give Noah a gift, even though they worked together. It wouldn't be considered proper. They would send Christmas cookies over to the family, and it would be fine for her to make something for the boys.

"That's a nice idea, Ruthie. Maybe matching green ones. They seem to like things that match."

Ruthie nodded. "I always thought it would be fun to have a twin. My sisters were so much older."

She made it sound like an enormous gap. As they all grew older, probably the gap wouldn't seem so great.

Mary held the book up to her mammi. "Story," she demanded.

"Yah." Ruthie took the book, pulling her a little closer, and began to read.

Soothed by the soft cadence of her voice and the rhythm of the double crochet stitches, Sarah let her mind wander. She'd sent a letter off to her sister in Saturday morning's mail after fretting over whether to call or write.

But writing, she'd finally decided, was safer. More private. She'd cautioned Nancy not to talk to anyone about this. It wouldn't do to let Janie's relatives know she was . . . well, snooping. Unfortunately there wasn't another word for it.

But if good intentions counted for anything, surely it wasn't so bad. She couldn't possibly mention anything to Noah without being sure Janie really was there.

Her thoughts cringed away from the outcome. If she did discover that Janie was living happily out in Indiana, would Noah want to know that? She didn't know, and until she felt more sure of the right thing to do, it was best that this stay locked in privacy.

Later, after lunch had been cleared away, Sarah's thoughts were still firmly on that subject. No matter what she learned from Nancy, she'd have to hide her feelings from Noah and pray to be shown the right path to follow.

She arrived at the workshop to find Noah hard at work

on the desk he'd been planning. A quick glance told her that the second rocking chair was gone.

"Did you take the chair to Mr. Portman already?"

"Actually, he came and picked it up on Saturday." He looked pleased with himself. "He paid me half the money, with the balance coming at the end of the week." He shook his head, sobering. "I guess I'm still not used to the idea of how this consignment thing is going to work. But Portman said he'd be paying me the rest as soon as he had payment from the buyer."

Sarah nodded. "I suppose that's right." She pulled out the ledger. "Did you enter the payment?"

For a second Noah looked like one of his sons caught in mischief. "Oops, sorry. I forgot."

Somehow she wasn't surprised. Flipping open the ledger, she entered the date of payment and what it was for. "Amount?"

"Four hundred. A nice amount with Christmas coming on."

"Yah, it is." She hesitated, but maybe it made sense to ask him. "Speaking of Christmas, is it all right if I make matching soft winter caps for the boys for Christmas? I'm doing some for other kinder, and I just thought . . ."

"That's wonderful kind of you, Sarah. I know they'd like that."

Well, apparently she hadn't made him uncomfortable. She was reminded again of how awkward their working relationship might be if she weren't careful. If Janie were in the farmhouse right now where she belonged, it wouldn't be an issue at all.

Somehow she couldn't imagine that. Her thoughts swung right back to the secret she was keeping, and she slammed the lid down on it.

A change of subject would be good about now. As she

glanced over the displayed objects, she realized that nothing besides the rocking chair was gone.

"Portman didn't offer to take anything else on consignment." Noah seemed to read her thoughts. "Maybe he'll pick something out the next time he comes. In the meantime, I seem to have a new outlet for selling something."

"Really? Another dealer?"

He shook his head, his eyes crinkling with amusement. "Don't you know? I'm certain-sure you put him up to it."

"Jacob, you mean." She could feel her cheeks grow warm. "He just told me about the opportunity. It was his idea."

"Inspired by you, no doubt." He chuckled. "Relax, Sarah. I'm glad to have such a go-getter as a part of my business."

That almost sounded as if he regarded her as a partner. He didn't mean it that way, of course, but it was still a good feeling.


NOAH KEPT TRACK of the time as the afternoon wore on. Teacher Dorcas was keeping the scholars a little longer today to try out the roles for different age groups before sending their parts home with the kinder.

He glanced at Sarah, only to find that she must have been watching the time as well, since she was straightening up her desk. She looked up and caught him watching her, responding with a smile.

"I'm not running off early. But I promised I'd help Dorcas with giving out the parts for the program after school. I can walk the boys home, if you want."

"Not necessary, since I'm going over to the school as well. I realized I'll need a few more measurements before I can start on some of the props." He smiled, shaking his head. "Do you know how tall fourth graders or sixth graders are? I don't remember."

"Depends on the fourth grader or sixth grader, I guess. But I understand. You don't want to make something and find it's too big for them to hold."

"Something like that." Finishing up, he reached for his jacket. "If you're ready, I'll walk over with you."

"Just give me a minute." She closed her desk drawers and took the coat he held out to her.

When they stepped outside, Sarah shivered and snuggled her coat a little closer. "Brr. It's gotten colder since this morning."

"Yah." He looked at the sky. "We might be looking at some more snow. That'll make the boys happy."

They headed off across the frosty lawn and onto the path that led to the school. Sarah kept step with him, striding along as if she enjoyed getting out in the air, even though it was chilly.

Before the silence became awkward, she spoke. "Have you decided on what you'll put on display in the harness shop?"

"Yah, Jacob helped me look at things while he was here. We both decided that the jelly cupboard was too big to take, but I'll take most of the smaller things."

"If you pick up a new customer or two, you might still sell the jelly cupboard." Her smile flickered. "I'd be sorry to see it go. If I had any possible place to put it, I'd buy it."

"Not going to fit in your bedroom at the grossdaadi haus, you think?"

She smiled. "I'm afraid not. And Grossmammi already has all of her things in the kitchen. I'm not complaining," she added hurriedly. "I love living there, and her things are ones I remember from my childhood. She even has some pieces that Daad left behind when we moved away."

Noah couldn't help noticing the trace of sorrow in her voice at that. "Sorry."

"Ach, don't let me pity myself," she said promptly. "I have much more happy things to think of, like getting the house ready for Christmas. And I'm going to help Dinah do some decorating at the bakery. It'll be fun to work together."

"I remember going out with my daad and brothers to cut the greens to decorate the house. I'd best find time to do that with the twins. I wouldn't want the tradition to die out."

"The thing I remember most was helping to set up Grossmammi's *putz*. She has the sweetest one, with the angels and shepherds and all carved from wood. And a real-looking stable. When we went out west, none of the Amish out there had a *putz*. I guess it's more of a Pennsylvania thing, ain't so?"

"I'm not a gut one to ask. I've never been anywhere but home at Christmastime."

Was Janie keeping up the Christmas traditions wherever she was now? He seemed to think about her more at times like Christmas.

Did the boys do that, too? It wasn't something he ever talked about with them, and maybe he should. This business of being the only parent wasn't simple, and he missed his mother's wise presence.

They reached the school to find that Dorcas had already started giving out the roles. She looked up, smiled, and waved them in.

"What do you need to know for the props, Noah? We'll get you started on that."

He felt awkward with all the kinder turning to look at him. "What about the candles? Which group will have those?"

"That'll be the fourth graders. Hold up your hands, boys and girls, so Noah can find your group."

Feeling as if he were back in school again, Noah headed for the kinder, aware of all those eyes on him. "So you're the candle holders, ain't so?"

The three girls and two boys nodded.

He pulled out his measuring tape. "So pretend you're holding up a very big candle, so I can see how tall they need to be."

Mindful of the weight of the candles, he measured from their hands to above their heads. Would that be too heavy? He'd have to experiment with the twins.

And thinking of the twins, he looked around to see what they were up to. Teacher Dorcas was handing the four first-graders papers—apparently their parts. He felt a sudden apprehension at the idea of Mark reading aloud before a roomful of people. But as long as Matty was by his side, he'd be all right.

Noah worked his way around the room, jotting down any notes or measurements he'd need. When he'd about finished, he glanced at the twins again. Teacher Dorcas had moved on, but now Sarah was coaching them as they read what seemed to be a good-bye poem—maybe the end of the program. He stopped behind the kinder, watching.

It struck him that the two little girls were quicker at reading than the twins were. Maybe that was always the case at this age. Anyway he hoped so.

Sarah coached the twins gently. Matty was nice and loud, but he stumbled over the words he was meant to read. Mark did better with the reading, but his voice was so low he could hardly be heard. Noah bit his tongue to keep from telling him to speak up.

Sarah listened patiently to the end. Gently she coaxed him to do first one part louder, then another. With his hand held in hers, Mark seemed to find the courage to speak up—at least so that Noah could make out most of the words. When he practiced with them at home, he could try to push Mark along.

Or should he? Sarah seemed to get results with gentle encouragement. Maybe she understood better than he did what Mark needed right now. He didn't want to admit it, but he couldn't deny the evidence in front of him. Sarah had a gift that he admired.

His thoughts flickered to what she had confided about her attitude toward marriage. It seemed an impractical viewpoint to him. Clearly she had a gift with children. Why wouldn't that be a consideration to the man who might propose to her?

Despite her age, Sarah seemed to have some romantic ideas of what love and marriage were. Like he had when he had married Janie—and look how that had turned out.

Falling in love might be the popular idea when a person was seventeen or eighteen, but folks could marry for a lot of other reasons. If Sarah could put romantic notions away, she might very well find someone who'd admire her many good qualities and prove to be an excellent husband to her.

Oddly enough, that thought didn't please him. Well, that was natural, he supposed. If Sarah married, she'd want to leave her job, and he'd hate to lose her. He'd become used to her, and when she wasn't there, he missed her quiet presence.

Still, he was right about the basics. Marriage took a lot more than moonlight and stolen kisses. She looked like such a sensible woman, and . . .

Sarah looked up then, catching his gaze. Her eyes widened a little, and she smiled.

It was as if she'd reached out through the intervening space and touched him. As if they were connected without the need for speech. As if they could understand each other's thoughts.

Horrified, Noah yanked his gaze away from her. He stared down at his notes, fumbling with them as if looking for something important.

What had just happened? He couldn't let himself think that way. He'd imagined that moment of communication between them. That was all. It couldn't be anything else.

At least he hoped not, because anything between them, between him and any woman, was impossible.

# CHAPTER TEN

Sarah stayed home again on Tuesday morning. The afternoon would be busier at the workshop because of getting Noah's finished pieces ready to take to Jacob for the open house tonight. She wanted to create some small placards to put out, naming Noah as the creator and giving his address. If only she'd thought of it in time, she could have made some leaflets to give out.

On the other hand, Noah might not have wanted that. She really had to be careful not to push too hard. She'd offered to go in with him this afternoon and help arrange the display, but he'd quickly refused. Almost too quickly. It had been after they'd worked at the school together, so possibly he felt he'd seen enough of her for a time.

Carrying a glass of juice, she tapped on and opened the door to Ruthie's bedroom. Ruthie was propped up in bed, with Mary once again snuggled up beside her. Exchanging glances with her grandmother, she smiled.

"Mary is being very affectionate. She must understand that you're not well."

Ruthie squeezed her daughter. "Maybe she knows that she'll soon have to share Mammi's attention with someone."

"Little ones always understand more than we think," Grossmammi added. She'd brought some mending up with her, and her needle never missed a stitch in the shirt she was repairing.

"Most likely." Sarah set the juice on the bedside stand. Somehow the younger ones seemed more sensitive to others than the teenagers did. When her siblings had hit their teens, it had seemed as if they were unaware of anything beyond their own thoughts and feelings.

Sarah glanced out the window. It was definitely more cloudy today than it had been the previous day. Perhaps they really were going to have the snow that the twins yearned for.

"Sarah, maybe while everyone's settled you can help me with something." Grossmammi stood, dropping the finished shirt on top of her sewing basket.

"For sure. What is it?"

"I'd like to go up to the attic to find some things for Christmas." She lowered her voice on the word, glancing at Mary.

Needlessly, Sarah thought. Mary wasn't old enough to remember anything about the holiday.

"You don't have to come up with me," she protested when Grossmammi headed for the door. "Just tell me what you're looking for and where it's likely to be."

"But that's just what I don't know. I know where I always did keep them, but Eli put things away last year. I should know the right box when I see it, though."

"But surely . . ." She had to hurry to catch up with her grandmother, and she may as well give up. No one ever succeeded in keeping Grossmammi from doing what she'd set her mind on.

The stairs to the attic were narrow and uneven. Sarah took the flashlight that hung on a hook next to the door, shining it on the steps. Grossmammi went up first and she followed close behind, alert to catch her if she stumbled.

But, as always, Grossmammi moved nimbly. Sarah had noticed that it was only when she was tired that she wavered. The attic was low ceilinged, but they were both able to stand up straight. Light came through the windows at either end, and with the aid of the flashlight they could see well enough.

"What are we looking for?" she asked. Everything was neat, but the boxes and trunks weren't labeled. She'd hate to have to open everything to search, especially as cold as it was up here.

"I want to get out the putz. And those candleholders I use in the windows with greens. You remember the putz, don't you?"

"For sure." Memory brought a smile. "How could I forget?" Grossmammi's manger scene, each piece carved of wood, had been a fixture of her childhood. Her grandmother had let the kinder play with the pieces, acting out the Christmas story again and again.

"Ach, you kinder always liked setting it up. It helped you learn the story of Jesus' birth, ain't so?"

"It did, that's certain-sure. And you always said we couldn't hurt it, but I remember one of the boys dropping an angel and chipping its wing."

"Jacob, that was." Grossmammi bent over a stack of boxes. "How that boy did cry over it. Now here's something I wanted to find."

"The putz?" Sarah went to her, focusing the light.

"Something that I always meant for you." Her grandmother took the flashlight from her. "There. The little dower chest. Pull it out. It's yours."

Sarah obeyed, her fingers lingering on the small wooden box. It was a half-sized version of the kind of dower chests girls filled with sheets and quilts in anticipation of marriage. The stylized birds painted on the top had faded, but they were still lovely, still typical of Pennsylvania Dutch folk art.

"Grossmammi, it's beautiful, but really, I don't need it. Why don't you give it to one of the younger girls? They'd love a place to store their treasures."

"It's for you." Her grandmother's voice was firm. "You were named Sarah, after my mother, and this was hers when she was a girl, and it has her name inside the lid. Don't argue now. And don't tell me you're not going to marry. That's foolishness."

"It's true," she said, smiling as she traced the shapes of the letters inside the lid.

"Sarah Grace, you have no idea what the Lord God has planned for you. Never forget that He promises you hope and a future. If that future includes marriage and babies, your age won't matter in the least little bit."

It was always pointless to argue when Grossmammi sounded like that. "We'd best get the putz before we catch cold up here. We can decide about this another time."

"You'll put it right there by the steps to bring down later," her grandmother retorted. "And there's the box with the putz in it, and maybe the candleholders, too. You can carry that down now. We'll let Mary help us unpack it."

Giving up, Sarah obeyed orders. Maybe Grossmammi would forget about the dower chest. Still, she couldn't deny that she loved the thought of owning something that had belonged to that earlier Sarah.

They'd reached the hallway when they heard the patter of running feet. Grossmammi bent and caught Mary before she could get to the stairs.

"Now, what are you doing, you little schnickelfritz? Mammi is calling you."

Mary tilted her head to look up at them, her cheeks

rosy with laughter. Seizing Grossmammi's hand, she tugged her toward Ruthie's room.

Surging into the room on a wave of giggles, they caught Ruthie halfway out of the bed, looking guilty.

"Where are you going?" Grossmammi hurried to tuck her in again, her tone gently scolding. "Mary's right here. I know what you need—you need a bell to ring for help."

"Good idea." Sarah swung Mary, still giggling, onto the bed. "Look who we found!" Mary snuggled against her mammi, looking as innocent as could be.

"Here's something that will keep that little one occupied." Grossmammi dusted the box and set it on the quilt. "Mary can help Cousin Sarah get out the crèche."

Ruthie caught Mary's hands as she reached for the box. "I don't want her to break anything. She's too little to understand."

"It's no use saying that to Grossmammi," Sarah said, opening the lid. "If she let the likes of Eli and Jacob and my little bruders do it, I doubt Mary can do any harm."

"That's right." Grossmammi sat on the edge of the bed, watching Mary's little face as Sarah drew the wrappings back. "They're carved of wood, so they're just right for little hands. Mary will learn the Christmas story with them, just like her daadi did."

Sarah drew out a paper-wrapped figure, feeling the shape of wings, and handed it to Mary. "I wonder what Mary will find."

The paper gave way to Mary's chubby hands, and the roughly carved angel emerged. "Angel," Grossmammi said, guiding Mary's hands over the angel's wings. "That's the angel who sang at Jesus' birth."

Patting it, Mary verbalized something that sounded a little like the word.

"That's right." Ruthie's face brightened with pleasure as she watched her daughter.

Sarah leaned back a little, watching the others as they shared the moment and built Christmas memories for yet another generation. Her throat tightened. This was what she'd tried to carry with the family each time they'd moved—this precious patchwork of family memories and family faith bound tightly together.

Had she done enough? And had she done the right thing in following her heart back home?

NOAH GAVE THE boys an early supper that night, having decided to take them with him to Jacob's shop for the open house. It was a school night, but it certain-sure wouldn't hurt them to stay up late once in a while. Selling was part of the business, as Sarah had to keep reminding him. They'd enjoy the unexpected outing.

They were excited—so excited that by the time they'd reached town Matty was about bouncing off the seat. Mark was snuggled up against his daad, looking around with his eyes wide and grabbing his twin's jacket when Matty got carried away.

Noah drew up at the hitching rail. "Hop down, you two, and get the mare's blanket. We don't want her getting cold out here."

"She'd like to come inside," Matty said, convulsing himself with giggles while his brother got the blanket and carried it to Noah.

The blanket secured, Noah caught the boys before they could run to the shop door. "Now then. Best behavior while we're in Jacob's store, yah? No running, and don't bother the grown-ups."

"We'll behave, Daadi," Mark said, and Matty nodded.

"All right, then." Trusting he wouldn't regret this, Noah led them to the door, pausing a moment to look down the street. The lights twinkled like stars, and every shop window had some sort of decoration. He smiled at the awestruck look on the twins' faces. Just because the Amish kept decorating to a minimum, that didn't mean they couldn't enjoy seeing the way others celebrated.

He opened the door, the bell on it jingling. Jacob looked up from where he was arranging some small leather goods on a counter. "Well, look at this—two new helpers for us. That's just what we need."

Noah smiled, looking from the boys' faces to Jacob. "Hope it's okay to bring them."

"Sure thing." Jacob gestured toward the right side of the shop door. "What do you think of your display?"

It seemed strange to see the products of his workshop in Jacob's shop, set up against a background of harnesses and saddlery hung on the wall. "Looks gut. Let's hope some customers think so."

Jacob stood next to him, frowning a little. "Let's get a woman's opinion." He looked toward the swinging door that led to Dinah's bakery next door. "Dinah? Can you come in for a minute?"

The door swung open, letting in a mixture of delicious aromas. Dinah appeared, with Sarah right behind her. He couldn't help staring.

"I didn't know you were coming, Sarah. We could have picked you up."

"I wasn't sure earlier, but one of Ruthie's sisters was there, so they had enough help at home."

"So instead, she came to help me," Dinah added. "Can we do something for you?" She had a gentle smile for the twins.

"Yah, have a look at Noah's furniture and tell us what you think of the arrangement?"

Both women looked at the pieces with identical expressions of dismay. Finally Sarah spoke. "I think it's not an arrangement at all." She and Dinah moved in and with what seemed like wordless cooperation, began moving things around.

Dinah seized a pair of small stands that his mamm had called *whatnot stands*. In a few minutes they'd displayed those on either side of a chair and added a few sprigs of greens in a jar on the shelves.

"You see," Jacob said, standing back with his arms crossed. "Turn it over to an expert."

Noah nodded. "Maybe they can figure out how to convince shoppers to buy harness."

"That would be beyond us." Sarah handed him a sheaf of cards. "When I realized I could come, I made these up to put on things or to give out if someone seems interested."

He found he was looking at hand-lettered cards giving information about his workshop and where to find him. *Noah Raber, Handcrafted Furniture*, it said. It looked oddly impressive to him.

"Denke, Sarah. I didn't expect you to do this." He supposed he should have thought of it himself. Looked like he had a ways to go as a businessman.

"No problem." The bell jangled in the bakery next door, and Dinah hurried off. "I'll need to help Dinah. We're giving away cups of hot cocoa and a cookie, so send the boys over whenever they need a break." She scurried in the wake of her friend before Noah could thank her again.

"Looks like we have customers coming, too." Jacob nodded toward the glass door. "Remember, you have to talk to people who stop to look."

"I know." He tried to sound more confident than he felt, and it wondered him how he'd let himself be talked into it. Then someone came up to him with a question, and he didn't have any more time to think.

To his surprise, he actually started enjoying it once

they got going. Some folks made foolish comments, for sure, but several seemed genuinely interested. Clutching the cards Sarah had made up gave him some confidence. At least if he couldn't think of anything else to say, he could hand a person one of them.

Eavesdropping on Jacob dealing with customers, Noah found he could learn a bit. Jacob's products might not be appealing to many Christmas shoppers, but he had a friendly way of talking that probably helped to sell a couple of belts and a leather key ring or two.

An Englisch woman stopped to look at a bookcase, smiling at the boys. "Did you make this?" she asked.

Matthew and Mark exchanged glances, and Noah hoped they'd learned enough Englisch in school to answer. "Our daadi did," Matty said at last. He sent his father a look that seemed to ask him to take over.

"The boys help me in the shop," he said. "If you have any questions, I can try to help you."

In a few minutes he found himself listening to a long story about a daughter who kept changing her mind about what she wanted for Christmas. He found he just had to smile, and nod, and hope the boys didn't get the idea that Christmas was about asking for presents.

In any event, the woman took one of the cards and said she'd decide soon, so maybe it was worth it.

As she moved off, Sarah murmured in his ear, "She was a talker, ain't so?"

"Yah, for sure." A tingle ran across his skin at her unexpected nearness.

To his relief, she stepped away quickly. "Maybe the boys can come and have cocoa now?"

The twins greeted the suggestion with eager smiles. "It looks like you have a couple of customers." He nodded to the boys. "But don't let them be pests."

"Never," she said, mock serious. "Komm, quick, before the cookies are gone."

Matty and Mark scampered to join her, Matty opening the door while Mark held on to her hand. He watched until the door swung closed behind them. Sarah was good to them—no doubt that was her nature. But he had to remember not to impose on that.

The evening seemed to last forever to Noah. Finally Jacob glanced at the clock, closed the door behind the last customer, and pulled down the shade. He grinned at Noah. "Not bad, was it?"

"Not bad at all." He looked over what he had left. "Both of the whatnot stands sold, and the small cabinet. And several other people said they'd be stopping at the workshop."

"I figured you'd make a hit, especially with those smaller things that folks could buy for Christmas gifts." Jacob looked as pleased as if they had been his sales.

"Denke, Jacob." He looked for words. "I'm wonderful glad you talked me into this."

Jacob clapped him on the shoulder. "Don't know why I didn't think of it before. Now that you've made a start, you can make some plans. Not much over the winter, but once spring comes, there's the mud sales, and the Spring Fest, and the big Craft Fair."

"Ach, I'm not looking to do everything that comes along," he said, laughing. "I'm just a carpenter, not a salesman."

"You'll be surprised what you can do when you get started." Jacob began replacing some of the small things he'd gotten out. "Look at Dinah. She never thought of half of what she's doing now before her man died. Now she's making a gut living."

That was most likely true. A person did what he or she

had to when the time came. Picking up the bookcase, he headed for the door just as Sarah came in from the bakery. She carried a large cardboard box, and the boys danced around her. A glance told him they'd probably crash into bed as soon as he got them home.

Sarah's glance met his and she smiled, as if thinking the same thing. She skirted the boys as she came toward him.

"This is for you and the boys. Dinah says such helpful boys deserve the leftovers. If you're loading your buggy, I'll bring it out."

"We can carry it." Matty's excitement took him right into Sarah's path, and he grabbed for the box.

Sarah lifted it over his head. "I don't think—"

"Not now," Noah said firmly. "You'll go back and thank Dinah properly. And see if you can help her clean up."

Matty made a face, but then his smile returned and the boys scurried back into the bakery.

Noah reached around his burden to open the door, and he held it while Sarah brushed past him. She was laughing a little as the door closed behind them.

"This box isn't the sturdiest thing. I'd guess the cookies would hit the ground in a minute if Matty carried them."

"I'm certain-sure of it." He walked next to her as they rounded the corner of the building toward the hitching rail. Immediately they stepped into the darkness beyond reach of the streetlights. He hesitated. "If you want to stay where you are, I'll put the bookcase in first and then take the box."

"Ach, it's fine. I've got it." Together they moved to the buggy, and she stood next to him while he lifted the bookcase. "You're pleased about the open house, ain't so?" Her face was tilted up to his, a pale oval in the shadows.

"Yah. And I know you're the one to thank." He slid the

bookcase into place in the back of the buggy. "Jacob wouldn't have thought of it if you hadn't put the idea in his head."

"I always did have to push Cousin Jacob a tad." The laughter in her voice was clear. He'd think she'd be tired after the long day, but she didn't show it.

"Let me help you." He reached for the box, and together they lifted it into the buggy, their hands tangling together in the process. Awareness of her closeness flooded through him as they stood together in the dark, quiet alley. She was so close he could hear her breathing. He felt the shiver that went through her.

"You're cold," he murmured, putting a hand on her wrist. Her breath caught, and her skin warmed under his touch.

"I'm fine," she began, tilting her face up to his. But her voice trembled on the words, and her eyes looked huge and dark in the dim light.

She was so close. He felt again what he had in that moment when he'd looked at her across the schoolroom and sensed a connection running between them, linking them. But this time they really were touching, and her lips seemed to call his. He bent his head, unable to control the movement, longing to—

Noah jerked away, horrified at what he'd so nearly done. He saw the same feeling reflected in Sarah's face as well. And then she spun around and fled for the shop.

STARING AT THE ceiling and pounding her pillow all night hadn't done a thing to help Sarah cope with what had happened. She had to face it.

In another moment Noah would have kissed her. Worse, she'd wanted it. It would be convenient to blame Noah for the whole thing, but she couldn't. She'd known, even if she hadn't wanted to admit it, that there was a strong attraction underlying their growing friendship.

It was impossible. They both knew it. Noah already had a wife. He was tied for life to a woman who'd deserted both him and her own babies. Sarah couldn't suppress a surge of anger at the very idea.

The straight pin she was using to fasten the front of her dress ran into her finger, and she sucked away a drop of blood. Was that a reminder not to judge others? Because she certainly had been guilty of that particular sin where Janie was concerned.

Smoothing her hair, she pinned her kapp into place and took an assessing look at herself in the mirror. Not good—she looked like a woman who hadn't slept all night. It didn't help to realize that she still hadn't decided what to do about the situation with Noah.

He'd be feeling as guilty as she did. Somehow, before she saw him, she had to decide what to say to him. But in the meantime, there was work to be done. Slipping quietly down the stairs in the dark, she headed toward the farmhouse to start breakfast.

But by the time she walked down the lane to the workshop, Sarah had an even bigger problem. Eli had picked up the mail and handed her a letter—a letter from Indiana. Her sister had written back, and there seemed little doubt that Janie Raber was living . . . or at least staying . . . near the community where her sister lived.

Sarah fingered the letter she'd tucked inside her mitten. Tell Noah or not? The question made last night's event fade in significance.

Noah was already at work when she entered the workshop. He glanced at her and gave a short nod, his face unreadable. Maybe that meant he intended to ignore the whole thing. She had a cowardly hope that it was so.

But Noah proved her wrong before she'd even reached

her desk. "Sarah." He put down the tool he had been holding and stared at it, not even glancing in her direction. "About last night . . . I'm sorry. I don't know what got into me. It was all my fault. I'm ashamed . . ."

"Ach, Noah, don't." She reached out to him and then let her hand drop. "It was mine, too."

He was already shaking his head. "You've never done the least thing. I'm to blame."

Sarah took a deep breath. "Let's start over again. It's no use arguing whose fault it was. Nothing happened. We were just foolish. Can't we forget it?"

Finally Noah met her eyes, and she could read the shame and confusion in his face. "I don't know if I can forget."

If they were being honest, she wasn't sure, either. The warm grasp of his hands on her arms, the feel of his breath against her cheek . . . No, that wouldn't fade easily. But maybe pretending would make it true in time.

"We were both wrong," she said firmly. "I want to put it aside and get on with work. Can we do that?"

Doubt flickered in his eyes before he turned to stare again at the work in front of him. "All right. Denke."

The constriction that had seized her chest relaxed, and she could breathe again. Instinct told her to say nothing more, so she sat at her desk and opened the ledger to enter the previous night's sales. That was one issue settled. Unfortunately there was another, more difficult one.

Taking advantage of Noah's involvement in his work, she slipped the letter from its envelope and read the paragraph again.

*Dearest Sarah,*

*I'm sorry if I upset you about the Burkhalter family. I don't remember them myself, but it's differ-*

*ent for you, knowing the little boys. I did ask some
questions, and it is Janie's father who is in our
church district. He lives with his brother and family.
I asked Daniel's mother, because she knows everyone. She says Amos Burkhalter goes to Standish to
see a relative there, but that relative never comes
here.*

"Sarah? Did you hear me?"

She blinked, jolted back to the here and now. "Ach, I'm
sorry. Did you want me to do something?"

"I'm making a couple more whatnot stands, since they
sold so fast. They'll be quick to make, especially if you
could do the finishing coats. Jacob says he'll display them
in his shop for me."

"That's wonderful gut." She tried to show the appropriate enthusiasm. "I'd love to. Just show me what to do."

He nodded, but her voice must have given her away,
because he was studying her face as if for a clue to her
thoughts. "What's wrong?"

She started to deny that anything was wrong, but it was
no good. She couldn't keep this from him. She had to
tell him.

Finally, unable to find the words, she held the letter out
to him. "You'd better read this. It's from my sister, Nancy.
I . . . I think you need to know."

His gaze still fixed on her face, Noah grabbed the letter. When his head bent to read it, she turned her chair
away, instinctively sure it would be wrong to watch him.

She heard the thud of his feet as she stared fixedly at
the calendar on the wall. Noah thumped the letter down
on her desk in front of her, forcing her to look at him.

"How long have you known this?" His voice was so
harsh she hardly recognized it.

"Nancy mentioned the name in the letter I got last

week, but I wasn't sure it was the same family. I didn't want to say anything until I was sure."

He drew in a rasping breath. "So Amos knows. All this time—Amos has known where she was."

"I'm sorry." She choked out the words. "I wish . . ." What did she wish? That he'd never have had to know? Or that someone else had been the one to tell him?

He stared down at the letter for another moment, his face dark with anger. Then he turned. Before she could guess what he was about, he'd slammed his way out of the shop.

# CHAPTER ELEVEN

Noah hadn't returned by the time Sarah had to leave for the school. She'd told Dorcas she'd be there for the last hour of the school day to help with the practice, so she left a brief note for Noah and headed out.

She couldn't help wondering where he was, but she suspected he'd found a method to help him deal with his feelings. Had she done right in telling him? She didn't suppose she'd ever be sure.

The schoolhouse was abuzz with activity as groups of scholars clustered around different projects. The excited humming sounded like a swarm of bees, and she felt a moment of gratitude that she'd never considered going into teaching.

Dorcas was as immaculate as always, but even she had a slightly frazzled look in her eyes, and she greeted Sarah with enthusiasm.

"I'm wonderful glad you didn't forget about me. The mother who was supposed to help me today is home with a sick child, and my scholars are so excited about the program that I don't know how they'll last until the big day."

"I can see that—or, rather, hear it." Sarah hung up her

coat and bonnet. "I'm here and I'm ready to help, so just give me a job."

"Lifesaver, that's what you are." Dorcas squeezed her hand. "Each group needs to run through its lines and movements. You can take the younger ones again. Do you realize that some of their mothers were actually in rumspringa with us?"

Sarah counted years. "I guess it's possible, but it seems so unlikely. How can you be sure enough about marriage when you're that age?"

Dorcas looked at her in amusement. "That was apparently the ideal age for falling in love. I don't know how we escaped the bug."

"Did you never feel that way? Don't I remember you raving about one of the Esch boys at one point?"

"Probably." She grimaced. "Luckily if I fell in love, I fell out again just as fast. What about you?"

"I guess I didn't like the idea of trusting my happiness to a man." That didn't sound as light as she had meant it to, and she found Dorcas was studying her expression.

"Are you talking about males in general, or your father?"

Sarah shrugged. "Sorry. I didn't mean to be obvious."

"It's all right." Dorcas squeezed her hand. "You've kept lots of my secrets. I'll keep yours. I suppose the truth is that we haven't found someone we're willing to give up enough for."

Sarah pressed her hand in return. It was good to know that their relationship was as strong as it had always been.

A glance at the twins suggested Matthew was ready to launch himself into the air. "What do I do with the ones I'm not taking through their parts? Maybe you have some rope handy?"

Dorcas's face lit with a smile. "It does seem necessary sometimes, doesn't it? But each group has decorations they're working on, so they should keep doing that. Just let me call them to order."

Far better for Dorcas to do that, she decided. She was fine with a few kinder at a time, but not this large a bunch.

Sure enough, Dorcas had each group separated out in a matter of minutes. "First and second, third and fourth graders, Sarah will help you with your parts. Give her your attention, and when you're not practicing, you can keep going on your paper chains. Let's see if you can make enough to go all around the room."

They seemed to welcome the challenge—maybe that was the way to motivate them. Taking a breath, Sarah plunged right in.

To her amusement, the scholars were more than ready to focus on their parts. She handed out scripts and got the older ones practicing while she checked on what the first graders were doing.

Apparently making paper chains required vast amounts of paste, most of which seemed to have found its way onto Matthew and Mark's clothing. She looked from them to the two little girls, who seemed spotless in comparison.

"Matty and Mark, I'm not giving you scripts until you've washed the paste off."

"Paste?" Matthew inquired. They inspected each other while the girls giggled. "It's just a little bit messy." Glancing at Sarah's face, he grabbed Mark's arm. "Come on, Marky. We'll wash up."

"Boys are messy," one of the girls observed. "Why is that?"

Sarah shrugged. "I don't know. It's a mystery, isn't it?" She handed scripts to the two girls. "You start practicing your parts, and I'll come back to hear you read them."

Revolving back to the oldest ones, she listened, coached, and listened again. When she was satisfied with one group, she sent them back to work on their projects and moved to the next, keeping an eye on the schoolroom clock. She'd have to leave enough time for cleaning up—that was obvious.

Every now and then her mind flickered back to what Dorcas had said. It didn't really seem to her that she'd have trouble giving up other things for a happy marriage. Her problem would be trusting her own judgment to find a man who wouldn't let her down.

Strange, how the truth about her parents had only become clear when her father had done the same thing to her that he'd done to her mother all those times—broken his promise. She should have seen it earlier. Maybe you never did understand a thing until it happened to you.

Now—well, where did that leave her now? She'd hate to think she'd go through life comparing every man she met to her father.

The young scholars finally worked their way to the good-bye piece in which the twins each had a large part. She listened, encouraged, listened again. Matthew forgot some of the words, but he plunged ahead without any sign of dismay. When it was his turn, Mark was the opposite— he knew his lines but spoke so softly she could hardly hear him from two feet away.

They came to the last line and looked at her hopefully. "Very nice," she said. "You can take your parts home with you tonight, to be sure you know your lines. And Mark, remember to talk in your biggest, loudest voice."

Mark nodded, looking apprehensive. She drew him close to her, speaking softly under the cover of the other children's chatter. "I've heard you talk much more loudly than that at home, so I know you can do it. Will you try?"

"I'll try," he murmured.

With a look at the clock, she sent them back to their chain-making activity. She turned away to check on the other groups, but turned back at someone tugging on her apron.

"What is it, Matthew?"

"It's a secret," he whispered.

Smiling a little, she sat in one of the low chairs and pulled him close, as she'd done with his brother a few minutes earlier. "Okay. Whisper it in my ear."

Needless to say, Matty's idea of a whisper wasn't really very soft. "It's about Mark. He really doesn't like to talk in front of people. He says it makes him feel all hot inside."

"Lots of people feel like that sometimes. It's nothing to worry about."

"But I thought maybe I should do his part for him. 'Cause it doesn't bother me and it does bother him. Okay?"

Sarah eyed him. She suspected Matthew was moved primarily by a desire to protect his brother, but at least part of it was the fact that he liked being the center of attention. She considered how best to respond.

"I'm glad you want to help your brother," she said slowly. "But you see, if you take over and do it for him, Mark doesn't have a chance to learn to do it himself."

"But if he *wants* to . . ."

Sarah upped the possibility that Matty was thinking about his own time to shine. "Yah, I understand," she said. "But what happens if Mark doesn't do his part this time?"

He looked puzzled. "I . . . I don't know. He feels glad, I guess."

"He feels glad right now, but what about the next time he has to talk in front of people? Each time he doesn't do it, it gets harder to do it the next time. Sounds funny, I know, but that's how it is. When we get out of doing something because it's hard, we find it's even harder the next time and the time after that. You see?"

That was a big lesson for a small boy to get, but it

would probably be better for both of them in the end. It wasn't always good to be the one for whom things came easy. You got to expect things always would.


NOAH WASN'T SURE how far he'd tramped into the woods before common sense began to take hold. He stopped finally, aware of being cold, his fingers feeling numb even inside his gloves. He'd been heading along the top of the ridge. The shortest way home would be to cut downhill until he reached the old railroad bed and then walk along it back toward home. An old log drag made for easier walking downhill.

It was clouding over, making it difficult to guess at the time. But the boys would be getting home before long, and he had to be back there for them. He hurried his steps, lost his balance, and slid several yards on the dry leaves before catching himself.

He got up, annoyed at himself. He'd let his anger take control, and look at the results. He couldn't afford anger—he had his sons to think of. Too bad Janie hadn't bothered to think of them. As for Amos—

The truth was that he didn't understand. How could Amos know about Janie and keep it to himself? How could he write to ask about the boys and not bother to mention where their mother was?

Anger took control again, and he had a struggle to master it. The church had an answer—forgive. Forgive no matter what the sin, no matter what the pain.

He could say the words. But he couldn't feel it.

Clearing his mind with an effort, he strode along more quickly once he hit the railroad bed. It had been a long time since trains whistled their way up and down the valley, but the level trail they had made still existed.

Finally he saw the house below him and headed down again, once more hurrying his steps. What would the boys think if they reached home and he wasn't there? He was always there, or else he'd arranged for someone else to be. Concern for his sons wiped out his anger, at least for now. What if they decided to go look for him? How could he be so thoughtless?

Noah was nearly running by the time he reached the bottom. He raced across the yard and pounded up the steps to the house, grabbing the door and charging into the kitchen. The twins were sitting at the kitchen table, mugs in front of them, looking at him with identical hot chocolate moustaches.

"You turned on the stove? How many times have I told you—"

"Ach, no, they wouldn't do that." Sarah stepped out of the pantry, a package of cookies in her hand. "I explained that you'd be a bit late, so we decided to have hot chocolate while we waited for you."

She'd been talking, he supposed, to give him time to compose himself. Or maybe to keep him from more foolishness.

"Denke, Sarah." He made an effort to smile normally at the boys. "It looks good."

"Have some, Daadi," Matty said, with an air of wanting to share his treat.

Sarah was already pouring another mugful. "You look as if you need something warm."

Their fingers brushed as he took the mug. He should be grateful to her, he knew. Too bad his feelings were in such a tangle.

Wrapping his hand around the warm mug, he took a seat at the table, trying to remember what they'd been going to do today. The rehearsal, of course. Sarah would have been helping with that after school.

"How is the Christmas program coming along? Did you have a good practice?"

"Yah, and we made green and red paper chains to deco-rate the classroom for the program. I'll bet we made about a mile of paper chains already, don't you think, Mark?" Matty looked at his brother.

Mark considered, head tilted to the side. "How far is a mile?"

Sarah's lips twitched. "About as far as from here to the schoolhouse, I'd say. Do you think it's that long?"

"Maybe not quite," Matty admitted. He turned back to his father. "Mark and me practiced the poem we're doing. Teacher Dorcas said it's the finale of the program."

"That means it's the end. So it has to be good." Mark looked a little scared at the idea.

"I said I'd do it by myself if Marky didn't want to, but Sarah says it's better if Mark does his part himself. So he won't be scared next time."

That didn't quite make sense to Noah, but Sarah was already rising and taking her mug to the sink. He stood, too, following her to the door. "I'll walk out with you."

Sarah didn't seem surprised. She nodded and slipped on her coat. When they reached the porch, he stopped, making sure the door was closed solidly behind them.

His mind was on what she'd found out about Janie, but the first thing out of his mouth was something else en-tirely. "What did you really say to Matty? If he wants to help his brother, he ought to do it, yah?"

Sarah pulled her mittens on, smoothing them over her wrists. "I told him that it's better for Mark to do his own part, because otherwise, it will be even harder to do the next time."

His instinctive reaction was negative. "I'd protect them from the hard things, if I could. There will be enough of those when they're older."

"Yah, and how will they cope with big hard things then

if they haven't had any practice with little ones?" Her gaze was steady on his face.

Was she pitying him, left alone to figure out how to raise his boys?

"They are my sons," he reminded her.

"Of course. You have a natural urge to protect them."

His face twisted involuntarily. "Too bad their mother didn't have that instinct."

"I'm sorry. Maybe I was wrong to tell you, but . . ."

They each seemed able to interpret what was behind the other's words.

"You couldn't do anything else. At least now I know I can't trust Amos." Bitterness was an acrid taste in his mouth. "All those times he wrote to ask about the boys, and he knew all along where their mother was."

"I know you're angry with him, but maybe he thought he was doing what was right for his child."

"Janie wasn't a child. She was a grown woman." He spat out the words. Janie had been so excited about marriage and babies. Right up until she'd had them. "I know what the church says. The church says to forgive. Too bad it doesn't tell us how, because I certain-sure can't do it."

A spasm of pity crossed Sarah's face. "Noah, don't. It's hard, especially when someone we love is hurt, but we have to try."

His anger erupted, out of control. "Don't tell me what to forgive or what to feel. And don't you dare pity me. You don't understand one thing about me."

Sarah paled, as if he'd hit her. Without a word, she turned and headed for home, leaving him standing there in the cold, ashamed.

What was he doing? There might be some excuse for his anger, but there was none at all for taking it out on Sarah.

———

SHE HAD MISHANDLED everything, Sarah told herself as she scurried down the lane toward the farm. A cold wind cut across the field, buffeting her as if in agreement. Everything—the twins, Noah's anger, even giving him that letter to begin with.

Well, no, she couldn't really say that with any conviction. Once she'd received Nancy's letter, she'd had no choice. Keeping secrets never worked—they came out in the end. Sooner or later Noah would have found out, and he'd have blamed her.

But the rest of it—she'd let her sympathy carry her too far into his affairs. She'd interfered, and she could hardly blame him for his anger at that. Managing and interfering, that's what she'd been. Well, no more. From now on she'd mind her own business.

She was cutting across the yard to the grossdaadi haus door when Eli fairly flew out of the farmhouse, yanking his coat on as he came.

"Eli? What's wrong?"

He caught her by the arms, propelling her toward the kitchen door. "You're just in time. I can't abide that woman another minute. You go to Ruthie before I explode."

"Wait a minute. Calm down." Sarah planted her feet to prevent being shoved into the kitchen, astonished to see the normally cheerful Eli in such a state. "What woman? What's wrong with Ruthie?"

Eli focused on her face and made an obvious effort to calm down. "Ruthie's all right. She didn't want me to cause trouble, but I couldn't—"

"Yah, I know. You couldn't abide somebody any longer." She gave him a quick shake. "Now start making sense. Who's doing what?"

"Ruthie's sister. Emma." He said the name as if it

tasted bad. "She's supposed to be helping, but all she's doing is upsetting Ruthie. She doesn't listen to Ruthie, she just insists on doing everything her way. She's like a . . . like a bulldozer!"

Sarah suppressed a laugh, but it wasn't really funny. Poor Eli. And poor Ruthie, trying to deal with it.

"You go up to her," Eli said, urging her toward the door. "You'll know how to handle Emma. The woman's driving us crazy. You get rid of her."

In other words he wanted to set one interfering woman to deal with another. She supposed it made sense. But what about her resolution to stop?

She studied Eli for a moment, his young face torn with worry and indecision. "It's all right." She patted his cheek. "You go on with your chores. I'll take care of Ruthie."

Grossmammi was in the kitchen, stirring something with unnecessary vigor. The sound of voices floated down from upstairs . . . It sounded as if Emma was scolding someone. Exchanging glances with her grandmother, Sarah hurried upstairs.

Mary came running down the hall toward her, clutching something in her hand, with Ruthie's sister in pursuit. "Naughty girl. Give that to me."

Sarah caught Mary, scooping her up in her arms and teasing a smile out of her. "What are you up to, little girl?"

Stopping at the sight of her, Emma frowned. "Sarah. I didn't know you were here." She reached for whatever Mary held so tightly.

Mary responded by clutching it more tightly, snuggling against Sarah.

"Give me that at once. It's not a toy." Emma held out her hand commandingly.

"Show Sarah, Mary. Come on. Please?"

Shielding the object with her little body, Mary gave her a glimpse. As she'd assumed, it was the wooden angel.

"That's quite all right, Emma. Didn't Ruthie explain? It's Grossmammi's wooden manger set, and she lets the kinder touch it all they want."

Emma dismissed the words with a sweep of her hand. "What if Mary broke it? Maybe when she's a bit older she can have it. I don't believe in letting kinder have their own way."

Sarah didn't doubt it. She didn't think it would be much fun to have Emma for a mother.

"But it's not Mary's way, it's Grossmammi's." She kept her voice calm, but very firm. "She gave Mary the angel when we unpacked the putz. You're not saying that Grossmammi can't do that, are you?"

Emma stared at her for a moment, openmouthed. Clearly she didn't have an answer for that.

"Maybe you misunderstood," Sarah said, pressing her advantage. "I'm sure you didn't mean to argue with Grossmammi's decisions."

"No, no, of course not." Emma seemed dumbfounded. Maybe she'd never considered what she was really saying in her determination to do things her way.

"It was so nice of you to come and help. But I'm here now, and my grandmother has supper under control. So we'll let you get home to your own family."

"Yah, well, since you're here." Emma sidled toward the stairs. "Denke, Sarah."

Not waiting to see her go down, Sarah turned her attention to Mary, getting her to giggle by the time they reached Ruthie's bedroom. Ruthie reached for her daughter, seeming torn between laughter and tears.

"There, now, everything is fine, ain't so?" Sarah plumped up Ruthie's pillows and urged her gently back against them. "Are you warm enough?"

"Yah, I'm fine." Ruthie's voice cracked, and her eyes filled with tears. "Ach, there's no reason to cry." She brushed her eyes with the back of her hand. "I don't know what's the matter with me."

"You're frustrated is all," Sarah said, hoping to soothe her without venturing to say what she thought of Sister Emma. "It's only natural you want to be up taking care of things yourself instead of letting someone else do it."

Sarah could see it clearly enough. It was like that moment when Ruthie showed her fear that Sarah would try to take over her house and her kinder.

A delicate balance was called for, since at this moment someone had to take over. But not someone like Emma, with her determination that everything be done her way. That had already riled Sarah. How much more must it upset Ruthie to be treated like a child in her own house?

Ruthie seemed to be relaxing, the tightness fading from her face. She looked as if she could drift off to sleep, in fact.

"Why don't you take a little nap before supper?" she suggested. "Mary can help us in the kitchen. And when it's ready, why don't we bring Eli's meal up here along with yours? That way the two of you can have a quiet supper together."

"It's too much trouble," she said, but not before Sarah had seen the pleasure in her eyes at the idea.

"Not at all. We'll pull the little table over by your bed, with a chair for Eli. All right?"

Ruthie let the smile come. "Ach, that's wonderful kind of you, Sarah. Denke." She hesitated. "I'm sorry about Emma. I mean, if she hurt your feelings with her way of talking."

"Don't be ferhoodled," Sarah said, keeping it light. "She's like my Aunt Anna. Nobody can do anything right unless it's done her way. Every family has someone like that."

"You don't let her run over you like she does with me. I heard you dealing with her. I wish I could do that."

Sarah patted her hand. "That's different. She's your big sister. I'm sure you don't want to hurt her feelings."

Ruthie shook her head. "It's not that. At least, not all of it. I should have stood up to her the first time it happened after I got married. But I didn't, and now . . ."

"Now it seems even harder." Here was another example of doing the hard thing. Like Mark, Ruthie struggled to speak up for herself.

Sarah held out her hand to Mary, determined not to give any unasked-for advice. "Komm. We'll go help Grossmammi with supper, yah?"

Mary hesitated for a moment. Then she nodded and took Sarah's hand.

As they reached the door, Ruthie's voice stopped them. "Denke, Sarah," she said softly. "I'm wonderful glad you're here."

# CHAPTER TWELVE

Apprehension weighed on Sarah as she walked down the lane the next morning. After the way they had parted the previous day, she wasn't sure she was right to come today. Still, she had said she'd be here this morning. What else could she do?

She reached Noah's place and set off across the yard to the shop, the frost whispering under her shoes. It was colder this morning, and a few snow flurries during the night had left sprinkles of white here and there on the brown grass. Eyeing the shop, she wondered if Noah was at work already. And if so, what would they say to each other?

Should she apologize? Even though she thought she'd been right, that didn't mean she should have spoken out.

But she had been right, she argued. Mark did need to have confidence to speak for himself, and she'd had no choice but to tell Noah what she'd learned. But she couldn't get the bitterness in his face out of her thoughts. Her instinctive reaction was to reach out, to attempt to banish the pain.

This wasn't a scraped knee or a broken arm. A pain

this deep required more healing than she could give. And even her sympathy had been rejected. Noah couldn't seem to recognize the difference between sympathy and pity.

Taking a deep breath, she opened the shop door and stepped inside. The breath came back out in a sigh of relief as a glance told her Noah wasn't in the shop. He had been, though, because the stove was throwing out enough heat that she could take off her coat. She retained the black cardigan that would ward off the drafts that whistled through a few cracks in the paneling.

After starting the coffee she headed for her desk, detouring along the way to look at the props for the Christmas program on a bench by the front wall. Noah must be close to being finished with these. Even as she touched a wooden candle, the door opened and Noah came in.

Sarah looked up, tongue-tied for an instant. Noah gave her a short nod, not speaking. Judging by the closed look on his face, she wondered what it would take to get him to say anything.

She didn't have to babble, but she did feel the need to say something. "The props look great. They must be almost ready."

"Yah." For a moment it seemed he wouldn't say anything else, but then he went on. "Teacher Dorcas wants them by Monday, so the scholars can practice with them several times before the program."

"You must have been working evenings." Every word seemed stilted to her, but surely it was better than staring at each other in silence.

"The boys are helping me." His eyes warmed, as they always did when he spoke of his sons. "It's been good, working together."

"Good for them and for you," she ventured, hoping she wasn't going too far.

He nodded, smiling faintly as if picturing it. Then he shrugged. "It's put me a bit behind."

Sarah glanced at the workbench where the whatnot stands were waiting for finishing. "I'm caught up on the book work, so I'll get to work finishing these."

"Yah, that'll help. I'll get you started and you can get on with it."

Noah hurried through explanations, making Sarah think he was eager to be finished with talking for the day. Fair enough. She was here to work, not to chatter.

Still, she was glad he'd talked about the boys so naturally to her. It seemed he'd dismissed what he'd said yesterday about her interest.

*They are my sons,* he'd said.

For much of the morning they worked in the same room with nothing more said between them. She ought to be relieved that things seemed to have returned to normal. Yet how could it be normal when she had the sense that too many things were left unsaid between them?

She stole another glance at his strong-featured face, his dark eyebrows two straight slashes that emphasized its strength, his jaw set. Stubborn. Determined to keep his problems to himself.

Not that she expected him to confide in her. But she hoped he talked to someone. His daad, maybe, or even Jacob. Or perhaps his mother—at least she was returning soon.

Was she trying to manage the situation again? She hoped not.

Finally she could stand it no longer. "Noah, about yesterday—I want to say I'm sorry."

"Forget it," he said shortly. "You meant well."

She winced, remembering Ruthie saying the same thing about her bossy sister.

"But won't you let me apologize if I feel the need? I'm afraid it's true—I'm too managing, like Jacob said. And what with raising my brothers and my sister, I guess I got too much in the habit."

"Forget it," he said again, but this time both his face and his voice had softened. He took a step closer to her, then another, as he seemed to struggle with the need to say something more. "I know it was just because you care about the boys."

*Not just the boys,* she thought but didn't dare to say.

He reached past her to touch the piece she'd been sanding, letting his hand slide along the side panel. "There's one spot that needs a bit more, and then you can move to the emery cloth to get it really smooth."

Sarah ran her fingers along the wood. It seemed to warm under her touch, almost as if it were alive. "Where . . ."

"Here. I'll show you." He took her hand and guided it along the panel. He leaned closer, close enough that she felt his breath across her cheek and the tickle of his beard against the nape of her neck.

Her breath caught, and she fought not to show what she was feeling.

"Feel that?" His voice seemed huskier. He moved her fingertips across the patch. "You need to use touch a lot in finishing. You want it smooth as . . . as a baby's skin."

"Yah, I see." She wasn't sure how she got the words out. Did he feel her reaction or was he totally oblivious? She ought to make some excuse, move away, say something . . .

"I . . . I'll finish that up before I go on to the emery cloth." She'd seen him using it, seen him smoothing it along his creation as if pouring his love into it.

She moved, intending to step away from his touch, but he moved at the same time. His shoulder bumped her head, sending her kapp askew.

"Ach, I'm sorry." He reached for the kapp as if to right it and then snatched his hand away. "I . . ."

Her face tilted up to his, and in an instant he was cradling her cheek with his palm, his touch so gentle, so warm, that it made her heart melt.

"Sarah." It was the softest murmur, coming out on a breath. His face bent to hers, their lips barely touched, and the world spun dizzyingly around them.

They both heard it at the same time—the sound of a car pulling up in front of the shop. Before Sarah could get her mind working again, Noah had backed up until he'd bumped into the other workbench.

It didn't help, she thought. They were still connected, no matter how far apart they were.

HORRIFIED WITH HIMSELF, Noah hurried toward the door, striking his hip on the workbench in his blundering haste. How could he have done such a thing? Sarah . . . was she frightened, angry? How could he make up for this?

Car doors slammed, and Noah opened the shop door, trying to compose himself in the face of the two Englisch women, probably out for a day's shopping.

"Komm in." He stepped back, holding the door open for them. He tried to assess them, but he found it impossible to guess the ages of Englisch women. These two looked very like the people he'd seen that night in Jacob's shop—prosperous and ready to spend.

"Are you Noah?" The one who asked stripped off her gloves with an air of getting down to business. At his nod, she went on, "We saw your ad in *Happenings* magazine and thought we'd like to have a look around." She hesitated, as if expecting him to say something. "You're open, aren't you?"

"Yah, yah, for sure." He tried not to stumble over his words. He gestured. "Look all you want."

They looked at him sort of expectantly, but when he didn't say anything else, they began moving toward the far end of the room.

They couldn't know how thankful he was for their arrival at that exact moment. He'd been on the edge of committing a grave sin—if indeed, he hadn't already committed it in his mind.

But it seemed to him that his mind hadn't had anything to do with it. The urge to touch Sarah had come out of nowhere, short-circuiting his sensible brain.

The two women walked around, seeming a little lost. He realized Sarah was looking at him. She frowned, jerking her head toward the shoppers. When he looked at her blankly, she shrugged and went over to the women.

"I'm Sarah," she said, smiling in welcome. "May I help you find what you're looking for?"

The two women exchanged glances and seemed to share a joke. "We're shopping," the one who'd appointed herself spokesperson said. "We don't have anything specific in mind, but it's Christmastime, so there are presents to find." She hesitated. "I'm not sure—do you Amish exchange gifts?"

"We do. Often it's something small and handmade. Or useful. I've been making wool hats for all my little cousins. That's the kind of gift we usually give."

"Not toys for the children?" The other woman looked shocked.

"Yah, usually the parents decide on a toy and leave the practical things to others."

"Like doting grandmothers?" the first woman said. "I'm expecting my first grandchild in the spring, and I've already started buying presents."

Feeling awkward, Noah turned away and busied himself at the workbench.

"Then it sounds as if you'll need a rocking chair,"

Sarah went on, undismayed. "This is a very nice one—the only one we have left in stock right now. Babies always like to be rocked."

"I remember." She sounded as if she were smiling.

Noah edged around the corner of the bench so that he could watch them without their noticing.

"Go on, sit in it. Try it out." Sarah patted the chair. "It's the perfect size for rocking a baby."

The woman sat. And rocked. "Very nice. Do you and . . . and Noah have any children?"

He was struck dumb, but Sarah didn't seem ruffled at all. "We're not married to each other." Her voice was calm. "But Noah has two little boys. Twins."

"Oh, how sweet." The woman looked at him with renewed interest, and Noah turned away from her gaze.

Where had Sarah gotten all this skill and poise with Englischers? She must be a born salesperson, in addition to being friendly and outgoing. Everything he wasn't, in other words.

Keeping his head down, he avoided questions, but he listened. Sarah was tireless. She must have shown the women everything in the shop before she was finished. But in the end she sold the rocker and a small bookcase, as well as one of the whatnot stands, which the woman agreed to come back for the next day when it was completely finished.

There was a slight holdup when the women realized they couldn't take credit cards, but eventually they scraped up the amount in cash between them. He carried everything out to the car for them, loading it carefully.

"Thank you." The woman stopped him to shake his hand. "I'm glad we came in." She laughed. "And we hadn't expected to actually buy something today. Your helper is a very good saleswoman."

He stood where he was, watching the car pull out of the

driveway. Yah, his helper was a very good saleswoman. Sarah had one priceless gift—her genuine interest in people. It was real, and people felt that without question.

If he lost her because of his offensive act . . . Panic swept through him. He didn't want to lose Sarah. She'd become an important part of his business and his life in such a short time. But he couldn't blame her if she walked away.

Maybe that would be for the best, no matter how he might hate it. At least then she wouldn't be nearby to tempt him. But that was so unfair to her.

All he could do was leave that up to Sarah. That, and apologize. Again. And he'd best do it now, before he lost his nerve. Squaring his shoulders, he marched back inside.

Sarah was at her desk, entering the sales in the ledger. She looked up at his approach, but he found her clear green eyes unreadable.

"I'm sorry." His voice sounded as strained as he felt. "I don't know what came over me. Can you ever forgive me?"

She was shaking her head, and his heart sank. Their friendship was over, then. Maybe that was for the best. He'd see her again, of course, but—

"No . . . I mean, there's nothing to forgive."

He gaped at her. "How can you say that? I touched you, I tried to kiss you—I'm a married man. I can't . . ."

"I know, Noah. I understand what you're feeling. But you have to understand something as well." Her hands clenched each other so that the knuckles turned white. "What happened . . . it was both of us. Maybe you didn't realize it before, but I did."

"Both of us?" His head spun. "You mean you felt it, too?"

The rich color came up in her cheeks. "I have felt attracted to you. I . . . I hope I didn't do anything to show it. But I felt it. So if anyone's guilty, it's me."

It took some processing for him to get it. She was

saying that he hadn't been the only one to feel that . . . whatever it was between them. That didn't make his behavior any less inexcusable, but oddly enough, it made him feel a little better about it.

"You felt something, too," he said, trying to get it clear in his mind. "But we can't."

"I know we can't." Her voice took on a sharp edge. "Don't you think I know that? But this hasn't happened to me before, not even when I was a teenager."

He blinked at that. "Never? No moonlight rides home from a singing when someone stole a kiss along the way?"

"No." The question seemed to relax her, and her lips twitched a little. "Is that what you did?"

Noah had to nod, remembering a certain night when the moon was full and the air chilly. Janie had snuggled against him in the buggy, and he'd kissed her and told her he loved her.

"I'm sorry." She seemed to sense his spasm of pain. "It made you think of Janie."

"Yah." He took a breath. "Now Janie is gone, and I'm not free. I don't suppose I ever will be. But you—"

"My mamm's illness and death hung over that time in my life. And now I've stopped expecting anything romantic to happen." Her lips twisted. "Life plays tricks on us, I guess. It happened."

"What are we going to do about it? Do you want to quit working for me? You could probably get another job. I'd pay you the rest of the month, but you could leave now, today, if you think that's best."

Sarah closed her eyes briefly, and when she opened them again, she had a look of decision.

"No. I don't want another job. I like working for you, and I like the convenience of being able to walk here and only work a few hours if that's what's needed. I'd hate to make a change."

Irrationally relieved, he nodded. "And I would hate for you to leave. I couldn't find another person with your interest and ability. But . . ."

"But." She shrugged. "We both know the danger now. Maybe that will make us on guard against it. We can't help being alone sometimes, but surely we're adult enough to resist temptation."

He certainly hadn't done a good job of it today. "I will try, if you will."

Noah hoped this was the right decision. He knew that the only other option was to have Sarah wiped out of his life, and he couldn't face that. He watched her expression. Eventually she gave a nod.

"I agree. If either of us starts to feel uncomfortable, we speak up. Anytime you say the word, I'll find another job."

"Right. Gut." He almost offered his hand for a handshake but he thought the better of it. No use flirting with temptation. "We have a deal."

BY THE END of the following day, Sarah was feeling very glad it was Friday. Friday . . . which meant she'd have the weekend to get over this ridiculous tendency to blush every time their gazes met.

The day had been busier than usual, with their customer from the previous day coming to pick up her whatnot stand and two other sets of customers coming in. She couldn't help but be gratified that the ad she'd talked him into was seeing such a good return.

Noah, she'd realized, really was reluctant to talk to the customers. That natural shyness of his stood in the way of his being a good salesperson. It wondered her how he'd ever imagined his business growing without seeing he'd have to put effort into selling.

Still, he was a craftsman, not a salesperson, and if that

meant she needed to do the selling, it was fine with her. She enjoyed it. As for how the idea of running the business with his sons went, he had a natural salesman coming along in Matthew. That boy could talk the birds from the trees if he tried.

"Something funny?" Noah's voice startled her. She hadn't realized she was standing there smiling at her own thoughts.

"In a way. I was just picturing Matty selling the work you and Mark produce. That's certainly his natural gift."

Noah considered it and then smiled. "Yah, you're probably right about that. The two of them make a gut team."

He hesitated, making her wonder if he intended to bring up what he saw as her mistake in insisting that Mark take his part in the school program. If so, he apparently decided against it.

"Maybe on Monday you could work on the finishing of this table." He tapped the drop-leaf table he'd been putting together.

"Yah, for sure, if you trust me with it." Remembering what had happened when he'd shown her the technique for finishing something was not helpful. That was best forgotten.

Sarah was just cleaning up her work when footsteps sounded and the twins burst through the door, bringing a blast of cold air with them.

"Daadi, Daadi!" Matty, as usual, was in full cry. "Grossmammi is coming home tomorrow, remember?"

"Quiet down, Matty. I'm right here, so you don't need to shout. And you didn't greet Sarah, did you?"

Matthew grinned, unrepentant. "Sorry. Hello, Sarah."

Mark echoed him with a softer greeting.

By then, Matthew had turned back to his father. "Remember, Daadi? Grossmammi—"

"Yah, for sure I remember. We'll be wonderful glad to see her after all this time."

Matty nodded so vigorously that his hat tipped over his eyes. "We think we should get greens and decorate. To wilkom her back, ain't so, Mark?" He didn't wait for a response but hurried on. "Can we go cut some greens? Please?"

Noah finished hanging up his tools before he turned back to his son. "Don't you want a snack first?"

"No, now." Matty was jiggling with impatience. "Can't we go now?"

"I suppose so." Noah lifted his jacket from its hook. "Coming, Mark?"

Mark seemed undecided. "I . . . I want to ask Sarah something."

"Go ahead, then. Hurry." Matty was already reaching for the door.

Sarah gave the boy an encouraging smile. "What is it, Mark?"

"Would you . . . would you stay and help me with my poem?" The words came out in a rush.

She tried to control her surprise. "Yah, for sure. Now?"

He nodded.

"Don't you want to come with us?" Noah asked. "I can help you later."

"Now." He was surprisingly firm. He gave her a pleading look. "Please?"

"That's fine." She put a hand on his shoulder, feeling how slight he was under the heavy wool coat. She glanced at Noah. "You're going to the stand of pines and hemlock along the lane? Mark and I can walk together to join you. It's right on my way home."

Noah seemed doubtful, but he nodded, and he and Matty went on out the door.

Sarah sat down in her desk chair, pulling over a stool for Mark. "It's warm in here, so you'd best take your coat off." She waited while he shed the coat, letting it slip to the floor.

"Now, then," she said when they were settled. "I'm happy to help you. Why don't you read it to me first, just the way you would talk?"

Mark clearly didn't need the bedraggled paper he pulled out. He said the whole piece from memory, not missing a word, but Sarah had to strain to hear him.

"Very nice. You know the whole thing, ain't so?"

His shy smile warmed her heart. "I need to be louder. Teacher Dorcas said so. But when I try, it gets really tight here." He indicated his throat.

"Ach, I see what's the matter. People who have naturally soft voices have to learn how to be louder. You have a soft voice just like Daadi."

Mark blinked, as if surprised, and then a slow smile grew on his face. "I'm like Daadi," he said, as if trying out the words.

"You are. So what you can do is give a great big yawn before you start. Like this." She demonstrated. "See? Now you try it."

He tried, giggled, and tried again, this time producing a creditable yawn.

"Gut. Feel how that makes your throat relax?" She put her fingers on her neck to show him.

Mark yawned again, mimicking her actions, and grinned. "It works."

"Sure it does. Then the next thing is to think about bringing your voice up from way down in your chest, not up in your throat. Try saying it again that way."

Fascinated now, Mark produced another yawn, smiled, and began to speak, his volume increasing as he went along. He ended with a huge grin. "That was better, ain't so?"

"That was much better." She resisted the impulse to hug him, not wanting to move too quickly with such a shy child. "Let's try it one more time. And don't be afraid to giggle when you yawn. That always makes me feel better."

Mark tried it again, standing up this time, and looking very pleased with himself. "Denke, Sarah. That's a wonderful gut trick."

"It is, isn't it? I'll bet if you keep practicing that way, you'd be able to make Daadi hear you all the way to the woods."

He giggled again at that, hesitated a moment, and then flung his arms around her in a hug. "Denke," he whispered in her ear.

Sarah's own throat felt tight as she hugged him back, and she had to blink away tears. Such a special little person—it blessed her to be able to help him.

Coats on again, they headed down the lane. The clump of evergreens was about halfway along, near the border between Noah's property and the farm. As soon as they came within sight of Noah and Matthew, Mark darted ahead.

By the time Sarah reached them, Mark was busily engaged in helping his brother heap armloads of evergreen into the wagon. Some of them looked rather odd sizes for decorating, but probably Noah intended to trim them into shape. She picked up a piece that Matthew dropped, inhaling the spicy scent of it.

"Smells like Christmas, ain't so?"

The boys stopped to copy her, nodding. "But I like the smell of cookies better," Matty said.

"You'll get plenty of that when Grossmammi comes," Noah said. "You can help her make cookies."

"Will we do that right away?" Matthew was obviously in a hurry. "The minute she comes?"

"Maybe not the first minute she's back," Noah cautioned. "She'll be tired from her trip, and she'll want to spend time with Grossdaadi and the rest of the family, too. But I think sometime soon she'll come over for cookie baking."

Matty tried to hide his disappointment, and Sarah found herself exchanging a laughing glance with Noah. Unfortunately that meant she reacted too strongly to the warmth in his eyes. Maybe she'd best go home.

"Have fun with your decorating." She raised her hand in a wave.

"Don't you want to help us?" Mark's expression was exactly like Matty's when he'd reacted to the news that cookies weren't immediately forthcoming.

Her heart winced, but she really shouldn't spend any more time with them. It had begun to feel too . . . too right.

"Sarah has to go home." Noah came to the rescue. "She has things to do there."

"Yah, I do." She managed to produce a smile for the boys. "Have fun." She walked off quickly before she could be tempted any further.

It was definitely good that it was Friday, she thought again. Definitely. She wouldn't see Noah and the boys at all for two days, except at worship. And by Monday, she'd have conquered this ridiculous feeling that they belonged together.

# CHAPTER THIRTEEN

"Higher, Daadi, higher." Matty was about to climb on the table in his eagerness to decorate the next day.

Noah removed him firmly. "That's high enough. The greens need to go under the light fixture, not on top of it. You don't want to start a fire, do you?"

"No." But he still looked yearningly at the top of the lamp. "But it would look pretty."

"Looking pretty isn't an excuse to risk a fire."

"What would we do if our house burned down?" Mark's eyes widened with fear.

"That's not likely to happen."

"Never? Are you sure?" Mark was being unusually persistent. Noah got down from the step stool to focus on him.

"Nobody can say never about something like that. But if it did happen, we've talked about how to get out of the house quickly, yah? Once we were safe, then we'd depend on God and our gut neighbors to help us build again."

"Like when Daadi helped build that barn for Joey Fisher's daadi," Matty said. "That's right, isn't it, Daadi?"

"Yah, it is." He'd sometimes thought the twins would be easier to take care of when they were older. Maybe that was true as far as diapers and bottles were concerned, but their constant questions about anything and everything really kept him on his toes.

Matty stood back, looking at the greens they'd put up in the kitchen. "Grossmammi will like the way it looks. It will make her want to bake Christmas cookies."

Noah chuckled. "You have a one-track mind." He ruffled Matthew's hair. "It's always on your stomach, isn't it?"

Matty grinned. "I like Grossmammi's cookies. And she lets us help with the snickerdoodles."

"Yah, she does." He looked thoughtfully at his sons. Was this the right time to bring up his determination not to rely on his mother so much? Maybe it wouldn't hurt to give the boys a hint, anyway.

"Grossmammi has always done a lot for us," he said. "I'm thinking now that you're older, we can do more for ourselves."

"But she likes doing it," Matty said, his face serious. "She does. She told us so."

Mark's forehead crinkled. "I don't remember her saying that."

"Sure she did. One time when Elizabeth came over. I heard her say that Grossmammi shouldn't have to do so much at her age, and Grossmammi said she wasn't that old and besides, she liked doing things for us."

Noah struggled to hide his amusement. If folks realized how much kids heard and repeated, they'd be more careful of what they said. Matty's voice had mimicked both women perfectly.

"I'm sure she does," he said, trying to get back to the point. "But that doesn't mean we should take for granted all that she does. We should show how much we appreciate it, and we should do things for ourselves as much as we can."

Matty wore his mulish look that said he was about to

argue, but Mark spoke first. "Grossmammi does things for us because she loves us. So we should do things to show we love her, too."

"That's right." Mark had simplified it perfectly. Raising kinder was a challenge, but it was wonderful satisfying when something went right.

They worked their way through the rest of the downstairs, and he listened to the twins' chatter, thinking how fortunate he was to have them. Did Janie have any idea what she was missing? He'd like to be able to forgive and wish her well, but he suspected he'd be struggling with that for a while yet.

He tuned back in to the boys' talk in time to hear Mark saying that Sarah had taught him a special trick to help him talk louder.

"She did? What is that trick?" Noah asked, intrigued.

"This one." Mark stood up very straight and gave a big, exaggerated yawn. Then he said the first line of his poem so boldly Noah could hardly believe it.

"That is amazing," he said. "You mean, just yawning like that makes you able to talk in a big voice?"

Mark nodded, solemn as could be. "It works. Sarah says it relaxes your throat."

"Wonderful gut." Noah patted his shoulder. He wasn't sure whether Sarah's trick relaxed Mark's throat or gave him confidence. But either way, it had worked . . . yet another reason to be glad Sarah had come into their lives and to do what he must to keep her there.

Helping the boys carry the discarded branches out of the house, Noah headed on to the workshop, surprised to find the twins following him.

"You can go and play until lunchtime," he pointed out.

They exchanged glances. "We'd rather help you," Matty said, apparently speaking for both of them. "It's more fun."

After an instant's surprise, warmth swept through

Noah. Wasn't that what every father hoped—that his sons would want to be like him? For the moment, at least, that was true.

"Gut, come on, then. We've got a little more work to finish today."

Once in the workshop, he set them a couple of simple things to do, trying to imagine what would appeal to them. Matty, he knew, had less patience than Mark did, and he smiled to think about Sarah's prediction that he'd be the salesman of the family. Every business needed someone to handle that side of it, he supposed.

It was nearly noon when he heard a car pull up at the shop and looked out to see Jeff Portman coming toward him. Opening the door, he welcomed him in.

"I'm wonderful glad to see you. Did the folks seem happy with the pair of rocking chairs?"

"What? Oh, yes." Portman frowned. "That's not why I'm here. I heard that you're letting that harness shop in town sell your things for you. What's the idea of that? We agreed that I'd be your sales point."

The belligerence in Portman's voice knocked him off his balance. Was that true? Had he broken the agreement they'd made?

A moment's thought was enough to reassure him. They hadn't even discussed such a thing. What's more, he had Sarah's written account of their agreement to prove it.

"I . . . I'm sorry if you think that." Was he doing the right thing? He didn't want to risk losing Portman's business. It might be the best outlet he could find. "But we didn't talk about that at all. I have the agreement we signed if you want to look at it." He gestured toward Sarah's file drawer.

"Agreement?" Portman's voice rose. "We had an oral agreement. How do you think I felt when I saw you advertising your stuff and putting it in other stores? It doesn't pay me to put in the effort to sell your things if you're going to sell things out from under me."

Noah took a step back, startled by Portman's vehemence. What could he do in the face of that?

And then he saw his sons watching them. Seeing the man push him into an agreement he didn't want to make. Mark had learned a lesson on how to speak up for himself. Did he have the nerve to do the same?

He took a deep breath, wondering what the man would think if Noah yawned in his face. Amusement trembled in him at the thought.

"I'm sorry you feel that way." He said the words quietly. "And I will regret not working with you."

For an instant Portman stared at him. Then his eyes dropped, and he shrugged. "Worth trying, anyway. Let me count out what I owe you, and then we can pick out a couple pieces to take back to the store." He pulled a wad of bills from his pocket.

Noah gave him a receipt for the money, trusting Sarah would be satisfied with it, and Portman signed one of the consignment papers Sarah had made up. When Portman drove away a few minutes later with a bookcase and a small stand in the back of his car, Noah still felt a little stunned. He had nearly given in to the man, not wanting to risk one opportunity for another. He should have known that bargaining was part of any transaction. He shrugged, grinning, and pulled the boys into a hug.

"Denke," he said.

Mark looked up, blinking. "For what, Daadi?"

"Your good example," Noah said. "Komm, let's fix our lunch."

SUNDAY SUPPER WAS often a little later than during the week, at least on worship Sundays. Sarah had tried to persuade her grandmother to let her fix the meal, but that never seemed to work. Instead they worked around each other in harmony in the farmhouse kitchen, prepping the vegetables to go in with the pot roast that already simmered slowly on the stove.

". . . so many people wanted to talk to you after worship," Grossmammi was saying. "I should have stayed home with Ruthie so you could go and visit with them."

"I enjoyed having a little more time with Ruthie and Mary." And she felt quite sure that Grossmammi had enjoyed the inevitable chatter that took place among the women while they served the meal after worship. "She's wonderful happy the midwife said she could sit in the chair a few hours a day."

"We'll have to keep even more of an eye on her," her grandmother warned. "She'll not be content until she can come downstairs."

"No, I suppose not. She wants to get back to taking care of this little girl." Sarah smiled down at Mary, who sat at the table engrossed in rolling out a piece of noodle dough with her tiny rolling pin.

The much-handled dough was turning soft and sticky from the warmth of Mary's hands. She gave it a pat as she'd seen Sarah do, and it came away, clinging to her fingers. She grabbed at the dough, getting it onto her other hand so that they stuck together. Mary stared at her hands in perplexity for a moment and tilted her face up to Sarah, lighting up with laughter.

Sarah's heart turned over, and yearning welled up in her. Where had it come from, this sudden longing to have a child of her own? She'd thought when she came home that she'd be content to live single, independent, and on her own.

Noah slid into her thoughts despite her determination to keep him out. Maybe that was all of a piece—her growing affection for the twins, the fierce attraction that had led them so close to an embrace, even this yearning for a child.

Sarah yanked her thoughts away forcibly. She'd had her two days away from Noah and had thought it was helping. And then it jumped out at her when she wasn't looking, all because of Mary's laugh.

"Let me help, sweet girl." She took the sticky hands and rubbed some flour into them, peeling off the dough. No sooner had she gotten it into a ball than Mary snatched it, eager to do the whole thing again.

"Sarah? Did you hear what I said?"

"Sorry, Grossmammi. I was helping Mary. What was it?"

Her grandmother dropped a couple of handfuls of potatoes into the pot and turned back to her. "I said, did Nancy tell you that Janie Burkhalter's daad and cousins are part of her community?"

Sarah's mind raced. How much to admit?

Her grandmother saved her the trouble. "Don't you go thinking you can pull the wool over my eyes, Sarah Grace Yoder. I can see you heard about it."

"Yah, Nancy did tell me. It makes me wonder if Janie is out there someplace, too."

"Did you tell Noah what Nancy said?" Her grandmother was determined to know the whole story, but at least she was safe. No one would hear anything from her.

"I felt I had to. Now I don't know if I did the right thing or not. Maybe he'd have been happier not knowing."

Her grandmother shook her head. "He'd have heard anyway, what with Margaret Esh knowing about it through her cousins. That woman has a tongue that won't quit. But she said something else." Her clear blue eyes clouded. "She said folks have noticed that Amos has been going to the hospital over in Standish."

Sarah's startled gaze met her grandmother's. "It doesn't have to have anything to do with Janie. It might be Amos is going for treatment, or tests, or something."

"Yah. Or it might be Janie."

"There's no way of knowing if Janie really is there," Sarah argued. "It's all just speculation, ain't so?"

Grossmammi shrugged. "Gossip, and plenty of times it's all wrong. But sometimes it's true."

Sarah's throat went tight with strain. "I don't want to be the one to tell Noah. Not again."

Her grandmother rounded the table to put an arm around Sarah's waist. "Tell me, child. You have feelings for Noah, ain't so?"

Sarah turned her face away, unwilling to meet those wise old eyes. "We're friends. I . . . I care about him and the boys. I know it can't go beyond that." *Please, don't ask me anything else. Please don't read my heart.*

"It's hard sometimes to understand God's doings." She gave Sarah a squeeze. "This is one of those times. All we can do is trust His plan."

Sarah nodded, her heart full.

"Anyway, most likely you won't have to tell him. His brother's wife was right there in the kitchen when Margaret's tongue was wagging. She'll tell him soon enough."

She'd think that would make her feel relieved, but it didn't. How could it, when she knew this news would make the grief in Noah's life even worse?

As SOON AS she reached the shop on Monday, Sarah realized that Noah knew. He glanced in her direction without meeting her eyes, gave a curt nod, and turned back to his work. Feeling as if she were walking on shattered glass, Sarah hung up her coat and went across to her desk.

A note, scribbled in Noah's hand, lay atop the ledger.

It was a consignment form signed by Jeff Portman for two more items.

Ordinarily she would make some comment on that, but a glance at Noah's face discouraged her from speaking. He looked as if he wore a mask—a stiff, solid mask that froze his features and hid whatever he felt behind an implacable barrier. No, it was best just to get on with her work. He'd have to figure out how to handle this situation himself.

But her heart ached for him.

She filed the note about the consignment pieces and brought the ledger up-to-date with the sales he'd recorded on Saturday. Then she was free to return to the finishing work.

That was proving far more enjoyable than she'd thought possible. The lure of bringing out the beauty that existed in Noah's fine work was incredibly strong. Seeing the grain of the wood glow under her polishing gave her a sense of accomplishment that book work could never do.

When she'd finished the fine sanding on the current piece, she paused. Ordinarily she'd ask for instructions before moving on, but Noah's expression still didn't encourage it.

He looked up abruptly, as if he'd felt her gaze on him. "What is it?"

"I thought you'd want to check this before I go on to the emery cloth." She took a step back away from the workbench, giving him space.

She needn't have taken the precaution. Noah obviously had firmly in mind the need not to touch her. He came to the other side of the workbench, running his hand slowly over every inch of the small cabinet. His eyes closed at one point, as if he were reading the wood through his fingers.

"There. You'll need to give that another going-over. Then you can go on to the emery."

Sarah touched the place he'd indicated, feeling the slightest roughness he'd caught.

"Yah, I see what you mean. I'll take care of it." Did she dare venture something light? "That's what it is when you have untrained labor."

The slightest tremor seemed to break through his barriers. "You're doing all right," he muttered, and went quickly back to his work.

Sarah followed suit, thinking she should have kept her mouth shut. But how could she know whether it was better to let him brood in silence or try to speak normally?

As they continued to work, she eyed Noah covertly from time to time, her heart hurting from the pain that was obvious in his shuttered face. How could he have reacted to learning not only that his wife might be ill but that everyone in the community was talking about it? For such a private person, that would be doubly painful.

Sarah tried to focus only on the movement of the emery gliding along the grain of the wood, but it seemed she was extraordinarily sensitive to Noah's every movement. She wouldn't have thought his face could tighten any more, but it had, and even his movements, usually so sure and deft when he worked, had become taut and jerky. Even as she watched the tool in his hand slipped. He let out an involuntary sound.

She had crossed to him before she realized what she was doing. "You're hurt. Let me see."

Noah turned away, hunching over his injury like a child unwilling to have a cut tended. "It's nothing. Leave it alone."

If he wanted to act like a child, she'd treat him like one. "Stop that. I can see the blood, and you're not helping by grabbing it that way. Now come to the sink and let me wash it off." Grasping his arm, she piloted him across to the small sink in the corner. He could have pulled away, but he didn't, which was a small gain, at least.

Taking his left hand in hers, she ran water over the cut gently, wiping away the blood, and gave a sigh of relief. Not deep, thank goodness. Experience with the many ways her brothers had found to damage themselves told her it wouldn't need stitches.

"That's not too bad." Quickly she made a pad from a small towel and pressed it firmly against the cut. "Can you hold that on? Do you have a first aid kit?"

He actually managed the beginnings of a smile. "In a workshop? For sure. It's on the bottom shelf." He nodded toward the cabinet that held the coffee fixings.

Sarah managed to persuade Noah to sit down by the simple expedient of pushing the chair against the back of his legs. Carefully she removed the pad just enough to see if the cut was still bleeding. It seeped blood, but the initial flow had stopped, and the edges of the cut didn't gape. Good news, she knew, but probably small consolation. Even a minor injury could be a problem to someone who worked with his hands.

Returning the pad to its place, she opened the first aid box. Iodine seemed to be the only choice, but there was an assortment of bandages. She held up the bottle. "What do you think? Are you ready for this?"

He gave a short nod, and she went on talking as she wiped the cut and then dabbed it with iodine. He jerked involuntarily but didn't speak, and she hurried, hating to hurt someone who was already hurting. Then for the bandage. Mindful of the way Noah used his hands, she folded a thick pad to cover the area, holding it in place with tape.

"There, that should do it." Sarah began putting things back in the first aid box.

He turned his hand, flexing it as if to be sure he still had movement despite the bandage. "You a nurse in your spare time?"

"I told you—my brothers were experts in damaging

themselves, and my mother taught me early how to cope. Sometimes I've wondered if she sensed I'd be taking care of them." A flicker of regret went through her.

Would it be worse for the twins, never having known their mother, than it would be to lose a loved one? She couldn't tell.

"It's useful, anyway." He started to rise. "I'd best get back to work."

"How about a cup of coffee first?" She gestured toward the pot on the stove. "Give it a few minutes so we know it's not going to start bleeding again."

To her surprise, he nodded without arguing, and she fixed the coffee quickly, bringing his to him and then fixing a mug for herself. She tilted it up, inhaling the warmth. She didn't know about him, but she certainly needed a moment to relax. Taking care of his injury had been an intimate action. She hadn't felt it at the time, engrossed in what had to be done, but now she replayed the feeling of his hand in hers.

They drank without talking, mainly because she couldn't think of anything to say that didn't risk showing what she was feeling.

"Denke," he muttered finally. "Sorry I acted like a child."

"We all revert when we're hurt, I think." She hesitated, wondering if she ought to bring up the subject that was on both of their minds.

"I guess you heard what folks were saying at worship yesterday." He brought it up for her.

"Yah. Well, I was home with Ruthie, but my grossmammi was in the kitchen, so she heard. She says some folks just can't help babbling anything they hear."

He nodded, staring absently at the bandage on his hand. He didn't speak again for a long moment, but eventually the words seemed to spurt out as if a dam had been breached.

"That's what it was like when Janie left. Talk, talk, talk. All the time. Everybody asking questions, telling me they were sorry, wanting to comfort me. I just wanted them to leave me alone. And now it's happening again."

"I'm so sorry." That was inadequate, but it was all she could find to say.

"I figured it was over with finally." He didn't seem to be aware of her. It was as if he were speaking to himself. "People got used to it. They stopped talking. I figured we could just go on with our lives and maybe someday I'd hear something about Janie. But I didn't expect it now."

It would have been hard on anyone, of course. But for a man as private and self-contained as Noah, it must have been twice the nightmare.

"I . . ." She didn't want to repeat that she was sorry. "It must have been so painful when she said she was going away."

Noah seemed frozen for an instant, and then his face came alive with anger. "She didn't tell me. That would have been bad enough, but she never said a thing. She just left. I was in the shop, working. I came in for lunch never imagining such a thing. I heard the babies crying upstairs. I went up, wondering why she wasn't going to them. And they were all alone. She wasn't there."

Her heart twisted at the thought of the twins crying and no one hearing. "How . . ." *How could she*, that was what she wanted to say, but better not to.

"I didn't realize at first." He seemed to take it as a question. "I called to her, tried to comfort the boys, and finally went all over the house carrying them. She wasn't anywhere. I panicked. Thought she was hurt, abducted, who knows what. The family came right away to help. Mamm and my sister took the babies, and the rest of us searched, thinking she was somewhere fallen, hurt . . . Then Mamm said I should check the bedroom, just to see if there was any clue. So we looked. All Janie's clothes were there. All of them. And I found a couple of plastic bags. They had receipts for clothes—Englisch clothes. She'd gone."

Her heart seemed to be breaking in tiny pieces for him. "She didn't tell you why?"

"Nothing. Not a note, not anything. Her daad seemed as much in the dark as any of us." His face changed. "But maybe that wasn't true. He knows now, anyway, doesn't he?"

"I guess so."

She wondered what kind of a man Amos was. She tried and failed to remember him. Most likely he hadn't known then—it was hard to believe anyone would connive at that sort of disappearance—but certainly it seemed he knew now. Noah would have trouble forgiving that.

Noah rose suddenly, startling her. He moved his shoulders as if shrugging something off. "Funny. I haven't told anyone that story in the past five years. Feels good to get it out."

Sarah managed to smile. She was glad Noah was relieved to shed a little of his burden. But now it seemed to be settled on her.

# CHAPTER FOURTEEN

In mid-afternoon, Noah began picking up the props that he and the boys had made for the Christmas program.

"Do you need some help?" Sarah moved toward him.

He paused. "I told Dorcas I'd bring them to the school this afternoon. Guess there's too much to carry, so I'll take the buggy."

"She'll be wonderful grateful to you, I know. Why don't I put these on the steps while you're harnessing the buggy? Then they'll be ready to load."

"Yah, gut." Noah reached for his jacket. "I'll bring the boys home with me. Just leave the lamps and stove when you go. I'll take care of closing up later."

Sarah nodded, relieved that they were back to talking normally with each other. She suspected Noah felt the same, maybe longing to forget the things that had turned his life upside down.

But as she moved the props to the small landing at the top of the outside steps, she found herself wondering if normal was even possible. It seemed to her that Noah was cautiously avoiding one big question. What could or should he do about the knowledge that had landed on him? If Amos or Janie was ill, perhaps seriously, what action did he take?

She didn't know the answer to that, and even trying to imagine herself in his place was impossible. Any action at all seemed fraught with pitfalls, but to do nothing felt impossible, too.

Noah returned with the buggy at that point, and she was glad to have that chain of thought disrupted. She picked up one unwieldy wooden tree only to have Noah take it from her hands.

"You don't have a coat on. Go back inside. I'll handle this."

She had a natural tendency to question orders, but the cold wind went right through the cotton of her dress. "Yah, all right. I'll just finish up what I was working on."

Noah nodded, seeming to dismiss her from his thoughts as he worked. With a slight feeling of envy for his ability to do that, she scurried back inside.

The piece she was working on was soon at a good stopping point, and she stood back a little, looking at it with satisfaction. One final polish tomorrow and it would be ready for Noah's approval. As she started to clean up, she heard a buggy pulling up out front. Startled, she headed for the door. Noah couldn't be back that fast, could he?

It took her only a second to identify the woman climbing nimbly down from the buggy—Miriam Raber, Noah's mother. Funny how memory worked. She'd barely remembered what Noah looked like when she came back, but there was a clear picture in her mind of Miriam, sitting at a quilting frame with Grossmammi at the first quilting bee at which she'd been allowed to help.

"Miriam." She held out her hand in welcome. "How nice to see you. I'm Sarah . . . Sarah Yoder."

"Ach, do you think I'd forget you, Sarah?" She envel-

oped Sarah in a hug and then urged her back into the
workshop. "Komm, let's get in the warm. I hoped I'd get
here before you left."

Closing the door, Sarah looked at Miriam and smiled.
She had hardly changed since those quilting bee days. A
few more wrinkles, maybe, but still with a round, rosy
face that wore a constant smile.

"I'm afraid Noah isn't here. He'll be back soon, though.
He took some things to the school, and he'll bring the
boys home with him."

"All the better." Miriam hung up her coat and bonnet,
moving toward the stove with her hands spread out to the
heat. "It gives us a chance to have a little talk. Tell me,
how is Ruthie doing? I heard you stayed home from worship to be with her yesterday. Bed rest, someone said."

"Yah, the midwife and the doctor both thought it best
for a week or two. She's doing well, though, and is allowed to sit up in a chair part of the time now."

"She'll be impatient to get back to normal, but it's best
to take precautions. With Christmas so close, there's a
lot to do."

"Grossmammi and I have convinced her to focus on
the scarves and mittens she's been knitting for gifts. Fortunately little Mary loves to sit up on the bed with her
mammi and look at books or listen to stories."

"Ach, not like the twins at that stage, then." Miriam's
face crinkled with amusement. "They were never still a
minute. Still aren't."

"That's certain-sure." She returned the smile, her
thoughts on the twins. How would Mark have done at
practice today?

"I saw them before they left for school this morning,
just for a few minutes. They had plenty to tell me about
you, you know. Sarah this and Sarah that. Sounds as if
you found a way into their hearts awful fast."

Sarah's smile softened, thinking of them. "I don't know about that, but they certain-sure found their way into mine. They're so alike to look at and so different inside."

"You do know them, then." Miriam beamed. "Most folks only see how alike they are. The two of them are just like my two oldest were from the day they were born. Isaac always lively and chattering, leading the way into mischief like as not. And Noah so quiet, intent on his thoughts, not giving away his feelings to anyone."

Sarah's heart twisted. That was Noah, for sure. "I'd thought about Mark being like his daadi. I don't know Isaac as well. So Matty is like him?"

"Yah." Miriam's eyes glowed with love for her grandsons. "It takes some doing to get to know Mark, but it's worth it to find all the sweetness in him. Like his daadi, ain't so?"

"I . . . I guess so." That question, with its implication that she'd found that in Noah, made her nervous. "I should get on with cleaning up my work, I think."

"Ach, I shouldn't keep you here talking. You'll want to be away home."

"I'm not in that much of a hurry, but I did want to cover this piece." She drew out the cloth she intended to put over the cabinet she'd been working on. "I don't want the dust to settle on it."

"So you're helping with the furniture, along with keeping the books."

Aware of Miriam's eyes on her, she felt her every movement was awkward. "Only the things that don't need much skill," she said.

"Gut. I've always thought Noah needed more help. He works so hard to keep a home and future for the boys." She hesitated. "And now this gossip is going around, making it even more difficult. You heard, I'm sure."

Sarah nodded, keeping her gaze on the workbench.

"Grossmammi heard the talk after worship. It's upsetting." Her feelings got the better of her discretion. "Things happen and it's all in God's hands, I know. But it's hard, all the same, to have this worry about Janie come up again after all these years."

"Noah is taking it hard." Miriam moved to the workbench, taking over the dusting Sarah had been doing. "But you know that, I'm sure." Sarah felt her glance. "He talks to you, I think."

A question she didn't know how to answer without betraying her feelings for Noah. She didn't dare do that, so she nodded, hoping there'd be no more questions.

Maybe Miriam sensed that. "Forgiving is difficult, that's for sure. Janie did a terrible thing in walking away from her family. I try to forgive, but the anger still flares up from time to time—when I look at those beautiful boys, and when I see Noah having to live his life alone."

Sarah could only nod her agreement. She felt the same, and if she tried from now until forever, she'd never understand a woman walking away from her babies.

"At least he has a friend in you now, my dear." Miriam spoke very deliberately, and Sarah understood what she was asking. She wanted to know whether there was more than friendship on Sarah's part.

Sarah fought down a flare of anger. Miriam was his mother. She was concerned about him.

She forced herself to meet Miriam's gaze, reading nothing but sympathy there. "I'm glad Noah feels I'm a friend." She wouldn't say more. She couldn't. They both knew, only too well, that there wasn't anything else she could be.

NOAH'S MAMM AND daad stayed for supper—provided by his mother, Noah was happy to see. No matter how much practice he had, he didn't seem to be turning into a good cook. Maybe one of the boys would inherit the gift from Grossmammi.

One of his nephews had dropped Daad off, and he'd drive Grossmammi home in their buggy. She hadn't liked to drive after dark since her cataract surgery a couple of years ago.

They sat around the table after finishing dessert, Daad having another cup of coffee. He claimed it never kept him awake, though Mamm had been known to press her lips together and shake her head over that claim.

Noah looked at the circle of faces, glowing in the soft light from the gas fixture. They looked so relaxed and happy, with the twins taking turns trying to claim the attention of one or the other. He'd missed this since Mamm had been away, and he'd guess Daad had found it even worse. His gaze kept returning to Mamm with a glow of contentment at being reunited with his other half. That was how a marriage should be.

Mamm rose from her chair with the air of being ready to get on with things. "Komm along, now. That's enough coffee. I'm certain-sure the boys would like to play a game with Grossdaadi before bed. Noah can help me with the dishes."

Daad glanced toward the window. "Ach, it's dark already. I'll play a game another time. We'd best get along home before it's any worse."

"Nonsense," Mamm said briskly. "It's dark now, and we'll have to use the buggy lanterns anyway. You boys run and set up a game with Grossdaadi."

She gave Daad a look that he seemed to have no trouble interpreting, and he got up, following the boys. Noah could interpret it, too. Mamm had something to say to him, and she wouldn't be satisfied until she'd said it.

Once they had left the kitchen, she seized a stack of

dishes and put them in the sink, starting the water running. He began clearing the table, knowing there was no getting out of hearing what Mamm wanted to say. Where her kinder were concerned, Mamm still treated them all as if they were about ten or twelve.

At first she seemed engrossed in getting the dishes underway, but then silence fell, punctuated by the clink of plates and silverware. Noah plucked a towel from the drawer and began drying.

"Well, Mamm? You'd best get started on the lecture." He may as well start on a light note, because this was probably going to get serious, given everything that had happened.

"Lecture? Nonsense," she said, but her lips twitched. "Can't I just want to have a chat with my son?"

"You can, but not this time, ain't so?"

"Ach, you're too suspicious." She reached out a warm, soapy hand to clasp his for an instant. "I'm wonderful glad to be back with you and the boys."

"And Daad?" he teased.

She smiled, flicking some soapsuds in his direction. "Always." She paused. "It was wonderful gut to see Sarah Yoder again after all this time. She's grown into a fine woman, ain't so?"

"She has." On that subject, he and Mamm were agreed. "It wasn't easy for her, with that father of hers."

"No, I'm sure not." His comment seemed to have confirmed something in his mother's mind. "The twins have taken to her right away, even Mark, and he's usually so shy with strangers."

"I guess it's from raising her brothers and sister, but she certain-sure knows how kinder think." He thought about Mark, practicing his piece. "I don't know how she did it, but she helped Mark get over being afraid to take part in the Christmas program."

"Mark is like you, that's certain-sure. Quiet, self-contained, willing to stand back and let others speak for him." She darted a look at him. "But you're a grown man."

"Yah." This was the thing she'd wanted to say, he decided. "I know, Mamm."

"Do you, Noah?" Her gaze grew serious, studying him. "It was a shock, yesterday, hearing all that talk about Janie."

"I know. I'm sorry. You and Daad have had too much grief already from my choices."

"Ach, don't be ferhoodled." She clasped his hand again, and this time she didn't let go. "You weren't to blame for what Janie did."

"She was my wife. I should have known—should have seen things were going wrong."

She shook her head sadly. "None of us saw. I was around her as much as anyone, helping with the little ones. We just never imagined it. A mother doesn't run away from her babies. Who could guess such a thing?"

"I was her husband. I should have," he said stubbornly, clinging to his guilt.

She shook the hand she held in sudden emphasis. "Enough of thinking about the past. The good Lord doesn't want us to live in the past or in the future, just in the now. And now you must decide what to do."

Noah had feared she was headed in that direction. "What can I do?" He tried to suppress a flicker of anger—not at Mamm, but at the circumstances he'd been plunged into. "I've heard from Amos from time to time, asking about the boys. He never once hinted he knew where Janie was. Should I go to him now, asking for news about my own wife?"

His mother just looked at him, letting him find his own answer. He didn't want to. He wanted to ignore the whole thing, to pretend he'd heard nothing of Janie, that she had stayed vanished.

Mamm's silence seemed to demand an answer from him.

"If Amos wanted me to know anything, he'd get in touch. He knows where I am."

Finally his mother shook her head. "We trust you to do the right thing, Noah. Right for you and for everyone else."

Those words continued to reverberate in his head all through saying good-byes, getting the boys ready for bed, hearing their prayers, and tucking them in. They were still there when he went back downstairs, the old house creaking gently around him.

He touched the greens the boys had put up with such enthusiasm. If only he could go back to the worries he'd had that day they'd cut the greens. They seemed so minor to him now in comparison.

Reluctantly he went to the jelly cupboard and opened the drawer. Writing paper, envelope, stamps, pen, address book—he took them all to the table, sat down, and began to write.

"THERE YOU ARE, all settled." The next day, Sarah spread a lap quilt over Ruthie where she sat in the padded rocker Eli had brought upstairs for her. "All right?"

Ruthie looked mutinous. "I want to be downstairs."

"I know." Sarah squeezed her hand in mute sympathy. "Soon, I'm sure. Meanwhile, ring your bell if you need anything. And don't try to get up without help, or you'll have Grossmammi and Aunt Anna both after you."

"Aunt Anna?" Ruthie's voice had a note of dismay at the mention of her aunt by marriage. "She's here today?"

Sarah read her reaction easily. Ruthie had heard Anna exercising her opinion on Sarah. "Don't worry. She doesn't know you well enough to tell you what to do."

Ruthie's giggle cheered her. Her sweet cousin was growing more dear to her every day.

"I'm off to work. Behave yourself."

"I don't have a choice, ain't so?" But Ruthie was smiling when she said it.

Sarah hurried downstairs, intent on getting on her way before Aunt Anna had a chance to ask her a hundred questions. But her aunt and grandmother were both in the kitchen when she reached it, and Aunt Anna swept her into a strong hug.

"Ach, Sarah, we don't see enough of you lately. How are you?"

Sarah tried to dismiss her instant guilt over having made fun of Aunt Anna. She had a good heart, in spite of her sometimes annoying ways.

"It's gut to see you, Aunt Anna. I've just been so busy with helping take care of Ruthie and the little one, in addition to my job, that I don't seem to have a minute."

"And I'm sure you're working too hard." Her aunt patted her cheek. "Won't Noah give you some time off? He certain-sure ought to. Maybe if I mention it to him—"

"No." She practically snapped the word. "Thanks, but we've been so busy that I wouldn't take time off if I could. And he did offer, I promise." Hugging her again, she hurried toward the coatrack. "I must be off. It's wonderful kind of you to come over."

Grabbing her coat, she fled.

By the time she reached the lane, she was laughing at herself. No doubt she disliked seeing Aunt Anna at her bossiest because it was like looking in a mirror. But she honestly didn't think she'd ever been quite that bad, had she?

Sarah snugged her scarf tighter around her neck to block the cold wind that found every chink in her clothing. Her bonnet made a good windshield on a day like today, its brim protecting her face. There was a damp feeling to the air, and the sky was nearly covered with low gray clouds.

Snow? Every child in the community would certain-sure welcome a layer of white stuff. They'd been looking for it for days. Just enough to let them ride their sleds would do nicely.

Noah was already at work when she reached the shop. He glanced up and nodded, turning his attention quickly back to his work. The tension was still in every line of his face. Hardly surprising, she supposed. Nothing about this situation would be resolved quickly or easily.

Sarah wondered, fleetingly, if he'd done anything about the rumor. She suspected he'd rather ignore it, im-possible as that seemed. However much you might want to stop thinking about someone who'd hurt or disap-pointed you, that person still lurked in the recesses of your mind. You couldn't help half expecting him or her to burst back into your life, upending your hard-won peace.

Taking off her coat and bonnet, she decided that pre-tending this was any normal day was her only option. "Cold out this morning." She moved to the stove, holding her hands out to warm them. "Those clouds look like snow, ain't so?"

Noah looked up, seeming startled by her words, as if he'd been so deep in thought it hadn't quite registered that she was here. He glanced toward the window. "Could be."

The terse comment didn't encourage further talk, but she decided to risk another remark. "It was wonderful gut to visit with your mamm yesterday. I'm sure she's as happy to be home as all of you are to wilkom her."

"That's for sure." He seemed to concede the need to speak. "My sister would have kept her longer, but Mamm had promised to be home for the Christmas program. She wouldn't miss that."

"No, I'm sure not. I can understand your sister's feelings, though. It's not easy to move away from everything you know."

Noah did actually look at her, perhaps because of the emotion that colored her voice. She ought to be over showing that reaction by now, she lectured herself. But he didn't speak. Taking that as an indication that conversation time was over, she moved to her workstation.

But no sooner had she given a finishing wipe-down to the cabinet she'd been working on than Noah cleared his throat. She looked a question at him.

"Yah, I know it's hard to move away. I tried to explain to the boys that their aunt needed Mamm more than we do, but I'm afraid it didn't make much impression."

"No, I can see that." She smiled, thinking of Matty's probable reaction. Mark, being a little more sensitive, might have tried to understand.

"Mamm and Daad stayed for supper last night. The boys thought it was just for them, but I knew better." He gave a slight grimace. "Mamm wanted to point out my duty. No hiding from that when she's around." He hesitated, and then forced the words out. "I wrote to Janie's relatives, since I don't know where Amos is staying. They'll get it to him."

She searched for something helpful to say and didn't find it. "I know that was difficult, but—"

"But you think it was best." He bit off the words, but she suspected it was only because he was forcing himself to talk.

"Yah, I guess I do. I think it's always better to know."

He nodded, turning his face away. The conversation was over.

Her mind still fretting over the possibilities, Sarah tried to sink herself in work. Eventually the fascination of seeing the wood come to life under her hands took over, and she forgot everything else.

It had started snowing by the time they took their lunch break—big fat flakes that drifted lazily down but covered the ground quickly. Noah still seemed disinclined to talk, so aside from a comment about how much the children would enjoy a snowfall, she kept her peace.

The afternoon passed quickly, as once again she became engrossed in what she was doing. She and Noah didn't talk, but it was a comfortable silence, as working side by side grew more familiar every day.

The sound of children's voices brought her back to the present. "Sounds like the boys are home. Goodness, look at the snow."

Noah blinked and tore his attention away from work. "Piling up all right. I think—"

But she didn't have a chance to hear the rest of the sentence, because the door flew open and the twins rushed in, covered with snow themselves and letting in a drift of flakes that swirled and dissolved in the warm air.

"Shut the door," Noah ordered. "Let's keep the snow outside."

"It's snowing—really, really snowing, Daadi!" Matty seemed to be talking in exclamation points. "I'm so excited. Komm and play. You want to play in the snow, don't you, Sarah?"

He gave her a pleading look, and Mark came over to lean against her, confidingly. "Don't you love the snow?" he murmured.

Tenderness swept through her, and she hugged him. "How could I help it? It makes the world look all fresh and new, ain't so?"

Solemnly he went to the window and looked out, as if that hadn't occurred to him, before he nodded agreement with the sentiment. She had to suppress a smile. All the caution destined for the twins seemed to have gone to Mark.

"Komm, hurry." Matty tugged at his father's arm. "Komm outside and see."

"Cleaning up comes first," Noah reminded him. "A good craftsman always leaves his tools put away and his work protected."

"I'll help," Matty said instantly, and seized a couple of hand tools to hang up, while Mark helped Sarah cover the piece she'd been working on.

It didn't take long with everyone working. Snuggling into her coat and pulling her muffler around her neck, Sarah stepped out into a wonderland of snow. *Stepped into* was definitely the case. Even on the steps, she sank to her ankles.

"Let's build a snowman. Even bigger and better than the last one." Matty jumped up and down, apparently trying to see how deeply he could bury his feet.

"You'll want to get home before it's any deeper." He gave her a look of apology. "I should have suggested you go earlier. I didn't realize how deep it was getting."

"But Sarah wants to help with the snowman." Mark's face drooped.

"You mean you want her to help." Noah tapped Mark's hat brim.

"I'd love to, but . . ." She let that trail off, moved by the disappointment on two identical faces.

"I have a better idea," Noah announced. "We'll get the sleigh out. You boys can help, and then we'll have a sleigh ride and take Sarah home at the same time."

Her protest that he didn't need to take her home was drowned by the boys' cheers. They each grabbed an adult by the hand and began tugging them.

"You can wait here . . ." Noah began.

"I wouldn't dream of it. I haven't had a sleigh ride in years, and I want to help." She went on down the steps.

The walk to the barn was a challenge in the snow, but Mark tugged her along, seeming to have no difficulty despite the fact that it came nearly to his knees. The sleigh, it turned out, was stored in the far corner of the barn and carefully covered to protect it . . . just another indication of the meticulous care Noah took with everything belonging to him.

With the boys' eager assistance, getting the sleigh out and cleaning it off was accomplished in a matter of minutes. They dragged it out into the snow, Noah sent the twins for the harness, and he led out the buggy horse.

The mare tossed her head and pranced at stepping into the snow, sniffing at it suspiciously.

"Silly girl." Noah patted her. "You've seen snow before, ain't so?"

Apparently taking him at his word, she allowed herself to be hitched to the sleigh. The boys danced around, getting in the way until Noah sent them to the house to collect a couple of blankets.

The sleigh had two seats, and Noah helped her into the seat next to him as a matter of course. The boys scrambled into the back seat and snuggled under their blanket. Noah climbed into his own place, the mare dancing a little as she felt his movement.

"Go, Daadi, go," Matty urged.

Noah took his time, shaking out the blanket and then tucking it around her as carefully as she imagined he tucked the boys in at night. Warmth filled her heart, and for a moment she could almost imagine a life of which that would be a normal part.

Noah slapped the lines, the sleigh hesitated for an instant as if reluctant to move, and then they slid easily forward and down the slight slope that led to the lane. The boys clung to the sides, leaning out to look down at the runners sliding along the snow.

"Look at us go. Faster, Daadi, faster," Matty urged.

"Let Daisy get used to it first. It's not like pulling a buggy for her."

The lane wasn't plowed yet, but they sailed along anyway. "It'll take some time for the township to get to all the lanes, I'd guess," Noah said. "We might have to travel this way for the next day or so."

"I don't think I'd mind that at all." She lifted her head, feeling the snowflakes touch her face. "It's so quiet—no buggy wheels creaking, barely even a sound from Daisy's hooves."

"Peaceful," Noah suggested. "Let's see if we can pick up a little speed. Not that I'm in a hurry." His lips lifted in a smile.

She glanced back at the boys. Matty laughed out in his exuberance, while Mark sat still, his face awestruck. The woods slipped smoothly past, the snow gathering on the ground as it found its way through the bare branches.

The plantation of evergreens came into view, and her breath caught at the sight. Every branch was bent with the weight of the snow, every single needle frosted with its coating of white.

"It's so beautiful," she breathed. She looked at Noah, wanting to share the sheer joy she felt at the moment.

He returned the look, as if taking it for granted she'd share his feelings. His face was transformed by pure happiness, wiping away the pain and regret and changing him into the man he'd once been. Her heart swelled until she thought it would burst with joy. If she never had anything else with Noah, at least she'd have this one perfect moment.

# CHAPTER FIFTEEN

Snow or not, Sarah found that the Christmas program was progressing full speed ahead, with the big production happening on Friday, the last day of school. Dorcas had asked for her help on Wednesday afternoon, so she headed out early from work, relieved that the township plow had made it down the school lane.

She arrived at the schoolhouse to find Dorcas conducting a spelling bee with the older scholars, while the younger ones looked on and clapped at each success. She slid into a back seat, watching their faces . . . the contortions as the speller struggled with the longer words followed by the triumphant grin when the word was right.

It was competition of a sort, she supposed, but there was a nice spirit about it. The other scholars seemed to want each speller to get it right, and they joined in the clapping with enthusiasm. It was a nice balance, she thought, between striving to do your best and letting that spill over into hoping someone else would fail.

The spelling bee ended with one of the fourteen-year-old girls successful, and Sarah loved her smile as her classmates surrounded her. Dorcas obviously had a gift for inspiring her young scholars both with a desire to learn and with the Amish attitude toward what the world called *success*.

Dorcas waved Sarah to the front of the room as the children began putting their books away, buzzing a little with their eagerness to start rehearsing.

"I'm wonderful glad you could make it through the snow. This is our last chance to have a full rehearsal, so we have to make it count."

"What about tomorrow?" She'd assumed their final practice would be on Thursday, since the production was Friday.

"You didn't hear about our trip? I thought the twins would be full of it. We're going over to the Rock Glen school to have a fun day together with Margaret Ammon's scholars. It's only five miles away, but we hardly ever see one another."

"That's something new, isn't it?" They put books back on the bookshelves while they talked, and she paused to look again at the cover of *Little House in the Big Woods*, always one of her favorites.

"This is the first time. It seemed like a great idea when Margaret and I talked about it back at the fall teachers' meeting, but now that it's here, I'm thinking we should have done it earlier. It's always impossible to get any work out of the kinder this close to the holiday as it is."

"In that case, maybe it's just as well," Sarah said, smiling. "They'll have a busy day elsewhere instead of frustrating you when they can't concentrate on work."

"Always finding the bright side, aren't you?" Dorcas teased.

"Not quite always." Her smile slipped away as she thought of the situation with Noah. It was never far from her, and the least hint brought it flooding back. She'd come home and found love, and now it was breaking her heart.

"I know." Dorcas clasped her hand in a comforting grip. "It's Noah, isn't it?"

She nodded mutely.

"I'm sorry. But . . ."

"But what? Go on. You're not going to hurt my feelings."

"I was thinking that you have found love, at least, even if it seems impossible. Not like me. Never even a hint of it. Guess I was born to be a maidal."

"Both of us," Sarah said, trying for a lightness she didn't feel. "At least we still have a gut strong friendship."

"We have to, remember? We know all each other's secrets." Dorcas laughed, her good humor restored. "Komm, let's get this practice underway."

Rehearsing was more of a challenge now that the scholars were actually working with their props. When the third and fourth graders came out with their candles held above their heads, the paper flames drooped lower and lower until the classroom dissolved in laughter.

"All right, stop." Dorcas was giggling along with them. "Sarah, will you help the scholars fix their candle flames? I guess we should have painted the flames, but I think some double-sided tape will hold them. Drooping candles don't get the message of the poem across, ain't so?"

Sarah gathered the kinder at the table that had been set up for refreshments after the program, and they got to work. When they'd finished, the first and second graders had completed their poem. Sarah's gaze sought out Mark, to find that he looked satisfied and happy.

Good. Now he just had to get through the good-bye poem with his brother.

Alas, that was where things fell apart. Sarah could see it happening in Mark's sudden tension and the panicked look that came over his face. His voice dropped to a whisper when it came to his solo part.

At least he hadn't forgotten the words. Sarah tried to console herself, but she knew it wouldn't console Mark, and her heart ached for him. As soon as the rehearsal ended, she found him fighting back tears in the corner of the room.

"Ach, Mark, don't. It's all right." She put her arm around him, and he leaned against her, letting his tears wet her skirt.

"It's not. I can't do it."

"Yah, you can." She knelt next to him so that she could look in his eyes. "You do it at home nice and loud, ain't so?"

"That's different." He wiped tears away with the back of his hand. He seemed to struggle to explain it. "It's nice and quiet there. Not like here."

"That's true. You're the kind of person who doesn't like having lots of people and noise around when you're trying to concentrate."

"Matty does." His lips trembled. "He just gets better."

"You're different. Remember when we talked about it? Some people like one thing, and others like something else. Matthew gets excited about being with people, but he's not really great at concentrating on something, is he? And you're not comfortable with a lot of people and noise, but you can focus on what you're doing and stay with it until the job is done."

"I'm more like Daadi," he said, obviously remembering their talk. "Do you think Matty is more like our mamm?"

The question, coming out of the blue, rocked her. She'd

never heard either of the boys mention the woman who'd been gone for all the years they could remember. What should she say?

*Don't lie, whatever you do.* The little voice in her heart was firm.

"I'm not sure," she said slowly. "You see, I didn't know your mother very well." She thought of what she'd heard about Janie, how she'd had all the boys buzzing around her and how stunned Noah had been when she'd picked him. "But maybe so."

He nodded, seeming satisfied, and the hard knot in her chest began to dissolve. Whatever had led to the question, he didn't seem to be obsessing about the mother who'd left them.

The afternoon ended with Dorcas reminding the kinder of the treat in store for them the next day, and warning them to be on time. "The vans will be here to take us to Rock Glen at eight thirty sharp. And I'm counting on you to be on your best behavior. Remember, each one of you represents our school."

There were solemn nods from a few scholars who took her words to heart, but Sarah suspected that most of them were too excited to heed any cautionary words. They'd probably be sufficiently intimidated by a strange place to behave in any event.

She'd promised to walk the boys home, so once they were bundled up in their warm clothes and boots, they set out. The lane was easy walking with the snow piled into high, icy mounds where the plow had pushed it. Sunlight sparkled on the snow, making it glitter enough to sting the eyes. Cold as it was, the wind had died down enough to make the walk exhilarating, and they arrived at the farmhouse in good humor, with Mark's dismay apparently forgotten.

"Look, Grossmammi's here!" Matty pointed to the buggy drawn up near the house. "I'll race you, Mark."

They darted ahead, and Sarah followed more slowly. She thought just to greet Miriam and be on her way, but as soon as Miriam came out on the porch, she knew something was wrong.

"Ach, it's two snowmen come to see us," she declared, ushering the boys inside. "Go sit with Grossdaadi and warm up while I talk to Sarah."

To her surprise, instead of inviting her in, Miriam wrapped a shawl around herself and joined her on the porch.

"What is it?" Sarah's heart was in her mouth.

Miriam shook her head. "Bad news. Noah got a call this afternoon from Janie's cousins in Indiana. It's Janie. She's passed away."

It was almost a physical blow, and Sarah struggled to absorb it. "How? What happened? She was the one in the hospital, then?"

"Yah." Miriam's eyes filled with tears. "Near as Noah could make out, it was the same cancer that killed her mamm so young. They do say that some of the women's cancers can be inherited."

She nodded, understanding what Miriam was trying to convey—that at least they wouldn't have to spend their lives watching for the same thing in the twins.

"I'm sorry." The words were inadequate. "How is Noah taking it?"

"Holding everything inside, like always. He's in the workshop. I think it might be gut for him to see you." In her words Sarah glimpsed Miriam's acceptance of Sarah's place in her son's life.

She wanted to help. Of course she did. But what was there to say?

"Yah. I'll go now." But she doubted Noah would be any more willing to talk to her than he was to his mother.

NOAH STOOD AT the workbench, staring down at the piece of oak that was destined to become a desk. Usually he could lose himself in his work, no matter what was happening. Not now. He felt as if the oak panel had lifted up and struck him in the head.

He heard the door and sensed that it was Sarah before she spoke.

"Your mamm told me. I'm so sorry about Janie."

He winced at the name. "I don't want to talk."

"I understand. Some things are too deep to talk about." She turned, heading back toward the door.

Before she could reach it, the words burst out. "They didn't even get my letter yet. She died on the day I wrote it. I should have done something sooner."

Sarah moved closer, not touching but letting him feel her presence. "How could you? The news only reached here on Sunday. You couldn't have done anything."

He shook his head. "Doesn't feel that way. They buried her today already. It's over, and I didn't know."

"That must have been the way she wanted it, ain't so? They knew where you were if they wanted to reach you."

Sensible words, as always from Sarah, but somehow they didn't help as much as she probably hoped. Words couldn't erase the guilt he felt . . . guilt for never understanding, for not knowing what was building up in Janie to make her run away, guilt for not trying harder to find her.

"You're feeling guilty." Sarah seemed to read his thoughts. "When people die unexpectedly, or even if you know it's coming, there's always something we wish we had done. Or said."

Noah rubbed the back of his neck in a futile attempt to ease the tension there. "I know. It doesn't help that I feel . . . angry. I shouldn't. That's wrong, I know it."

"It's human," she said, her voice very gentle.

"How do I tell the boys?" The question spurted out like water under pressure. "How? What can I say to make sense of it for them?"

Sarah was silent for so long that he knew she didn't have an answer. There wasn't one, he guessed.

"They'll take it better than you think." Her words startled him, and he swung to look at her.

"Why would you say that?" The anger was directed at her now, striking anyone and anything that came too close.

"Because I know them." She spoke calmly, ignoring the anger. "They rarely think of their mother, and when they do, they speak of her as someone they've heard about but never known. She's never been part of their lives. And that was her choice, not yours."

It all came back to that in the end. Janie had walked away. He'd like to be able to put the blame on her, but he couldn't. He had vowed to love and cherish her until death, and somehow he had failed.

He shook his head. "I wish I could think that. They shouldn't have to be hurt like this."

"They'll take their cue from you—you know that, don't you? They'll take it the way you do. If you can be calm and practical about it, they will be, too."

"Not so easy," he muttered.

"No, it isn't." He could read what she didn't say in her voice. She was wishing she could take the pain away from him and carry it herself.

How strange it was that they both wanted to absorb the hurt for another. Not strange, for sure, that he wanted that for his sons. That was part of being a father. But Sarah . . .

Sarah loved him. He couldn't give her what she wanted, but she loved him anyway. Longing built up in him. To turn to her, to accept the comfort of her embrace . . .

But he couldn't. Alive, Janie had stood between them. And now that she was gone, it didn't seem to make any difference. She still barred his way to loving anyone.

"So what do I do now?" He slammed his fist on the workbench, welcoming the pain. "Play the part of the grieving widower? Go through the motions and accept sympathy from everyone who knows me?"

Sarah closed her eyes briefly, as if his pain caused her physical pain. "Everyone will know already what the circumstances are. You won't have to tell them or explain." She fell silent for a minute. "You are the grieving widower, ain't so? You're grieving for what might have been."

He nodded, knowing it was true. What might have been was gone, swept away by time. But that didn't really seem to help. Nothing would.

SARAH TRUDGED TOWARD home, fearing she had done more harm than good by trying to talk to Noah. This situation had no prescribed response, as so much did in Amish life. Somehow Noah had to get through it until he could accept and forgive the past, and that might be a long time coming.

As soon as she came within sight of the house, Sarah realized something was happening. A strange buggy was drawn up by the barn, its horse apparently already stalled. A visitor who was going to be here awhile, apparently.

Seeing movement through the kitchen window, she hurried to that door, to be instantly grabbed by Eli, who clutched at her hands.

"It's coming. The baby is coming." He sounded like a

small boy anticipating Christmas and hardly able to believe it was near.

Sarah glanced to Grossmammi for confirmation, and she nodded. "The midwife is here, and she says she'll stay. Sometime tonight, most likely."

"What can I do?" She shed her coat and bonnet as she asked.

Grossmammi sent a sideways look at Eli. "Take care of Mary. And the new daadi. And you'll have to finish getting supper ready."

"For sure."

She suspected that as an unmarried woman, her job was going to be fetching and carrying, with little admission to the actual birthing process. It was what she'd expected, but she did long for a moment to be part of what was going on upstairs.

Grossmammi gave a satisfied nod, and then a second look that appraised Sarah's face and registered something amiss. There would be questions later, no doubt, but at the moment, Grossmammi was in her element with a new baby about to arrive. She scurried toward the stairs.

Eli followed her as far as the door and turned back, his expression a mingling of disappointment and joy. "I can't go into my own bedroom to my own wife unless the midwife says. That's a fine state of affairs."

"Komm, now. Would you really like to take over the birthing?"

He gave a shamefaced shrug. "No, I guess not. I've helped with plenty of calves coming into the world, but when it's someone you love . . ."

"We'd best follow orders, ain't so?" She patted his shoulder, thinking how young he seemed at this moment. "I'm shut out, too, I'm afraid."

"You're not in the club," he said, recovering his spirits

with a grin. "Guess we have our work to do, though. I'll get on with the milking while you watch Mary and work on supper. Yell if you need me, or ring the bell."

The bell hung on the back porch, and it had always been used to summon the men from the fields. A couple of repeated clangs meant a meal was ready, while a loud clamor of the bell said, *Komm at once!*

The block tower Mary had been building toppled over with a clatter, making them both jump. "Boom!" she declared, clapping her hands.

"Boom, indeed, little girl." Sarah bent to kiss her on the head, and then turned back to Eli, catching him on his way out the door. "What about Ruthie's kin? Should I plan on extra for supper?"

"They're all over in the next county at a funeral, so there's no reaching them at the moment. They thought we had at least another week, but . . ."

"But babies come on their timetable, yah?" She finished it for him. Smiling, he headed toward the milking shed.

Sarah, with Mary occupied with her blocks, checked on the supper preparations. Grossmammi had put a chicken to roast, so she went to the pantry, seizing potatoes, a jar of green beans, one of applesauce, and a packet of dried corn. As in any Amish household, Ruthie's pantry was well stocked and ready for any number of unexpected visitors.

Time wore on with no news from upstairs. Sarah, waiting for a call that there was something, anything, she could do, was disappointed. She began to sympathize with Eli. With such exciting things happening, it was hard to be shut out.

At least her mind had been thoroughly distracted from Noah and his grief. Brooding about that would do no good, and as Grossmammi had always said, *Just do the*

*next thing that needs doing. God doesn't want us brood-*
*ing about the past or anxious about the future. Bear the*
*current burden. That's enough.*

Grossmammi had it right, for sure, but it wasn't easy.

Eli came back from the milking, and she heard him
clattering in the mudroom before coming in the kitchen.
When he did, he looked at her questioningly.

"Nothing new," she said in answer.

But his expression didn't change. "James Esch stopped
over. He's heard that Janie Raber died. Did you know?"

She nodded. "Miriam told me when I brought the boys
home from school. She was so young."

"Cancer, like her mamm, Jim said. Ach, that's a bad
thing. Hard to know what to do or say, ain't so?"

"Yah." She hesitated, but suspected he'd ask if she
didn't say. "I spoke to Noah briefly, just to express sympathy. He was worried about telling the boys, I think."

He shook his head. "They didn't know her. Hard to say
if that makes it easier or harder." He hesitated. "Should I
go over? Offer to help or anything?"

Sarah understood his feeling. That was the first, the
natural thing any neighbor would do.

"I don't think so. His family is there, so they'll take
care of things for him."

"Good." He flushed. "I mean, I wouldn't know what
to say."

She thought of what she'd told Noah about folks already knowing and understanding. "I'd say just extend
sympathy when you see him and get back to normal talk.
He wouldn't wilkom anything else, and this way is easier
on him."

He looked relieved. "I'm glad you told me. Better to
say nothing than to say the wrong thing, ain't so?"

"Yah." Most of her regrets came from rushing into
speaking too soon.

Footsteps on the stairs had them both hurrying to the
hall. Grossmammi smiled and shook her head. "Nothing
happening yet. Sarah, you can go up and sit with Ruthie
so the midwife can come down and have a cup of tea."

"What about me?" Eli said.

Grossmammi patted his arm. "Your turn next, but wait
and talk to the midwife in case there's anything she needs
you to fetch."

Eli subsided, apparently grateful that he was to be
allowed to help in some way, and Sarah headed quickly
upstairs.

Elsie King, the midwife, was the younger of a mother-
daughter pair who had been delivering babies in the valley for years. She smiled and rose from her chair by the
bed when Sarah appeared, and Sarah reflected that even
her smile radiated calm and confidence in the face of new
life.

"Here's Sarah to sit with you, Ruthie. Don't worry,
now. It's going to be a bit longer."

Ruthie nodded, leaning back against the stacked pillows. "I remember."

"This one may come a bit faster than Mary once he or
she gets going. It's often that way." She slipped out, unhurried, and Sarah took the chair she'd vacated.

"Elsie makes you feel calm just looking at her, ain't
so?" She reached out to touch Ruthie's hand. "How
are you?"

"Fine. A ways to go, like Elsie said." Her assurance
gave her a gravity beyond her years, and Sarah almost felt
as if she were the younger of the two.

"I'm sorry we couldn't reach your family. We'll try
again later."

Ruthie shook her head. "It's all right. Not that I
wouldn't be glad for Mamm to be here, but she'll bring
my sisters, and that's . . . well, too much fuss."

Her grip tightened on Sarah's hand, and she realized Ruthie was having a contraction. She seemed to focus on what her body was doing or saying, and Sarah thought the best thing she could do was stay silent and hold her hand.

Ruthie's face relaxed as the contraction eased. "That was a stronger one. Gut. Maybe we'll make some progress."

Sarah nodded, flexing her hand. "I see why they call it labor. It's a lot of work, ain't so?"

"Yah." Ruthie chuckled. "But worth it."

Sarah almost envied her that calm absorption in her task. For the time being Ruthie would be intent on the job at hand, and nothing else would intrude—no thoughts of tomorrow or regrets about yesterday, as Grossmammi said.

The small table with the putz on it had been moved against the bed, she noticed. "Do you want me to shift that table?"

"I like it there. I've been thinking about it." Ruthie's gaze was soft as she looked at the stable. "About how it was that night, you know. Was she worried, giving birth to her first in a stable far from home?"

Sarah looked at the carved wooden figure, curved protectively over the manger where the baby lay. The carver had given the face an expression of serenity and love.

"I don't know. I think the other women would gather round, even if they didn't know her."

Ruthie nodded. "Women do. I feel close to her tonight."

"She would have been happy, even in a stable." Sarah somehow felt very sure of that in this moment.

They sat quietly together through another contraction, and then the door opened. Elsie came in, followed by Eli, who was trying to tiptoe and not making a very good job of it. Smiling, Sarah gave up her chair, squeezed Ruthie's hand, and slipped out.

When she returned to the kitchen, Grossmammi already had Mary in the high chair. Mary was splashing her spoon in a bowl of applesauce until Sarah took her hand and guided it to her mouth. "This way, little girl. It tastes better on your tongue."

As usual, Mary followed her lead without protest. She was certain-sure an easy child, like Mark probably had been. She imagined Matty greatly preferring to splash applesauce in all directions.

Grossmammi came to stand next to her, resting a hand lightly on Sarah's shoulder. "We heard about Janie. Poor thing. I remember when her mamm went. Such a sad time that was."

She nodded. "The whole situation is sad. Noah is left grieving, but . . ." She let that trail off, not having any other words.

"Yah. But the future will be better. He can only trust in the good Lord now. And that's what you must do, as well."

"Me?" Sarah looked at her, startled. "Why me?"

"Ach, Sarah, do you think I don't know how much you care about Noah?" She smoothed her hand across Sarah's back. "Everything seems impossible now, but you must trust God. Your earthly father hasn't given you much reason to trust, I know, but your heavenly Father won't let you down. Just trust."

Sarah bent her head in agreement. There was no sense in burdening Grossmammi with her fears and worries. *Trust.* Well, she'd try.

Grossmammi went back upstairs, Eli came in, and she sensed that the pace of things had quickened. She served the meal without much attention and tried to keep Eli talking. His nervousness increased by the minute, it seemed.

Eating, cleaning up, and putting Mary to bed took time, but no calls came from upstairs. It was full dark now, and when she looked out the kitchen window Sarah could see the square of light from the window upstairs glowing on the snow.

They ran out of talk eventually, and she sat across from Eli in silence, waiting. Finally it came—the sound they'd been waiting for. It was a thin, plaintive wail that grew steadily stronger and louder, as if the new baby protested at being propelled into the world.

Together they bolted for the door and jostled each other up the stairs. Grossmammi met them at the top, closing the bedroom door behind her.

"It's fine. Ruthie is in wonderful shape, and we have a fine strong baby boy in the family."

Eli laughed and cried at the same time. "You hear that, Sarah? A son. I have a son, as well as a daughter."

Sarah hugged him. "Wonderful gut news, Eli. I'm so happy." Tears stung her eyes, but she, too, was smiling.

"Can I go in now?" Eli reached for the door, but Grossmammi stopped him.

"Ruthie wants you to wait until she's all cleaned up. It will just be a minute. Sarah, you go in and help while I talk to Eli."

Assuming Grossmammi wanted to give him time to calm down a bit, Sarah nodded and slipped inside. She found Ruthie exhausted but beaming, looking down at her tiny boy as he lay in her arms. Her face, the curve of her arms, and the protective tilt of her body . . . all of it was like that figure they'd been looking at. Sarah's tears spilled over again, accompanied by a fierce longing.

*Let it be me, sometime, please. Let it be me.*

It couldn't have been more than a couple of minutes before Grossmammi opened the door and let Eli in.

Instead of the headlong rush she'd expected, he advanced slowly, his expression awestruck. He slid onto the bed next to Ruthie, looking from her to his son with a devotion she'd never seen on him before. He put his arms around both of them, very tenderly, and held them close.

Sarah backed away, heart full, joy pushing out the pain and regret of Janie's passing and Noah's future. There was only room now to rejoice.

# CHAPTER SIXTEEN

Time passed in a haze of misery for Noah. He was aware of family coming and going, of Mamm taking over caring for the boys, of Sarah working quietly in the shop, but that awareness didn't seem to penetrate the essential pain and guilt inside him.

The only bright spot had been the reaction of Matthew and Mark when he told them the news. Sarah had been right about them. Matty repeated the conventional words he'd heard others say, but didn't appear to feel anything beyond that. As for Mark, his eyes filled with tears for a moment, but his reaction was to reach out and touch his father's face.

"I'm sorry, Daadi." He said the words, and Noah realized that Mark meant exactly what he said. He was sorry that his father was in pain, but that was all.

As Sarah had said, they had no experience with Janie to grieve over. She had never been a presence in their lives, so how could they miss her?

Had she thought about them? The question entered his mind and he slammed the door on it. He didn't want to think about Janie. He was sensitive to any thought, breath, or word of her—as if every part of his body winced away from it. The only safe way was to shut everything out.

He stared out the window of the workshop, his mind registering that the snow was still there. It had continued cold, and the world outside was frozen into stillness, just as he was.

The door opened behind him, and Sarah came in from lunch. He sensed her studying him for a moment before silently hanging her things up and moving to her desk. At least she didn't speak. He could stand her being there, carrying on with her work, as long as she didn't distract him from the effort of keeping his pain and guilt bottled up.

He'd been vaguely aware earlier that she and Mamm were talking about the arrival of Eli and Ruthie's baby— a boy, from what they'd said. He ought to go over, offer to help Eli with the chores since they had a new baby in the house. It was the right thing to do, the thing any neighbor would do automatically.

The duty came into his mind and slipped back out again, but it didn't compel him to move. *Frozen,* he thought again.

Sarah moved, clearing her throat as if asking for his attention. "Noah," she said when he didn't respond.

He stared at her dully.

"It's time to get ready to go to the Christmas program. Your mamm said to tell you she's packed up the snacks, and she kindly asked me to ride along with you folks to the school."

He turned it over in his mind. The Christmas program was on Friday. Surely it wasn't Friday already.

"Noah," she repeated.

"Yah, all right." It felt like shifting a tree trunk to move. "I forgot." He hesitated. "Will it matter so much if I stay home?"

He wanted to see the boys in their program—of course

he did. But it meant seeing everyone else, too. Feeling their eyes on him, probing for signs of emotion, signs of grief and pain.

"You can't miss your sons' first Christmas program." Sarah's voice was quiet but firm. "You know you don't want to disappoint them."

"No, I mean, yah, all right, I'll come." He ran a hand across the back of his neck, trying futilely to clear his head. "Just give me a minute."

Sarah waited, but before he had forced himself to move, the shop phone rang, jangling his nerves and tightening his scalp. He made a brusque, cutting gesture with his hand, but Sarah was already moving across the room. She picked up the phone, answering quietly.

"Put them off," he said abruptly. "Whatever it is, put them off."

Sarah ignored him, continuing to speak into the receiver, and gradually the sense of her words penetrated. She was expressing sympathy. His forehead furrowed. Who?

Covering the receiver with her hand, Sarah turned to him, holding out the phone. "You'll have to take it. It's Janie's daad."

He stared at her, outrage building until he thought it would blow the top off his head. Amos, calling after all this time, expecting him to talk. Amos, who had known all along where Janie was and lied about it, ignoring his grandsons' right to know.

"No!" The word exploded out of him. "I have nothing to say to him. Hang up."

"Noah, please. The man is grieving. At least hear what he has to say."

She held the receiver out to him, her expression pleading, and then hardening to something like a demand. "Noah," she said again.

"No, I said!" He grabbed the receiver from her hand and slammed it down on the phone.

Sarah winced at the sound, staring at him with reproach and what might have been disappointment in her face. "You have reason to be disappointed in Amos, but that's no excuse. You can't behave that way to a man who's just lost his only daughter."

"Don't tell me how to behave." He rounded on her, needing an outlet for the unaccustomed rage that surged through him. "Don't tell me what to think or what to do. That man lied to me . . . probably for years. He kept up a pretense of interest in my sons and all the time he was lying. I will not speak with him. I don't want to hear what he has to say."

"Oh, Noah, don't." She reached toward him. "Don't you know what your anger is doing to you? Listen to yourself. That's not you. That's not the Noah I know. What would your sons think?"

"My boys are not your concern. You just work for me, remember?"

Shaken by his own words, he swung around, then charged out of the shop into the cold.

SHOCK KEPT SARAH frozen where she was for several minutes. He'd gone out without his coat. Surely he'd come back. But when she looked out, there was no sign of him.

Wrapping her arms around herself, Sarah tried to suppress the pain. She cared so much—she'd only wanted to help. To let him see what he was doing to himself by his refusal. Now . . . well, now there was nothing left.

It was over. She realized, too late, that she'd been secretly hoping Janie's death would open the door for them to move into the future together. He cared—she felt sure he did. It wasn't just wishful thinking on her part. Given time, she'd thought he might be free to turn to her.

But he was never going to be free, because he couldn't let himself. He was so tied up in his anger and his pain that he couldn't see beyond it—couldn't even see that it was hurting the people who loved him.

Love. She wouldn't stop loving him. That was impossible. But there was no future in it. That hope was dead.

Stiffly, moving as if every separate cell in her body hurt, she put on her coat and bonnet. She couldn't just run away without telling Noah's parents what had happened. No matter how she might long to hide, it was impossible.

Miriam met her at the door, her face showing that she already knew something was wrong. "We saw Noah heading toward the woods. What has happened?"

"I'm so sorry." Tears stung her eyes as Miriam guided her into the kitchen, where her husband was putting on his jacket. "Noah had a call from Amos, Janie's daad. I answered, but Noah refused to speak to him." Her voice shook, and she forced it to steady. "I . . . I've never seen Noah that way. He was so upset that Amos would call him, and so angry with me for trying to persuade him to speak . . ."

"He ran off," Miriam finished for her. "That's what he did when he was a child. When he couldn't face something he ran off to the woods."

"He's not a child any longer." His father's voice grated. "It's not right."

"He's hurting, so he's run off to hide the pain," Miriam said, and Sarah reflected that she knew her son very deeply. "He's like an injured animal, Matthew. Don't blame him."

Matthew's face softened when he looked at his wife. "I don't, but he has to face things. It's not right to take his pain out on other people."

He glanced at her, and Sarah realized that her face was giving too much away. Still, it was obvious that they understood her feelings for their son.

"The Christmas program . . ." Miriam was dismayed. "We can't let the boys down."

"You two go on," Matthew said. "I'll find Noah and bring him. Go on now." When Miriam didn't move, he made shooing motions at her.

She nodded. "All right. But be understanding when you find him. Poor boy—I'm so sorry for him, but he has to forgive and accept forgiveness or he'll never be able to go on."

"Don't see why you think he needs to be forgiven," Matthew grumbled, pulling on his gloves. "He didn't do anything wrong. She left him, remember?"

"Yah, but he has harbored anger in his heart all these years. And now we see the cost of it. He's hurting himself and everyone who loves him."

Sarah half expected Matthew to argue the point, but he nodded. "Ach, he's hurting. Not making sense. Give him time. You two go on, now. I'll bring him."

Nodding, Miriam shooed Sarah out toward the waiting buggy. "It's all right," she said. "Matthew will find him. For all the disagreeing they do, Matthew understands him better than he knows."

Sarah nodded, feeling oddly relieved. Noah was fortunate in his parents, maybe more so than he realized. Their parenting was based on a good marriage—the thing she longed for but would never have.

As she followed Miriam into the buggy, Sarah wondered if she should look for another job. It would be painful to go, but equally painful to stay—to watch Noah ruin his life through his guilt and anger and be able to do nothing.

Miriam, maybe sensing her turmoil, began to talk

about the Christmas program as if nothing was wrong, forcing Sarah to respond. All the way to the school, she kept up a stream of chatter. Sarah could just listen, nod, and think her own thoughts.

It was only when they'd reached the school and turned the horse over to the teenage boy who was parking buggies that Miriam let her chatter lapse. They headed inside, and as they walked together she squeezed Sarah's arm.

"Don't lose heart," she murmured. "Never do that."

Sarah couldn't quite believe, but the words were enough to keep her moving forward.

Inside, the schoolhouse hummed with excitement. Parents, aunts, uncles, cousins, siblings, grandparents, and well-wishers filed in, laughing and chatting. From behind the improvised screen Dorcas had set up came murmurs, excited voices, an occasional nervous giggle. Once or twice the screen wobbled alarmingly, and Sarah's breath caught for fear it would come tumbling down.

But apparently Dorcas had everything under control. A couple of handpicked mothers were assisting her behind the scenes, chosen, she'd confided to Sarah, because of their unflappable calm.

She followed Miriam to a row of desks near the front, and they took their places. This was good—the twins would be able to spot them quickly, and she was close enough to watch for signs of panic on Mark's account.

Unfortunately, it meant that they couldn't see those filling up the seats behind them. Sarah felt as if they were the focus of many pairs of eyes, and she suspected Miriam felt the same. She was outwardly calm, but Sarah could feel the tension that radiated from her.

One scholar after another peeked out around the screen to check the audience. It wobbled, and Matthew looked out. He waved, irrepressible, at his grandmother, looked farther, and blinked with disbelief.

He disappeared, only to reappear a moment later with Mark. Mark scanned the audience carefully, looking first at Sarah and his grandmother and then coming back to them with an expression of disbelief. His lips trembled, and Sarah saw his eyes fill with tears before his brother yanked him back out of sight.

Sarah felt her own eyes tear up, and she clenched her fists until her nails bit into her palms. *Please come. Please.*

The twins would be so upset and disappointed if their father didn't show up, no matter who else was here. Surely Noah would realize it. He'd put his sons first, as he always did. He would, wouldn't he?

She tried to hold on to that assurance, but the back of her neck prickled, and she had to force herself not to turn around every few seconds and look at the door.

"He'll come," Miriam whispered, but she didn't sound sure. "Matthew will bring him," she added. "If Matthew finds him, they will be here." Of that she did sound confident.

"Yah," Sarah murmured, praying she was right.

People came up periodically to speak to Miriam . . . awkwardly, for the most part, seeming to feel their way through a maze of difficult responses to what had happened to her daughter-in-law. Miriam at least seemed prepared for it, ignoring anything that might be a question and accepting condolences with a solemn nod.

Then there were those intent on getting the latest news on the new baby from Sarah. She fielded questions, gave vital statistics, and accepted on Ruthie's behalf the offers of meals delivered, knowing the extra help would be more than welcome.

Sarah felt a stir behind her back, and someone's skirt brushed against her. It was Elizabeth Schmidt. Ignoring Sarah, she bent over Miriam.

"So glad to see you back safely." She pressed Miriam's hand. "We all did what we could, but Noah and those poor boys missed you."

Sarah, staring straight ahead, remembered the twins' response to Elizabeth's description of them. From what she could tell by Miriam's expression, she didn't like it any more than they did.

"Such a pity about Janie. But then, she never was very stable, was she? At least now Noah will be free to look for happiness."

Even Miriam's poise seemed disturbed by that comment, and she gave Elizabeth a look that would have shriveled someone less confident. "It would be unkind to think about that now, ain't so?"

Even Elizabeth seemed to get the message, because her eyes fell. "Yah, well, I'd best find my seat," she muttered, heading past Sarah again as if she weren't there.

The outer door opened behind them, letting in a swirl of cold air, and there was a moment's awkward silence. Sarah risked a glance over her shoulder. It was Matthew, and right behind him came Noah. Rather than stumbling through the rows of chairs and desks, they found a place to stand at the very back.

Sarah took only the briefest of glances at Noah, but his face was seared onto her mind—grim, as tight as if it had been carved out of stone, defying anyone to attempt to speak with him. It was a face that would surely repel the most determined busybody or the most devoted friend.

She stared forward, her throat tight. Glancing at Miriam, she realized that Miriam, too, knew he was there. She looked nearly as pained as Noah did. How it must hurt her to see her son's suffering and be able to do nothing about it.

As if at some invisible signal, the schoolroom fell silent. Anticipation trembled in the air as the screen was pulled away and the first group came out. They glanced around the room, each seeming delighted, terrified, or both, and began their welcoming poem.

This was familiar territory to most of the audience. They'd sat through any number of Christmas programs, and while the content of the individual presentations varied, there was a predictability about them. Each poem or skit or song would portray an Amish vision of Christmas—a time of giving, remembering, sharing, and putting others before yourself. Secure in the knowledge that all was going as it should, the audience relaxed in enjoyment.

Each class group stepped forward to do its part. Sarah, having helped with practice, knew the lines as well as the scholars. When the first graders came out, her anxiety rose. Mark should be fine in this one, she told herself. After all, all of them were reciting together, so he didn't have to raise his voice in order to participate.

One of the little girls stumbled over a line. Her lips formed an O of dismay, and then an engaging grin spread over her face as she hurried to catch up. Chuckles from the accepting crowd encouraged her. No one could want a more appreciative, understanding audience than this one, that was certain-sure.

Reaching the end, the first graders smiled at one another and at the crowd. Matty's wide blue gaze met Sarah's and he gave her an engaging grin. He, at least, had no doubts about his performance.

Some of the older scholars came next, with a series of skits about preparing for Christmas, including one about a grumpy grandfather that brought chuckles from all corners of the room. Miriam leaned over to murmur, "I wonder who's seeing himself in that one." They exchanged smiles, and some of Sarah's tension seeped away. Surely, after this success, Mark would be fine for their good-bye recitation.

After the last class had performed, all the children came out to sing familiar Christmas songs. One of the older boys gathered their attention with a glance and began singing the first line of a carol, and the others joined in. Their clear, childish voices rose to the ceiling in the much-loved song. Looking at their faces, Sarah suspected she was not the only one who was smiling through her tears.

At last nothing was left but the good-byes. The twins stepped out, looking identical in their black pants, white shirts, suspenders, and bow ties. Two identical faces turned to the audience; two pairs of blue eyes surveyed them.

They did their part together first. Aside from gripping each other's hands tightly, they seemed to have it under control. Then came time for the solo part, and in that instant, Sarah saw Mark falter. His solo piece came first. His eyes widened, panic-stricken, and he looked wildly around the room. He wasn't going to be able to do it; he was going to rush off the stage—

Sarah gestured, attracting his attention. Her heart thumping as if she were the one facing unimaginable fear, she gave him an encouraging smile. And then, deliberately, she yawned.

At first he didn't react. Then, slowly, his frozen expression started to melt. His mouth moved, as if he tried to speak, and then his lips opened in a huge, nearly jaw-breaking, yawn. The audience, affected, gave a kind of nervous giggle.

And then Mark began to speak, his treble voice coming out loud and clear, each word distinct. He went flawlessly to the end of his part, grinned at Sarah, and nodded to his brother.

Miriam nudged her, smiling. "That's for you," she whispered.

When they turned their attention to Matty, disaster struck. He stood there, his lips parted, his eyes staring, and nothing came out. The room was so quiet that the rustle of a paper was audible. He couldn't speak.

Dismayed, Sarah mouthed the first words at him. Poor Matty—he'd been so sure of himself. She should have practiced more with him, she should have—

Then, before the silence could last too long, Mark stepped forward. He took his brother's hand and began Matty's speech, giving him an encouraging smile. After a surprised second, the frozen look vanished from Matty's face. He joined in, shaky at first but gaining confidence as he went. They did the rest of the poem together, and Sarah had to blink away the tears when they finished.

This was far better than any individual success. Instead it was a beautiful illustration of relying on one another in love.

# CHAPTER SEVENTEEN

Sarah hardly knew how she'd gotten through the weekend. When Noah had walked away from the schoolhouse without a word to her on Friday, she'd accepted the fact that there was nothing she could do for him.

Although maybe *accepted* was too strong a word. Each time she thought she had it mastered, it flared up again— the desperate hope that something, somehow, would change Noah's heart.

She'd avoided any possibility of seeing him on Saturday and Sunday, staying busy with Christmas preparations and keeping company with Ruthie and the babies. When she had gone outside, she'd avoided so much as glancing in the direction of the Raber place. She couldn't set foot on the lane without feeling a moment of sheer panic at the thought of him.

But by this morning, she'd begun to realize she could no longer give in to her instincts of self-preservation. No matter how much it hurt to think of seeing Noah, she had to go over there. It was the day before Christmas, and her gifts for the twins were wrapped and ready. Grossmammi, perhaps thinking she needed a little push, had prepared a basket of Christmas goodies for the Raber family. Then she had rather pointedly handed it to Sarah.

"When you go in to work today, you can drop these at the house for Miriam."

"I . . . I'm not sure I'm going today." It sounded feeble, even to her.

"Nonsense," Grossmammi said briskly. "You mentioned there were a couple of pieces to be finished for Christmas gifts. People will be coming to pick them up. Given Noah's troubles, the least you can do is take that over for him."

Sarah tried to come up with an argument, but her eyes fell before Grossmammi's firm gaze. She didn't take the easy way out of anything, and she clearly didn't intend to let her granddaughter do so, either. Trying to swallow the lump in her throat, Sarah nodded.

A few minutes later she was bundled up and striding along the lane toward the Raber house, firmly ignoring the little voice that whimpered in her heart at the thought of seeing Noah again.

When she arrived she took a quick glimpse of the workshop and then hurried on to the farmhouse. It made sense to deliver the food and gifts first, didn't it?

Stamping the snow off the heavy shoes she preferred when it was wet out, she tapped lightly and opened the door, stepping through the mudroom and on into the kitchen. The aroma of baking cookies rushed out, enticing her, and Matthew and Mark greeted her with delighted cries.

"It's Sarah. Look, Grossmammi, it's Sarah. She came to bake cookies with us." Matty, kneeling on a chair pulled up to the table, waved floury hands.

Mark slid off his seat and came to tug at Sarah's hand, pulling her mitten right off. "We're making cutout cookies," he said. "I made stars."

"I made some, too," Matty said. "Look." He tried to

pick up the unbaked cookie he'd just cut out, only to have it break in half in his hand. "I broke my star," he cried. "Grossmammi . . ."

"Gracious, calm down," Miriam said, smiling at Sarah. "I'll help you fix it, but at least let Sarah take her coat off."

"It's fine," she said. "I really should get to work, but I wanted to leave this with you." She handed over the basket.

"Ach, how wonderful kind." She burrowed into the basket. "Presents for two noisy boys, I see." When Matthew made a grab at the package, she held it above his head. "For Christmas, not now. Ain't so, Sarah?"

"That's right. You'll open it on Christmas." She hadn't been able to resist getting small toys to put in with their hats. Carved wooden animals weren't much, but she thought they'd be pleased—a cow for Matthew and a sheep for Mark. They could add them to the animals in the stable of their *putz,* if they wanted.

Miriam removed the fruitcake and peppernuts Grossmammi had made, exclaiming over them. "No one makes a fruitcake so tender and moist as your grandmother does. You tell her how delighted we are."

"I will." She glanced toward the door. "I should get to work, I think."

"Stay a minute, will you?" Miriam seemed to have something on her mind. "That pan of cookies is ready to go in the oven. You boys go and wash your hands, and then you can go upstairs and find the things I helped you wrap for Sarah." Forestalling any argument, she lifted the cookie sheet and transferred it to the stove.

The boys rushed out, battling to be first as usual. The cheerful smile Miriam had been wearing slid from her face as soon as they were out of the room, replaced by a worried frown.

"Does Noah know you're coming today? He didn't mention it."

She shrugged. "We didn't talk about it, but there were a couple of things to be finished. So I thought I should. Would you rather I didn't—"

"Ach, don't think that," Miriam exclaimed, grasping her hand. "It will be gut for Noah to see you. Maybe it will make him pretend for a moment that he's all right."

"But he's not, is he?"

"He's moped the whole weekend," she said, her tone blunt. "At least he had sense enough to tell the boys what a wonderful gut job they did. I feared they might think, from his silence, that he was disappointed in them."

"He'd never feel disappointed in them." Sarah felt again that rush of happiness she'd enjoyed when the twins had completed their roles so well.

"Well, they don't know that, and I told him so." Her hands twisted in her apron. "I hardly know what to do with him. It's natural he should be shocked and upset, but he has to come to his senses and accept what's happened."

"I'm sorry. I wish I knew what to do for him." Sorrier than she could possibly say. It was a grief to her to see him in pain and be unable to help.

Miriam patted her hand. "Just try to be there for him," she said. "I don't have the right to ask it, but . . ."

"It's not a question of right." She blinked back the tears that tried to fill her eyes. "If I could take his pain away, I'd do anything. You know that."

So much had passed unspoken between them in the past few days that she couldn't doubt Miriam's knowledge of her feelings.

"We can just try," Miriam said softly. "And pray."

Nodding, Sarah brushed away a tear that had escaped. "I will."

The boys came rushing back, so they couldn't say anything else, but it was enough. Forcing a smile, she opened the presents the boys thrust on her—a small box of candy and a heart-shaped pincushion. She wrapped her arms around them.

"Denke." Her voice was husky. "They are just what I need."

Walking slowly toward the workshop a few minutes later, Sarah hugged her coat around her body, yearning for comfort. *Selfish*, she scolded herself. She didn't need comfort as much as Noah did. The pain came from knowing she *couldn't* comfort him, no matter how she might long to.

When she reached the workshop door, Sarah paused, breathing a silent prayer for wisdom. She opened it and went inside.

Although she didn't look toward him, Sarah sensed Noah's gaze on her while she took off her coat and bonnet and hung them up. When she turned toward him, he glanced away.

"You don't have to work today." He clipped off the words as if it were an effort to speak. "It's Christmas Eve."

"You're working," she said, pointing out the obvious. "I knew those two shelf units were supposed to be picked up this afternoon, so I wanted to finish."

Without waiting for a response, she went to the bench where the pieces still waited and picked up her dusting cloth to wipe off anything that had accumulated on them over the weekend.

"Besides, I'm not needed at home this morning, or so my grandmother informed me. She's in her element, making preparations for the Christmas Eve dinner in the kitchen where she did it for so many years."

She paused, giving him a chance to speak, but he didn't take it. If she'd thought his expression closed before, it was now barred and shuttered and nailed down. He wouldn't let any emotion out—maybe he couldn't.

Trying to ease the silence, she went on. "Ruthie's family

wanted all of us to come there, but Ruthie put her foot down. She wasn't taking a tiny baby among all those people so soon, or having them all come in on her. When it comes to her kinder, shy little Ruthie can be a mama bear."

No answering smile, of course. "So it will be just us tonight, and Aunt Anna is bringing supper to us tomorrow. Eli thinks in another week she'll be ready to have a few more of the family around, but it's up to her."

Still nothing. "I dropped off some gifts for the twins and a few other things at the house. Your mamm was busy baking cookies with the boys."

"Yah." Noah finally roused himself, to her relief. "They were wonderful excited about it." His voice died out, and she thought that was all.

But then his hands stopped their steady movement. "The twins . . . I haven't thanked you yet for helping them with their parts for the program."

His expression had eased, ever so slightly, as he spoke of them, and she murmured a silent word of thanks.

"It was my pleasure. I was wonderful pleased with them. To see them helping each other . . . that touched the hearts of everyone watching."

Noah's gaze flickered to her and then away again. "You were right. I see that now. It was gut for Mark to do his part. And to help his bruder."

She smiled, thinking of that moment. "They've stolen my heart, that's certain-sure."

Now he actually looked at her. His eyes were still dark with misery, but the rocklike impression eased when he talked about his sons.

"You've been gut for them. Especially now." His eyes closed for an instant before opening, looking at her with frowning intensity. "I didn't realize how much you'd become part of their lives."

He almost sounded as if he were accusing her, and she wasn't sure what to say. There'd been nothing deliberate about her friendship with his sons. It had simply happened. They'd been thrown together, and the twins had needed her. She'd never found it possible to resist that.

"That's a gut thing, ain't so?" She moved closer to him, trying to read his expression. "Surely kinder need to have people who love them. The more, the better, I would think."

Noah's jaw tightened. "If you were to leave, it would be hard on them."

So that was what it had come down to. Their own mother had left, so how could he believe that anyone else would stay? She felt a spasm of pain that he thought she'd ever hurt his children.

"I'm not going anywhere." That wasn't enough. She needed to say more, to make him understand what she'd learned to see so clearly in the past month. "But surely it's always better to have love, even if you lose it, ain't so?"

He stared at her, frowning, but she didn't think he was angry. The gaze seemed to last forever, and when he spoke, it was in little more than a whisper. "I wish . . ."

Need swept through her. She had to know. She couldn't turn her back on this chance. "What do you wish, Noah?" Reaching out, she clasped his wrist.

The touch seemed to galvanize something inside Noah. He moved convulsively, his gaze locked on her face. And then he grasped her arms and pulled her against him, his lips seeking hers in a kind of frantic haste.

Joy swept over Sarah. This was what she wanted . . . what she longed for. His hands were hard, his kiss fierce with pent-up longing and a kind of hungry intensity.

In the space of a heartbeat, it seemed, the fierceness faded, replaced by a tender wonderment that grasped her heart. His lips moved gently on hers, as if remembering what a kiss was. His hand moved to cup her face with such tenderness. The world receded until there was nothing left except her and Noah and loving him.

Suddenly, as suddenly as it had happened, it was over. Noah forced himself away from her, cannoning into the workbench behind him. "No!" He turned, bracing his hands on the surface, leaning over them like someone in the depths of pain.

"Noah . . ." There was a world of love and empathy in the word. She reached out to him helplessly. "Don't, please. Let me in."

"I can't. I just . . . can't."

Tears choked her throat, but she forced her voice out. "Why? Because you can't trust me? Is that it?"

He stared at her for a long moment, seeming to struggle for speech. And then . . . "No. Because I can't trust myself. Don't you see? I don't even know what I did that drove Janie away. How can I trust myself not to do it again?"

His face twisted and he turned away, shoulders hunched against her.

Sarah let out a long, shaky breath. So that was it. Behind all the anger and lack of forgiveness, there was the truth. Noah blamed himself.

Words flew into her mind . . . arguments, explanations, excuses . . . But none of them were any good. If Noah were to change, to get out of this cycle of blame and grief, he'd have to open up, and it seemed he couldn't.

Pressing her lips tight to hold back the sobs that threatened to overwhelm her, she grabbed her coat and fled out into the cold.


NOAH STOOD WHERE he was for what seemed a long time after Sarah left, struggling to regain control of himself.

He'd wanted, so much, to lose himself in Sarah's love and caring. She was the one woman who could make up for everything that was missing in his life and the boys' lives.

For an instant he indulged in the dream—Sarah as a loving wife, a loving mother to the twins. Sarah had the gift of creating a home. Given the chance, she would make a joyful home, filled with love and prayer and laughter. They could have more children. They'd work beside each other, sharing everything that came along, even growing old together in the kind of harmony his parents had.

But it was a dream. Just a dream. He hadn't fully accepted the truth about himself until he'd said it to Sarah. He'd failed Janie. He'd promised to love and care for her all their lives, but he'd failed, and he didn't know why.

The thought of failing Sarah ate at his heart like acid. He couldn't take that risk. He loved her too much for that.

He heard the door open behind him, and his heart leaped. Sarah . . . but it couldn't be Sarah.

"Noah." His mother's voice sounded, and he forced himself to straighten.

"Yah?" He met her eyes and saw concern mixed with . . . was it apprehension? "What's wrong?"

"Nothing's wrong," she said quickly. "But someone is here to see you."

"I'd rather not—"

"It's Amos Burkhalter, come all the way from Indiana to talk to you."

His stomach churned. "It's no good. I don't want to see him."

"He's come all this way just to see you. Surely you can listen to the man. He's not your enemy."

"He lied to me. He knew about Janie and he kept it from us, pretending he didn't. Now he wants to talk? He should have thought of that years ago."

"Noah Raber! Never would I think to hear such bitterness coming from one of my kinder. The man is grieving, and he's come all this way—"

"No!" It was the first time he'd ever raised his voice to his mother, and shame swept over him. "I can't. Don't you see, I can't?"

"I do not see." She snapped off the words in the way that always meant you were in trouble. "I'm ashamed of you."

But at least she didn't try to argue. She went out, closing the door with something just short of a slam.

Noah was too relieved to be left alone even to think about how he'd repair the damage he was doing. There were things a man could do and things a man couldn't do, and that—

The door opened again, and Mamm fairly propelled Amos, protesting, through it. Once again it slammed.

For a moment neither of them spoke. Then Amos cleared his throat. "A very determined woman, your mamm. I'm sorry, Noah. I would not force myself on you. I can't make you listen to me. I can only beg you to hear me out."

Noah stared at him, the words that would make Amos leave hovering on his tongue. But he couldn't seem to say them, not now that he had a good look at Amos.

Amos had grown old. It had been five years since he'd seen the man, and he looked as if it had been twenty. His beard was completely gray now, and his face was pale and drawn with pain and grief.

"You lied to me." That wasn't what he'd intended to say, but that was the most bitter thing. "All those times you wrote to ask about the boys, you never told me where Janie was."

"I didn't know. I promise, Noah. I never knew where she was until six months ago." He stopped, seeming to struggle for control. "She came to me when she knew she was dying."

Like a blow to the stomach, it knocked the wind out of Noah. "I thought . . ."

"No. Never. If I'd known, don't you think I'd have tried to make her see sense—for her babies, at least?"

Noah struggled to find solid ground. He couldn't doubt what Amos was saying—it was far too painful to the man to be a lie.

Noah put out a hand, steadying himself against the workbench. "After she came to you . . . she still didn't want to see us?" Not him, he supposed, but surely she should have wanted to see the twins.

"No. I'm sorry. It wasn't that she didn't want to see you, if just to ask for forgiveness. But she said she'd never given the boys anything, and she wouldn't give them the pain of seeing a dying mother just to satisfy her own needs." He paused, seeming to relive that moment. "I thought then that she'd finally faced what she did. Too late."

Noah rubbed the back of his neck, trying to understand what he felt. Not anger, at least. Maybe the beginnings of pity. "Tell me . . . did she ever find it? What she was looking for, I mean?"

Amos shook his head, sorrow dragging down the lines of his face. "No. How could she? She seemed to think happiness was something she could find by looking for it, like a lost coin. She never understood. Maybe, if her mamm had lived, she'd have known better what to do. I . . . I didn't."

Failure, that was what he meant. Someone else who felt he'd failed Janie. "Why?" He asked the question he'd never been able to answer. "Why did she run away?"

A spasm of pain crossed the old man's face. "I wish I knew. I asked her, but she couldn't answer. It seemed like her mamm dying so young did something to her."

"Other people have had to deal with that." He thought of Sarah, who'd made a home for her father and siblings.

"Yah, they do. It's not an excuse. It . . . it was something in Janie. She told me, toward the end, that she'd always believed she'd die like her mamm did. Maybe she was trying to run away from that." Amos shook his head. "That's all, I guess. I thought you had a right to know." Tears slipped from his eyes, and he turned his face away, maybe trying to hide them.

He ought to comfort the man. Ought to say something, at least. But he felt like he had when he'd fallen from the hayloft after his brother had dared him to balance on the edge. Neither his mind nor his body seemed to be attached to him.

Amos turned, opening the door and letting a blast of cold in. It seemed to rouse Noah, at least a little.

"Are you leaving?"

"I've done what I came here to do. I'd best go."

Noah sucked in a breath, trying to find something that made sense to say. And then he knew what it was.

"Why don't you stop at the house? You ought to meet your grandsons."

Noah watched joy sweep over the old man's face, wiping away the grief and pain. And inside himself, he felt something that had been frozen solid seem to shiver and crack.

# CHAPTER EIGHTEEN

S arah looked around the living room of the old farm-house, loving the gentle glow of candlelight on the faces of family. Mary, staying up a little late in honor of Christmas Eve, stared into the heart of the candle flame Grossmammi had just lit. She had set it carefully on the table behind the putz, so that it looked like the Star of Bethlehem shining over the stable.

Grossmammi drew a chair close to the table and sat, patting her lap for Mary to join her. She cuddled the little girl close, Mary's silky, fine hair against her cheek.

"See?" She murmured the word. "Here is the star shining in the night. And Mary and Joseph put Baby Jesus in the manger with nice soft straw to make his bed."

Mary touched each figure with care, as if realizing that there was something special about the story on this particular night. Sarah's gaze met Ruthie's where she sat in the rocking chair, cradling her baby boy against her breast. *Peace*, that was what Ruthie's sweet expression conveyed. There was peace and stillness on this night, perhaps as there had been on that night long ago.

The peace seemed to ease the pain of her broken heart. She'd never realized before how right that expression was.

Her chest ached, for all the world as if something inside was broken. Through the depth of her sorrow, the peace of the moment seemed to bring light.

All was not lost, even though what she longed for was denied. There was still the family's love and work for her hands. Maybe one day there would be joy again. She wouldn't have a happy ending to her story with Noah, but she had experienced loving him. Love had taken her by surprise, overwhelming her, and she could never regret loving him.

Grossmammi finished the story, Mary attempting to name each of the figures after her. She still clutched the angel that was her favorite, but when Grossmammi reached the end, her small hand reached out and put the angel in its place, overlooking the family in the stable. She looked up at Grossmammi as if for approval.

"That's right, sweet girl. That is where the angel belongs, watching over them."

Eli, the family Bible on his lap, began to read. Using the High German of worship, he read the familiar words of the Christmas story. Sarah listened, gazing out the front window to where an oblong of yellow light fell onto the blanket of snow that still covered the earth. Would Noah and the twins be at his parents' house tonight? That might be best for the boys, at least, to have other people around. It wouldn't matter to Noah, sunk as deeply in his grief and guilt as he was, but Matthew and Mark should feel surrounded by their family's love.

As Eli finished the reading, they sat quietly. It was probably time Mary was in bed, but she delayed saying so, not wanting to lose this moment. The others seemed to feel the same—Eli running his hand over the worn leather cover of the Bible, Grossmammi snuggling Mary close, Ruthie rocking gently with the baby asleep in her arms.

Then, as if they had been waiting for it, there was a knock on the back door. Eli looked up, startled, and rose. "Who can that be at this time of night? I didn't hear a buggy, did you?"

Sarah shook her head, rising to join him as he went toward the back door. The others came along after them, obviously curious. She was standing right beside Eli as he reached the door and threw it open. The yellow glow from the gas fixture shone on the faces—Noah, his parents, and the twins, the two men carrying lanterns.

As if the door opening had been a signal, the twins began to sing, their voices rising in a sweet treble with "Away in a Manger." At the end of the first line Noah and his parents joined in, the song rising on the frosty air. First Grossmammi and then the others sang as well, and they finished the carol together. Sarah's eyes stung with tears as she watched the boys' faces, so sweet and sincere. They looked at her, as if their song was for her, and her heart filled with joy, love, and pain mixed together.

"Komm in, schnell," Grossmammi exclaimed, reaching toward them. "What a lovely Christmas surprise to find dear neighbors on our doorstep."

Freed from their singing, the two boys rushed Sarah, wrapping her in their eager arms. "Did you like it?" Matty said. "Were we gut?"

"We sang it for you," Mark whispered.

She hugged them close, letting herself believe, just for a moment, that they were hers. "You were wonderful gut. Komm in, get warm."

"Yah, yah." Grossmammi ushered them in, and there was a confusion of laughter and voices.

Under cover of the chatter, Noah reached out to circle her wrist with his fingers. "Put on a coat," he murmured so no one else could hear. "Komm out for a moment."

She probably should just fade back into the kitchen and

cling to the safety of the group. But she couldn't. She slipped on her coat and stepped out into the cold, clear night with Noah.

The light from the kitchen vanished behind the closed door. They walked, side by side, a few feet along the path through the snow. Sarah felt as if she were suspended, caught between who she'd been and who she was going to be. She didn't feel the fresh pain of loss or the thrill of hope—she just waited. Above, the stars glittered against a black velvet sky, seeming close enough to reach out and touch.

Noah stopped, and she felt him look at her.

"It's cold out," he muttered. "You have to button up." With a gentle movement he drew her coat closer around her, fastening the top buttons she hadn't bothered with. His hands were gentle, the gesture one she'd use with a child.

"Denke." She said the word in a whisper, almost afraid to break the stillness of the night.

"I shouldn't bring you out in the cold, but I had to talk, had to tell you . . ."

He seemed to run out of words.

"It's all right." Both the cold and whatever he needed to say were fine.

"I had a visitor this afternoon. Amos came."

"Janie's father? But I thought he was in Indiana."

"Yah." His mouth twisted a little. "So did I. I guess he thought talking to me was worth coming all this way."

"You had to see him, then, ain't so?" She couldn't see where this was going, but he'd have to tell her all of it now.

"Yah, well, Mamm wouldn't put up with anything else." He had the ghost of a smile. "Amos . . ." He seemed to stall for a moment, but then he went on. "I was wrong about him. I was so angry, and here he didn't know where

Janie was at all until a few months ago—until she was dying." A spasm of pain crossed his face on the word.

"I'm sehr sorry." For Amos, for Janie, for everyone whose life was touched by this tragedy.

Noah glanced down. Almost without making a decision, it seemed, he took her cold hands, folding them within his as if that were a routine movement.

"Amos said . . . he said he felt like Janie had always believed that she'd die young, like her mamm did. He said it seemed like she kept running away, trying to outrun it. But she couldn't."

Sarah could ache for that unhappy, frightened young woman even while praying that knowing this could relieve Noah of the terrible burden he carried.

"There wasn't anything you could have done. Or that Amos could have done."

"No." There was a wealth of sorrow in the word. "We couldn't protect her from the fear that was in her own mind. Or from the disease that took her mother."

*Does it make a difference?* That was what she longed to know. *Does it make a difference to your future?*

Noah's shoulders moved slightly, as if he shrugged. "This whole day—I've felt like I was being tossed around in a storm, hardly knowing which way was up. Starting with knowing I love you."

Her heart gave a leap, but she was almost afraid to believe. "Because you kissed me, you mean."

"Because I love you," he corrected. "I love you, and I hurt you."

"Only because you were hurting so much yourself." Even with her heart singing in her ears, she needed to go slowly.

"I'm kind of slow," he said, as if echoing her thought. "I have to think things out in my head. But I don't give up.

And finally I saw that I've been blaming everyone—Janie, Amos, myself—for things we couldn't help. It was as if everything I thought I knew was blown up. And when the dust cleared, there was you."

He was looking at her in a way that made her heart thud in loud, insistent beats. "You," he said again. "Loving me when I least deserved it." His voice roughened. "I'm afraid even your patience might be exhausted by now."

Through the whirling in her thoughts one thing stood out clear and bright as the stars overhead. Love.

"That could never happen. You might infuriate me, but you can never make me stop loving you."

"Ach, my Sarah." He touched her cheek, his hand warm against her skin, his eyes shining with love. "We are going to be so happy together. With the twins, with the other kinder we'll have . . . we'll be a family, living and working and loving together all of our days. I could never ask for anything better."

"There's one thing I might ask," she said, lifting her face to his. "A kiss to seal the partnership."

"Partners," he repeated, and then his lips met hers, and they said nothing more at all.

Eventually, reluctantly, he drew back just a little so he could see her face. "Happy?"

"Very happy," she said, remembering her hopes when she'd come back home. She'd thought happiness would be in a place, but it wasn't. It was in people—the people she loved who loved her back.

She glanced toward the farmhouse, its lights glowing with welcome. "Should we go in and tell them?"

"Yah." He put his arm around her, snuggling her close to his side. "Let's tell the boys we are going to be a family. Forever."

Together they walked back to the old farmhouse.

# CHAPTER NINETEEN

Sarah couldn't think of a Christmas Day when she'd been any happier than she was right now. Dinner would soon be ready, with the aroma of roast turkey filling the air, and she could see Noah coming up the lane with the twins. She hurried to the door to greet them, knowing that her happiness was evident for all to see.

The two boys ran ahead, wearing the hats she'd made for them. It gave her an extra little bubble of joy to see it, seeming to affirm that they were hers.

"We love our hats," Matty exclaimed. "And Daadi gave us a farm set and a new bat and ball."

"That's wonderful," she said, hugging them. "Did you give Daadi a present?"

They nodded. "Grossmammi helped us," Mark said.

"We picked out a new winter hat for him," Matty added.

"And it's a perfect fit." Noah came up behind them, stamping the snow off his boots before stepping inside. He paused to put his arm around her and press his cheek to hers. His cheek was cold, warming when they touched, and his beard felt silky soft against her skin. "Happy Christmas," he whispered. "Mamm and Daad are expecting us for supper. All of us," he added, making sure she knew that included her.

"I hope you're awful hungry then." A bubble of laughter came with the words. "There's a huge turkey dinner waiting for you here."

"With pumpkin pie?" Matthew asked hopefully.

"For sure," she said. "Komm in where it's warm."

As they moved into the kitchen, Matty tugged at her skirt, stretching on tiptoe to whisper, "Can we call you Mammi now?"

"I told you we should wait," Mark said. "You made Sarah sad."

"No, of course you didn't make me sad." She brushed away the tear that had escaped. "These are happy tears, because there's nothing I'd like better than to have you call me Mammi."

She was instantly throttled in a double hug from the twins, and she looked at Noah, her heart full. "That's the best Christmas present ever," she said, and he smiled.

"For me, too."

Grossmammi came hurrying to give hugs all around. "Dinner will be ready in two shakes. But first—Noah, there's a present for Sarah just inside the pantry door. Would you bring it out for me?"

"For sure," he said, moving toward the pantry while Sarah looked at her grandmother suspiciously.

"You've already given presents."

"It's just another little thing for you," Grossmammi said.

Noah slid a large, oblong package from the pantry, and Sarah's lips twitched as she realized what it must be.

"Boys, will you help me take the paper off?" She knelt next to it, the twins on either side. Noah stood behind her, his hand resting on her shoulder, linking them.

Matty seized one end. "Ready?"

She nodded. "Go." They pulled the colorful paper away together, exposing the handmade dower chest that Grossmammi had insisted would be hers. Sarah felt herself tearing up again.

"Happy tears?" Mark asked.

"Yah, happy tears," she answered, looking at her grandmother. "You couldn't have anticipated that I'd be needing it now."

Grossmammi smiled, her eyes twinkling. "Maybe. Maybe not. But one thing I did know. I knew God created our Sarah to have a family, and look what He has provided—not only a loving husband but two sweet sons as well. You can always trust God to take care of the details."

Sarah looked up at Noah, putting her hand over his where it rested on her shoulder, and felt the happiness and love flowing between them.

Grossmammi was right, as always.

# GLOSSARY OF PENNSYLVANIA DUTCH WORDS AND PHRASES

**ach.** oh; used as an exclamation

**agasinish.** stubborn; self-willed

**ain't so.** A phrase commonly used at the end of a sentence to invite agreement.

**alter.** old man

**anymore.** Used as a substitute for "nowadays."

**Ausbund.** Amish hymnal. Used in the worship services, it contains traditional hymns, words only, to be sung without accompaniment. Many of the hymns date from the sixteenth century.

**befuddled.** mixed up

**blabbermaul.** talkative one

**blaid.** bashful

**boppli.** baby

**bruder.** brother

**bu.** boy

**buwe.** boys

**daadi.** daddy

**Da Herr sei mit du.** The Lord be with you.

**denke.** thanks (or *danki*)

**Englischer.** one who is not Plain

**ferhoodled.** upset; distracted

**ferleicht.** perhaps

**frau.** wife

**fress.** eat

**gross.** big

**grossdaadi.** grandfather

**grossdaadi haus.** An addition to the farmhouse, built for the grandparents to live in once they've "retired" from actively running the farm.

**grossmutter.** grandmother

**gut.** good

**hatt.** hard; difficult

**haus.** house

**hinnersich.** backward

**ich.** I

**ja.** yes

**kapp.** Prayer covering, worn in obedience to the Biblical injunction that women should pray with their heads covered. Kapps are made of Swiss organdy and are white. (In some Amish communities, unmarried girls thirteen and older wear black kapps during worship service.)

**kinder.** kids (or *kinner*)

**komm.** come

**komm schnell.** come quick

**Leit.** the people; the Amish

**lippy.** sassy

**maidal.** old maid; spinster

**mamm.** mother

**middaagesse.** lunch

**mind.** remember

**onkel.** uncle

**Ordnung.** The agreed-upon rules by which the Amish community lives. When new practices become an issue, they are discussed at length among the leadership. The decision for or against innovation is generally made on the basis of maintaining the home and family as separate from the world. For instance, a telephone might be necessary in a shop in order to conduct business but would be banned from the home because it would intrude on family time.

**Pennsylvania Dutch.** The language is actually German in origin and is primarily a spoken language. Most Amish write in English, which results in many variations in spelling when the dialect is put into writing! The language probably originated in the south of Germany but is common also among the Swiss Mennonite and French Huguenot immigrants to Pennsylvania. The language was brought to America prior to the Revolution and is still in use today. High German is used for Scripture and church documents, while English is the language of commerce.

**rumspringa.** Running-around time. The late teen years when Amish youth taste some aspects of the outside world before deciding to be baptized into the church.

**schnickelfritz.** mischievous child

**ser gut.** very good

**tastes like more.** delicious

**Was ist letz?** What's the matter?

**Wie bist du heit.** How are you; said in greeting

**wilkom.** welcome

**Wo bist du?** Where are you?

# RECIPES

## *Whoopie Pies*

*Makes two dozen*

**FOR COOKIES:**
1½ cups regular sugar
½ cup shortening
2 eggs
1 teaspoon vanilla
½ Tablespoon cocoa powder dissolved in ½ cup warm
   water
1 teaspoon baking powder
1 teaspoon baking soda
½ cup buttermilk

Preheat oven to 350°F.

Cream the sugar and shortening together until fluffy.
Beat in the eggs, vanilla, and cocoa mixture. Combine the
dry ingredients, then add to the shortening mixture alter-
nately with the buttermilk, beating each time. Drop by
tablespoons onto a greased cookie sheet, smoothing into
the traditional oval shape. Bake for 10–12 minutes, or

until firm to the touch. Remove from the pan and let cool on a wire rack.

**FOR FILLING:**
**3 Tablespoons flour**
**1 cup milk**
**¾ cup shortening**
**1½ cups powdered sugar**
**1 teaspoon vanilla**

Put the flour in a small saucepan and gradually stir in the milk. Cook over medium heat, stirring constantly, until the mixture is thick and smooth. Remove from the stove and refrigerate until completely cool. (Be sure the mixture is cooled, or the filling will not come together—something I know from personal experience!)

In a separate bowl, cream together the shortening, powdered sugar, and vanilla until fluffy and the sugar is completely dissolved. Add the cooled flour mixture slowly, beating for about seven minutes. At first the mixture may appear curdled, but continue to beat until it comes together and is light and creamy.

Spread the filling on half of the cookies, topping each with the remaining cookie half. Cover tightly in a container and refrigerate.

*Note: This is an old-fashioned filling, one that my mother used as both a filling and a frosting on cakes. It is very light and creamy while not terribly sweet. Though it's time-consuming to make, it is delicious. Easier fillings are sometimes used, including whipped cream or marshmallow crème.*

# Layered Hamburger Bake

*Serves 8*

8 ounces medium noodles, preferably Pennsylvania
Dutch style
1 pound ground beef
1 quart spaghetti sauce
8 ounces cream cheese, softened
½ cup sour cream
3 Tablespoons milk
2 Tablespoons chopped onion
10-ounce package chopped spinach (or the equivalent
of fresh spinach), cooked and drained
½ cup shredded cheddar cheese

Preheat oven to 350°F.

Cook the noodles in boiling salted water per the package directions. Drain and set aside.

Brown the beef, then drain off the fat. Add the spaghetti sauce and cooked noodles, stirring well. Set aside.

Mix together the cream cheese, sour cream, milk, and onion.

In a two-quart casserole dish, layer half the ground beef mixture, then half the cream cheese mixture, then the spinach, then the remaining ground beef mixture. Bake, covered, for 30 minutes. Uncover and spread with the remaining cream cheese mixture and the cheddar cheese. Bake, uncovered, for an additional 10 minutes.

## Dandelion Greens

¼ pound bacon
2 eggs, beaten
½ cup sugar
½ cup water
½ cup apple cider vinegar
2 quarts fresh dandelion greens, spinach, or leaf
    lettuce, washed and drained

Fry the bacon until crisp; drain, crumble, and return to the pan.

Mix together the eggs, sugar, water, and vinegar and add the mixture to the bacon, stirring over low heat until thick. Pour the dressing over the greens and serve immediately. If desired, top with sliced hard-boiled egg and/or sliced mushrooms.

# AMISH CHRISTMAS CUSTOMS

Christmas is probably the most important celebration in the Amish year. In fact, it's so important that it is actually observed by some Amish three times: Christmas Day, Second Christmas, and Old Christmas.

Christmas Day falls on December 25 for the Amish as it does for other Christians, a day when the miracle of Christ's birth is recognized with joy and awe. For such an important event, one day isn't enough, so while time spent with the immediate family is the norm for Christmas Day, the day after Christmas, also called Second Christmas, is a day to celebrate with the extended family. Visiting and sharing a meal can be an extraordinary event when your extended family is as large as that of most Amish. There might be more than fifty people there!

In many Amish groups, Old Christmas is still observed. Falling twelve days after December 25, January 6 is the celebration of Epiphany, the arrival of the wise men to visit Jesus, and in the Middle Ages this was the culmination of the Christmas feast. When the Gregorian calendar replaced the older Julian calendar, the Pope set December 25 as the official Christmas Day, but many Protestants kept to the old calendar, celebrating on

January 6. The tradition has hung on among some Amish who celebrate on both days, with Old Christmas usually being a more solemn and religious day.

Whether they recognize Old Christmas or not, an Amish holiday is one that most people in contemporary society would consider very plain. Amish children don't make lists for Santa Claus or pore through catalogs searching for the latest in electronic gear. Old Order Amish homes don't have Christmas trees or elaborate light displays. The Amish Christmas celebration, like all of Amish life, is focused on faith, home, and family.

Holiday customs vary from one Amish community to another. More conservative communities have low-key observances of the holidays. In Pennsylvania, the Amish are affected by the strong Pennsylvania German tradition, and they are more likely to have the customary Pennsylvania Dutch decorations.

Christmas decorations in a typical Pennsylvania Amish home may include lighting candles and placing them in the windows to symbolize the birth of Jesus. Many homes now use battery-powered candles that pose less threat of fire. Candles are sometimes also used with greens on the mantelpiece and tables. If you visit a home with young children, you'll probably find doorways and windows draped with strings of paper stars, angels, and sometimes popcorn. If the family receives Christmas cards, they'll probably be displayed so that they can be enjoyed time and again throughout the season.

Christmas cards are sent in some church districts and not others. With so many Amish working in jobs that bring them into daily contact with the Englisch, it has become more common for Amish families to send cards to Englisch friends, and the cards are almost always hand-made.

The putz, or manger scene, is an important part of the Christmas decoration throughout the Pennsylvania German communities. The putz developed very early in the church's history as a way of teaching children the story of Christ's birth. If you visit Bethlehem or Lititz in Pennsylvania during the holiday season, you can see some beautiful, elaborate depictions, sometimes including other Biblical scenes in addition to the familiar manger. The typical Amish putz is much simpler, using clay or wooden figures and possibly a stable. Some families embellish the scene with natural materials like straw and greenery. Using the putz, the Christmas story is told over and over throughout the days leading up to Christmas.

The Moravian Star is a twenty-six-point star, first used in Germany in the 1800s. The Moravian community that settled in Lititz has preserved the tradition of hanging the multi-pointed star, and many Amish homes also include the Moravian Star in their decorations as representing the Star of Bethlehem.

School celebrations are an important part of the Christmas season in most Amish areas. The children begin preparing their parts a month ahead, but their teachers have probably been busy since last year's program in collecting materials to use! The program, presented before as many family and friends as can cram into the one-room schoolhouse, typically includes readings of prose and poetry, the acting out of skits, and the singing of Christmas carols. Every child participates, and parents hold their breath until their little scholar gets through his or her piece. Teachers sometimes exchange skits and poems with each other, building up a collection so that each year they can provide something new to the audience, which has probably seen countless Christmas programs over the years. The theme of every poem and skit is that of gratitude for the gift of Christ and of the proper response of humility and love. This may be the only time when an Amish child "performs" in any way, but the audience is always uncritical and enthusiastic.

Gift-giving is part of the Amish Christmas celebration, but it bears little resemblance to the avalanche of gifts common to a typical American household. The presents are often handmade and generally something that is useful. Younger children typically receive one toy from their parents, while other gifts might be handmade clothing, cloth dolls, or wooden toys. An older girl might welcome something for her future home, while tools are popular gifts for older boys. The Amish school often has a gift exchange among the children, and usually the children take great pleasure in making a gift for the teacher.

The Amish home will probably be filled with the aroma of cookie-baking and candy-making for weeks before the holiday. While you can usually find home-baked cookies on any day, the holidays call for something special, and Amish cooks preserve family recipes for the cookies and treats, passing them on from mother to daughter. Most Pennsylvania Dutch are known for the quality and variety of their Christmas cookies.

In addition to celebrating with immediate and extended families, most Amish adults have various groups that plan Christmas lunches and suppers. In fact, there are so many of these that they might still be going on in February! Groups of cousins, people who work together, girls who went through rumspringa at the same time—all of these and more may share a special Christmas treat together.

But the focus of the Amish Christmas celebration, as of all Amish life, is the family. Gathered around a groaning table spread with roast chicken, all the trimmings, and an endless array of breads, cakes, cookies, and homemade candy, the family celebrates Christmas together with humility and gratitude to God for His amazing gift.

*Dear Reader,*

*Welcome to Promise Glen, a peaceful community located in central Pennsylvania, where the Amish and English strive to live in harmony with each other. To Sarah Yoder, Promise Glen has always been her Promised Land, but her longed-for return brings her surprises, conflict, and old friends. Promise Glen offers an opportunity for happiness she's only dreamed of, but first she'll have to surmount obstacles that challenge every bit of courage and faith she possesses.*

*It's my hope that you will enjoy my story and feel empathy for Sarah as she struggles to find her place in the world.*

*I'd love to hear what you think of this book. You can reach me online at mpjohn@ptd.net or at facebook.com/martaperrybooks, or you can write to me* Care of Berkley Publicity Department, 1745 Broadway, New York, NY 10019. *I'll be happy to respond and send you a bookmark and my brochure of Pennsylvania Dutch recipes.*

*All the best from Marta Perry*

Looking for more Christmas cheer?
Read on for an excerpt from

# NAOMI'S CHRISTMAS

*Pleasant Valley*
BOOK SEVEN

by Marta Perry

Available now
from Berkley

Naomi Esch froze in her seat at the family table, unable to stop staring at her father. Daadi had just tossed what felt like a lightning bolt into the middle of her thirtieth birthday celebration. Around her, she could feel her siblings and their spouses stuck in equally unbelieving attitudes.

"Ach, what is wrong with all of you?" Daadi's eyes narrowed, his beard seeming to bristle as he glared at his offspring. "This is a reason to celebrate, ain't so?"

Lovina, her brother Elijah's wife, was the first to recover, her calm face showing little of what she felt. "We wish you and Betty much happiness." She bounced Amos, her two-year-old, on her lap, hushing him. "Wilkom, Betty."

Betty Shutz, a round dumpling of a woman with a pair of shrewd brown eyes, nodded and smiled, but the glance she sent toward Naomi was cautious.

Isaiah, the youngest and most impetuous, said what everyone was thinking. "But what about Naomi? If you and Betty are marrying, what is Naomi to do?"

The question roused Naomi from her frozen state. What *was* she supposed to do, after fifteen years spent raising her siblings, tending the house and garden and her beehives, and taking care of Daadi?

Daadi's gaze shifted, maybe a bit uneasily. "Naomi is a gut daughter, none better. No one would deny that. But newlyweds want to have time alone together, ja? So we . . . I was thinking Naomi would move in with Elijah and Lovina. They are both busy with the dry-goods store and two young kinder besides. It would be a big help to you, ja?"

Elijah and Lovina exchanged glances, and then Lovina smiled at Naomi. "Nothing would please us more than to have Naomi with us, but that is for her to say, ain't so?"

"Denke, Lovina." Naomi found that her stiff lips could move, after all. "But what about my beehives?"

Odd, that her thoughts had flown so quickly to her bees in the face of this shock. Or maybe not so odd. The beehives were the only thing she could call truly hers.

"I've already talked to Dick Holder about the hives, and he'll be happy to give Naomi a gut price for them." Daad spoke as if it were all settled, her life completely changed in a few short minutes.

"I will not sell the hives." Naomi could hardly believe that strong tone was coming out of her mouth. Everyone else looked equally surprised. Maybe they'd never heard such firmness from her.

Daad's eyebrows drew down as he stared at her. "Komm, Naomi, don't be stubborn. It is the sensible thing to do. Betty is allergic to bee stings, so the hives cannot stay here. And Elijah's home in town isn't suitable. The money will give you a nice little nest egg for the future."

A babble of talk erupted around her as everyone seemed to have an opinion, but Naomi's thoughts were stuck on the words Daad had used. *Her future.* He clearly thought he knew what that future was to be. She should move from one sibling to another, helping to raise their children, never having a home or a life of her own.

She was engaging in selfish thinking, maybe, and it was unfitting for a humble Amish person. But . . .

She looked around the table. Elijah, two years younger than she, whom she'd comforted when bad dreams woke him in the night. Anna and Sara, the next two in the family, who had traveled by bus with their husbands from the next county for her birthday today. She'd taught the girls everything they needed to know to be Amish women, overseen their rumspringas, seen them married to gut men they loved. And Isaiah, the baby, the one whose first stumbling steps she'd guided. Were they to be her future, as they had been her past?

Much as she loved them, her heart yearned for more. Marriage might have passed her by during those years when she was busy raising her siblings, but she'd looked forward to a satisfying future, taking care of Daad, tending her hives, enjoying her part-time work at the bakery.

Amos slid down from his mother's lap and toddled around the table to tug on Naomi's skirt. A glance at his face told her he'd detected the strain in the air. She lifted him to her lap, running her hand down his back, murmuring soothing words. He leaned against her, relaxing, sucking on two fingers as he always did before going to sleep.

Lovina met her gaze from across the table and smiled. "Naomi is wonderful gut with children."

"For sure," Betty said, her first contribution to the conversation. "A widower with kinder would do well to have a wife like Naomi."

Somehow, that comment, coming from Betty, was the last straw. Naomi had to speak now, and quickly, before the rest of her life was set in stone by the family.

"You are all ser kind to give so much thought to my

life. But as dearly as I love my nieces and nephews, I have no wish to raise them. And I will not give up my beehives. So I think I must find this answer for myself."

She took advantage of the ensuing silence to move the drowsy child to his father's arms. Grabbing a heavy wool shawl from the peg by the back door, she walked out, closing the door gently behind her.

Mid-November, and it was ser chilly already, a hint of the winter to come. Even the hardy mums on the sheltered side of the house had succumbed to frost. Clutching the shawl more tightly, she walked across brittle grass to the gnarled old apple tree that had once held a tree house when the boys were young. It was a relief to get out of the kitchen, too warm from all the cooking that had been done today for her birthday. This day had certainly turned out far different from the celebration her sisters had so lovingly planned.

She stopped under the tree, resting her hand against the rough bark. No point in going farther—she couldn't escape her family, and she wouldn't want to. Soon someone would come out to talk to her, and she would have to explain and justify and try to make them understand. But for this moment she was alone with her thoughts.

The family had one thing right. She did have a gift with children, and she couldn't deny that gift. But to raise someone else's children again, to grow to love them so dearly, but to know that she always took second place in their hearts . . . no, she couldn't. But when she tried to think how to carry out that brave declaration she'd made, she found she was lacking in ideas.

It was Isaiah who came out to her. Maybe they thought the youngest would be most likely to soften her heart. But Isaiah was a man grown now, married for just a year, and so much in love with his Libby. Not a baby any longer, but he still seemed so young to her with his round blue eyes and his corn-silk hair. The beard he was growing as a married man was as fine and silky as his hair.

He leaned against the tree next to her, his eyes serious as he studied her face. "Are you all right?"

Naomi managed a smile, though it probably wasn't very convincing. "Ja. I will be, anyway. I guess Daad's news was a shock."

"For sure." Isaiah shook his head. "It wonders me that none of us saw this marriage coming, but we didn't. I guess we all figured that if Daad had been going to wed again, he'd have done it years ago."

"Then Betty would have had the raising of you." Her smile was more natural this time.

Isaiah seemed to shudder. "Ach, I'm sure she's a gut woman. But I'm glad it was you who brought me up, Naomi."

For an instant she was surprised almost to tears. "Denke," she whispered, her throat tight. She'd never say she loved one more than another, but Isaiah was especially dear, both because he was the baby and because of his sweet nature.

She tilted her head, watching him, wondering how he would react to the question she was about to put to him. "What about you, Isaiah? Do you think I'm being selfish not to do what Daadi wants?"

He blinked, eyes wide and innocent. "Ach, Naomi, everyone knows there's not a selfish bone in your body, no matter—" He stopped, looking as if he'd bitten his tongue.

So that was what someone had been saying, once she'd left the kitchen. Well, she wouldn't put Isaiah in the middle by noticing.

"I guess the first thing is to find a place for my beehives," she said, deliberately turning the subject. "It's not going to be an easy job, moving them all."

"I'll help," he said instantly. "And I was thinking that

I should ask Nathan King if you could have them on his farm. With Libby and me living right on the property, I could keep an eye on things for you."

Naomi hesitated. Isaiah enjoyed working for Nathan King on his dairy farm, and she didn't want to cause any difficulties between them by asking for something Nathan might not be so eager to grant. Nathan could have plenty of reasons not to want her beehives on his property.

"I wonder if that's wise," she said, careful to keep her voice neutral. "Ada and I were such close friends, and Nathan still mourns her so deeply even after two years. He might not want to have me around, reminding him of her."

Vertical lines formed between Isaiah's brows. "It's true he's still grieving for Ada. But as for reminding him . . . well, he seems to be thinking about her all the time anyway."

"Poor Nathan," she murmured. And poor Ada, gone far too early, it seemed, in such a freak accident, leaving Nathan and two young kinder behind. Naomi accepted it as God's will, but she couldn't help wishing it had been otherwise. As for Nathan—well, she doubted he would ever be able to accept his loss.

Isaiah straightened, pushing away from the tree. "Let me talk to Nathan about it, anyway. I won't push. I'll make it easy for him to say no, if that's what he's of a mind to do. But he might well say yes."

She was still doubtful, but she nodded. "I guess it can't hurt to ask."

"That's right. And if he says no, we'll find someone else." Isaiah put his arm around her shoulders. "You're cold. Let's go inside."

She hung back. "That's not a gut idea. Daadi will just start trying to persuade me again, and I don't want to provoke a family quarrel on my birthday." Although maybe she'd already done that very thing.

"He won't say a word." Isaiah sounded confident. "Betty told him it was best to let you think about their marriage and get used to the idea of moving out without him pushing you."

"And he agreed to that?" It didn't sound like Daadi at all. Once he'd made up his mind, he was like a rock.

"He did." Isaiah grinned, blue eyes twinkling. "Seems like Betty can manage him better than the rest of us put together. So don't lose heart. This is all going to turn out for the best, you'll see."

Naomi nodded as they started toward the house, not wanting to lay her burdens any more heavily on Isaiah. But she doubted this situation could possibly turn out for the best . . . for her, anyway.

NATHAN KING SLID the harness over the back of Coal, the sturdy pony standing patiently between the shafts of the pony cart. He'd promised Joshua and Sadie a ride in the cart this afternoon, and he'd best get at it. Days grew short in November here in Pleasant Valley.

His father moved out of the shadow of the barn door, glancing up at the weak sunlight. "Giving the kinder a ride, ja? Are you sure you don't want me to stay around to help you with the milking?"

Nathan shook his head, feeling an inward pang at the stiffness with which Daad moved. It was impossible to keep him from helping on the dairy farm, but Nathan tried to spare his father as best he could.

"You go on home before Sarah is scolding me for keeping you late." Since Daad was living with Nathan's sister, she could be tart with Nathan about Daad doing too much, but he'd noticed she didn't have any better luck getting Daad to slow down. "Isaiah said he'd be back in time for evening milking."

"They were having a birthday party for Naomi, ain't so? I must remember to wish her happiness." Daad shook his head, the wind ruffling his beard, more gray now than brown. "I can't see her without thinking of your Ada, that's certain-sure. They were gut friends, ain't so?"

Nathan nodded, feeling his face stiffen. He didn't like talking about Ada, not that he ever stopped thinking about her.

He glimpsed movement from the corner of his eye, and his heart jolted.

"Joshua!" He snatched his small son from under the pony, where Joshua was reaching for the harness strap. "What are you doing?" He held the boy close for a moment and then set him on his feet. "You know better than to mess around the horses."

"But I can help, Daadi. I watch you and Grossdaadi all the time. I know how to harness Coal. She likes me."

"Whether she likes you or not isn't the point. You are too young to be harnessing her."

Nathan could sense his father's gaze on him, no doubt disapproving. Joshua stared at him with changeable hazel eyes so like Ada's that it cut to the heart to see disappointment in them. But keeping Joshua safe was more important than anyone's approval.

"But, Daadi . . ."

"Go back to Grossmammi. I will bring the cart up to the house in a moment."

Joshua pressed his lips together. Then he turned and walked back toward the farmhouse, his small shoulders drooping.

"The boy is six already," Daad commented. "When you were his age, you were doing more than harnessing a pony."

Nathan's jaw set. "He's too young. When he's older, I'll

show him how." He turned to the patiently waiting pony and fastened the straps.

Daad put a hand on his shoulder. "Just because you lost Ada to an accident . . ."

"Don't." He was instantly sorry for the harshness of his tone, but he couldn't help it. He couldn't listen again to someone telling him that it wasn't his fault Ada died trying to get the horses out of the blazing barn. Or telling him, as people seemed to want to do, that after two years it was time he started living again.

He couldn't get over Ada. He couldn't undo the past. All he could do now was protect the children she had given him with all his strength.

"I'm sorry, Daad." His voice was tight.

"It's all right. You must deal with grief as best you can." Daad cleared his throat. "Have you settled on who is to take care of the kinder when Ada's mother is away?"

Worry settled on Nathan like a wet, heavy blanket. "Sarah will komm a couple of days a week. She offered to have Joshua and Sadie stay with her every day, but I don't want them away from home so much. I'm still trying to find someone to watch them here for the rest of the time."

He could hardly fault Ada's mother for going to help Ada's middle sister with her new baby, but how was he to get along without her? She'd cared for the kinder every day of the past two years.

Realizing that his father was looking at him with concern, he shrugged. "I will find someone. You best get on home. Isaiah will be here soon."

"Isaiah is here now," a voice announced, and Isaiah Esch walked toward them with his long, loping stride. With his lanky body and wide grin, Isaiah still looked like the boy he'd been when he first came to work for Nathan instead of the married man he was now.

Daad nodded to him. "You had a gut birthday party for your sister, ja? Give her my best wishes when you see her again."

"Ja, denke, I will." Isaiah still smiled, but Nathan thought he detected something at odds with the smile in Isaiah's normally open face.

"I will be off now," Daad said. "No need to make Sarah fuss more than she already does."

He walked toward his buggy horse. Nathan knew better than to offer to help him. Daad resented any implication that he couldn't do what he'd always done.

Nathan turned toward Isaiah. "Was ist letz?" *What's wrong?* He knew Isaiah well enough to realize when something wasn't right.

"Ach, you're not going to believe it." Isaiah patted the pony absently. "It's my daad. He's going to marry Betty Shutz. Can you imagine? Announced it right in the middle of Naomi's birthday party."

Somehow the timing of the announcement didn't surprise Nathan as much as it seemed to have Isaiah. Sam Esch had always struck him as someone who put his own wants ahead of everyone else's.

"So Betty said yes to him. Well, if anyone can handle him, she can."

Isaiah blinked at this way of looking at his news. "Ja, you might be right about that. But it doesn't help Naomi much."

"No, I suppose not." It hadn't occurred to him how this change would affect Naomi, and it should have. "Maybe it will be all right. With Betty taking over the house and your daad, Naomi will have more time for her job and her beehives."

"If only," Isaiah said, the Englisch phrase a hangover from his rumspringa years. "Daad expects Naomi to move out. He acted like it was all set without even asking her. He said she should move in with Elijah and Lovina to help with the kinder. And he'd even set up for someone to buy the beehives."

A vague idea drifted through Nathan's thoughts. "And will she?"

Isaiah shook his head, his expression one of surprise. "She says not. Says she'll decide for herself what she's going to do. Mind, it's how I'd have felt if Daad did this to me, but I didn't expect it from Naomi. Nobody did." He grinned. "Least of all Daad."

"I can imagine." Sam wasn't used to his children refusing his ideas. "So what is Naomi going to do, then?"

"She says the first thing is to find a place for her beehives. Then she'll worry about herself." Isaiah's forehead wrinkled.

"She can't keep them at your daad's place?" Surely not even Sam would be that unkind just because Naomi didn't like his plans for her life.

"Apparently Betty's allergic to bee stings. Not that she'd be likely to get stung, not with honey bees, unless she poked a stick in the hives. But there it is. Naomi has to move the hives." Isaiah came to a stop and looked at Nathan. Expectantly.

So that was where this conversation had been headed. Isaiah hoped he would offer to have Naomi's beehives here.

Well, why not? He had plenty of available land, and the beehives wouldn't have to be close to the house. The only deterrent was that he would be brought into closer contact with Naomi, with her inevitable reminders of Ada.

Still, as he'd thought when Daad had mentioned something about their friendship, he didn't stop thinking about his Ada anyway. And Naomi . . . the whole valley knew how gut Naomi was with children. He made a quick decision.

"Have Naomi stop by to talk to me about it. Maybe we can find a solution to that part of her problem, at least."

In fact, maybe he'd found a way to solve both of their problems.


NAOMI DISCOVERED THAT her stomach was tied up in knots when she drove her buggy up the lane to Nathan's place the next day. The lane was both wide and well-kept, since the milk truck came in to pick up milk from the dairy operation. Nathan had made a thriving business from his dairy farm, but Ada wasn't here to share it with him.

Thoughts of Ada and Nathan plummeted her right back to an incident she tried to hide, blocking even her own memory of it.

She'd been sixteen, of an age to start her rumspringa years, but shy and uncertain, unlike Ada, who hadn't been able to stop talking about it.

Ada had been everything Naomi wasn't . . . pretty, lively, full of laughter and eager about life. But it was Naomi whom Nathan had approached that Sunday after worship; Naomi who'd heard Nathan asking if he could take her home from the singing that night. She had looked into his golden brown eyes and felt herself sinking into their depths. She would have done anything to be able to say yes.

But she couldn't. She wouldn't be going to the singing. She'd be staying at home to take care of the young ones, and so she'd had to say no.

Nathan had taken Ada home from the singing that night, and they'd tumbled into love with a suddenness that made it seem inevitable. Certainly Ada had never had any doubts.

She had confided in Naomi, of course. They were best friends. And Naomi had suppressed whatever envy she'd felt and encouraged her friend. When the time came, she'd been the one to help Ada's mother with the wedding, she'd been one of Ada's side-sitters, what the world would call a bridesmaid, and she'd rejoiced when Ada started her new life with Nathan.

It was as it should be, Naomi reminded herself now, stopping the buggy horse at the hitching rail by the back porch of the farmhouse. Nathan loved Ada with single-minded devotion and still did, even two years after her death.

Other people thought Nathan should move on, that he should marry again and give his kinder a mammi, but he wouldn't. Naomi understood that. Nathan would never betray his first love.

Naomi slid down from the buggy seat, shaking her skirt to straighten it, and turned toward the porch to discover Nathan and Ada's two children standing there, watching her.

"Joshua. Sadie. I am ser happy to see you." She bent to give each of them a hug, her heart touched as always by their resemblance to Ada. Joshua had hazel eyes just like his mother's, while Sadie, almost five now, had her pert, lively expression, with a smile always tugging at her lips.

"How are the bees?" Sadie held on to her for an extra second. "Did you bring us some honey?"

"You shouldn't ask," Joshua chided. Then he darted a glance at Naomi, eyeing the basket she carried.

She laughed, and he grinned back, knowing she'd caught him. "For sure I brought you some honey. I would not forget you." She handed the basket to Joshua. "Do you think that's enough?"

He peered at the three jars of amber honey. "For a while," he said, making her laugh again. "Daadi says he will be out in a minute, and we should keep you company."

"I can't think of any better company," she said. She sat on the top step, and the children sat on either side of her, Joshua holding the precious basket of honey jars on his lap.

"So what have you been doing? Do you have your sled ready for the first snow?"

Joshua nodded, studying the sky earnestly. "I wish it would snow. Do you think it will soon?"

"Well, November is a little early to get much snow," she said, careful not to promise what she couldn't deliver. "But it is gut to be ready for when it comes."

Sadie leaned against her. "Grossmammi says I am ready for a saucer all my own this year."

"If Grossmammi says it, it must be so," Naomi said. She put her arm around the little girl, irresistibly reminded of sitting on the back step, heads together with Ada, exchanging secrets.

"Grossmammi is going on a trip," Joshua informed her. "She is going to stay with Aunt Elizabeth for a while, and she says we must be very gut while she is away." He sat a little straighter, as if accepting that responsibility, making her think how like Nathan he was in temperament.

"I don't know why she has to go away." Sadie sounded a bit fretful. "I want her to stay here."

Naomi knew why Ada's mother was headed for Ohio. Elizabeth, Ada's next younger sister, was about to have her first baby after several years of trying. Naturally she'd want her mamm there.

"Maybe your aunt needs her for a little while," she suggested. "It would be wonderful kind of you to share Grossmammi with her, ain't so?"

"I guess," Sadie said, her voice filled with reluctance. She nuzzled against Naomi's coat. "But we need her more."

Naomi smiled, even as her heart winced. For sure, Ada's kinder needed her mamm. Emma Miller had been the constant in their lives since Ada died.

"While she's away, you can write her a letter, and the postman will take it all the way to Aunt Elizabeth's house in Ohio," she said.

"But I can't write yet," Sadie protested, even as Joshua nodded at the idea.

"You can draw a picture for her," Naomi said. "I'll tell you what. While Grossmammi is away, I'll come over one day and help you make a picture and a letter to send her. All right?"

"Promise?" Joshua studied her face, as if measuring whether this grown-up could be trusted to do what she said.

"I promise." Naomi met his gaze.

Apparently satisfied, he smiled.

Warmed by that smile, Naomi put her free arm around him, hugging both children even as her heart hurt for their loss.

The door clicked behind them. Naomi looked up, to find Nathan watching her with an expression she couldn't interpret.